ALL
THE
BISHOP'S MEN

C. P. HOLSINGER

Foremost Press
Cedarburg, Wisconsin

Published by Foremost Press
www.foremostpress.com

ISBN-10: 1-936154-95-1
ISBN-13: 978-1-936154-95-1

This is a work of fiction. Any similarity of characters or events to real persons or actual events is coincidental.

To Anita, who gave up so much
for what she believed.

John

Good Luck

Good Friend

C.P. Alsman

6-5-13

CHAPTER 1

Mike Bradley's tires squealed as he turned into St. Michael's parking lot. His eyes scanned the rows of vehicles and white stripes and luckily caught the last open spot. He darted into it, killed the engine, and threw the SUV into park, all in one motion. He got out of the car, reached over his shoulder and pushed the remote lock button. The horn returned its short response as he scurried across the blacktopped parking lot and glanced at his watch: five o'clock.

Mike hated to be late for Mass, especially when he was scheduled to serve as he was tonight. Quickening his pace and hoping they hadn't started the procession yet, he stepped up onto the sidewalk that led to the church doors.

On his way out of his house the ring of the telephone had caught him. Something told him to answer it, and he was glad he did. It was his Aunt Teresa calling from Pennsylvania with bad news; his mother had been taken to the hospital.

He had phoned the hospital and spoke to the charge nurse who described his mother's condition as stable and reported that she had passed out at home. That was all she could tell him at the time, except that she was sleeping and shouldn't be disturbed. "She needs to rest. Can you call back in a couple of hours? When she awakes, I'll tell her you called," she had told him.

Stepping into the church breezeway, he was reminded that this was St. Patrick's Day. Many people were donning green and one of the greeters handed him a shamrock as he went in. The readers, eucharistic ministers, altar servers, and Deacon Tom were all gathered around the large, gray stone holy water font that sat majestically in the center of the vestibule. As he dipped his fingers into the water and crossed himself, he heard the familiar sound of his wife's voice as the choir sang what he thought was the processional hymn. He was about to find out just how wrong he was.

Hurrying over to the bulletin board and reaching up to the servers' schedules, he scribbled his initials next to his name and joined his fellow ministers. The looks on their faces told him that something was not quite right. Their normal joyful expressions of celebration were replaced with worry and disarray.

Dusti greeted him with her normal hug and whispered in his ear, "We have no celebrant."

"Huh?" Mike's eyes quickly scanned the vestibule. "What are you talking about?"

"No priest. No one showed."

"Again? Who's scheduled?"

"Supposed to be Father David, I guess."

"Why am I not surprised?"

Dusti grinned as she looked at him with understanding eyes.

"I wonder who he'll blame it on this time," he said.

They knew he'd been late several times since becoming their pastor a little over a year ago. There was always an excuse for his tardiness; it was never his fault. Either someone changed the schedule, or was to cover for him, or some other excuse. The truth was their pastor just didn't like to say Mass on Saturday nights. Mike thought the parishioners would have respected him more if he'd told the truth. Some pretended to believe him, but Mike found it hard to understand how the priest couldn't see beyond them. "Has anyone called or paged him?" Mike asked.

Dusti shrugged as Mike caught sight of Deacon Tom and walked over to him. "What's going on, Tom?"

Shrugging his shoulders, the deacon replied, "No priest."

Tom Fleming and Mike Bradley had been friends for over twenty years and Mike easily recognized the look of concern on his face. "I heard. You okay, Tom?"

He nodded, but his eyes betrayed the pain he attempted to hide. He loved his church passionately, but hated the way his leader represented it. But he, as did the rest of the staff, knew Father David was in charge and in total control and that they all must obey him.

Tom was in his fifties with thinning hair that still had its color. Once, when asked how he kept from going gray, he reached into the holy water font, sprinkled some water on his head and said, "Works every time." A sense of humor was something not lacking in their beloved deacon.

Tom was worried because he knew that somehow Father David would blame him for tonight's fiasco. The deacon posted the schedule and knew Father David would come down on him about it as he had done many times before.

"Has anyone tried to locate him?" Bradley asked.

"I paged him," Tom replied. "And I called his house. I left a message on his voice mail."

"What about Father Roman?"

"He's in Tucson. His niece's wedding."

"Oh, yes." Mike remembered that their associate pastor's favorite niece was getting married today and how happy he'd been that Father David allowed him to go and perform the ceremony. "Has anyone checked his house?" Mike asked.

"Like I said, we called—"

Mike interrupted, "Has anyone gone over there? Has anyone even knocked on his door? Maybe he's asleep, or passed out or something."

"No, I don't think—"

Again his sentence was cut short. "Well, I think . . . Be right back."

"Mike, do you think that's a good idea? You know what he's like."

Father David Mignanelli didn't like people coming to his home. He was known to refuse to let people who came to visit him inside the house. Folks wondered, but never understood why.

With his hands on his hips and his head cocked slightly, Mike said, "Frankly, Thomas, I don't . . . well, you can fill in the blanks." Seeing the faint start of a smile tease both corners of the good deacon's mouth, he walked away.

* * *

The residence was only about fifty yards from the church. Mike scurried over the north parking lot and crossed Desert Oasis Drive to the house in which Father David resided. The house was owned by the church, and the pastor lived there alone. The associate pastor lived in the house next door. Both houses had been acquired by the church years ago. One used to be a rectory, the other a convent. Since there haven't been any nuns there for several years, accompanied by the shortage of priests, each had their own private home. This was much to Father Roman's liking. He had once spoken to Mike and Julie Bradley of his fear of Father David.

The front of the house was encompassed on three sides by a small chain-link fence. Bradley opened the gate and walked along the sidewalk that was edged by a freshly manicured lawn. Thick green grass teased the sidewalk like a perfectly painted picture. Red, white, and yellow roses lined the wall of the garage next to the walkway. A sign on the front door read: Peace to all who enter here. He pressed the doorbell and heard a loud chime that somehow didn't seem like the type Father David would allow. After waiting for about thirty seconds, he pressed the bell again, still no response. The third try was also fruitless, but his ears caught the faint sound of music coming from inside, so he tried again. Nothing. He saw a small window above the rose bushes and being careful not to get stuck by a thorn, stretched out on his tiptoes and peered into the garage. The bright red Mustang convertible that he knew belonged to Father David sat there alone with the top down. Strange, he thought. Something's not right.

Giving in to his curiosity, he made his way across the front lawn. Checking the gate leading to the rear yard, he found it slightly ajar. Pushing it open he followed the sidewalk to the rear of the house, stepped onto the patio, and was surprised to see that the sliding glass door was open about a foot. He could hear the music louder now as he knocked hard on the large pane of glass. It sounded like a jazz station playing in the background.

After several unresponsive knocks, he decided to go in. The grinding of the glass door as it slid from right to left temporarily covered the sound of the music. He stepped into the room onto plush inlaid carpet.

Mike Bradley stood there in silence, momentarily stunned by the setting before him. There had been rumors their pastor had extravagant tastes, but this was a scene he had not expected.

As Mike stood there in awe, he now understood his pastor's reluctance to allow people inside this home. St. Michael's was far from being a rich parish, and the lavishness of this room would not go over well at all!

Directly centered against the left wall was a large plasma TV, flanked on each side by highly polished ebony wall units. An overhead track lighting system, perfectly aimed for maximum effect, reflected from their mirror finish. Blue and red lights from the stereo system were rising and falling with the music. Plush stuffed recliner rockers sat along each side of the room. Both were angled toward the TV making for a perfect view. Directly between them was a large sofa with recliners at both ends. The furniture was arranged in a comfortable U. This room exhibited the most in comfort, relaxation, and expense.

In the center of the room was a large round brass and glass cocktail table that sparkled like a Christmas tree as it reflected the lights from the stereo. The rest of the room was exquisitely accessorized with expensive imported lamps on tables that matched the one in the center.

Awed by the appearance, Mike felt like he was viewing an ad in *House Beautiful*. Perhaps it is true, he thought.

"Father David, hello." Waiting for a response and hearing none, he slowly walked across the living room into the dining room, again amazed at what he saw. The large dining table was also polished ebony and a perfect match for the wall units at the opposite end of the room. A large china cabinet stood centered along the wall to the right of the table, and along the adjoining wall sat a buffet which held a collection of angels. Both the china closet and the buffet matched the table perfectly. There were various items of silver and crystal visible through the glass doors of the china closet. The table was empty except for one half-empty bottle of whiskey.

Stepping into the hallway that led to the sleeping area, Mike stopped and called again. "Hello, anybody home?" Except for the sound of the stereo behind him, the house was silent.

Looking back at the bottle on the table, the thought that maybe the priest had passed out came to mind. Wouldn't be the first time a priest drank too much, he thought. Hesitating for only a moment he proceeded toward the rear of the house. "Hello!" he again called while passing a bedroom on the left. "Anybody home?" The door was open, so he peeked into the room. It, too, was well furnished and exquisitely decorated. The drapes in this one room looked like they had cost more than all the window coverings in the whole Bradley house.

Turning around to the room directly across the hall and seeing that the door was closed, he tapped on it, opened it, and said, "Anybody here?" The room was dismally dark; a complete contrast to anything he had seen in the rest of the house. The only furnishing was a futon that sat in the center of the room. It was covered with a large, navy blue blanket. The dark atmosphere of the room gave Mike an eerie feeling. How strange, he thought, maybe he just hadn't got around to this room yet.

Continuing down the hallway, he saw a room to his left. The door was closed so he knocked. When there was no response, he opened it. "Father Dav . . ." Stunned, Mike stood there. There he was, his back to the door, face down on his desk. Remembering the bottle on the dining room table, Mike thought the priest had passed out until he looked up and saw the condition of the room. The shock of what he saw would be forever etched in his memory. The off-white walls were splattered with red. He looked back to the slumped form before him. The scene was something he had only seen in movies.

Blood was everywhere; on the laptop computer and on the drapes. The desk, where his head rested, was drenched in blood that had dripped to the floor and formed a scarlet pool on the mauve carpet.

Swallowing hard and trying to compose himself, Mike rushed over to the slumped figure. His hands and arms were on each side of the laptop, almost like he was hugging it. Reactively, Mike reached to feel under his neck, the carotid artery was lifeless. It was then that he saw the hole in his pastor's head and the gun in his left hand. The first thought was to pick up the phone that sat on the desk next to the computer, but the blood on it warned him not to disturb anything.

Quickly leaving the room, Mike rushed down the hall to the kitchen. There must be a phone there, he thought, wishing he hadn't left his cell phone in his car.

His eyes caught sight of a phone on the wall above the marble counter top. Mike fished a handkerchief from his right rear pocket and removing the phone from its cradle, dialed.

"Nine-one-one. What is your emergency?" The voice at the other end was raspy and impersonal.

"Uhhh . . . I want to report a . . . a . . . a man's been shot. I think he's dead," he stammered.

"What is your name and address?" Her voice tone didn't change.

"Michael Bradley. I don't know the address. Fifty something Desert Oasis Drive. Don't you have it on your caller ID?"

There was silence for a moment, then she answered, "Sir, I have your location. Help is en route. Please remain right where you are until someone arrives, and stay calm."

"All right," Mike said as he returned the instrument to its cradle. Immediately he reached out, grabbed the phone again and dialed the parish office, knowing that on Saturdays the phones were answered by volunteers. He hoped it would be someone he knew.

He didn't recognize the female voice that answered, "St. Michael's Church."

If she said her name, Mike didn't hear it as his words covered hers. "This is Mike Bradley. I need you to go out to the vestibule and get Deacon Tom right away."

"I'm not supposed to—"

He cut her off midsentence. "This is an emergency! Please, get him now!"

Clunk was the sound in his ear as the phone dropped to the desk. He could hear the sound of footsteps as she followed his command.

The seconds seemed like hours as Mike pondered over what he was going to say to the good deacon. Finally, there was a voice on the other end.

"This is Deacon Tom." He sounded frustrated, and rightfully so, not knowing who would have the nerve to call him during what was supposed to be Mass time.

"This is Mike. You'll have to do a communion service, or something. You won't have a celebrant tonight."

"What happened? Did you find him?"

He didn't want to make the deacon's night any worse than it already was by telling him what he had just experienced. He knew Tom Fleming was very capable, but he needed to concentrate on the task before him. Mike said, "You don't wanna know; at least, not now. You'll just have to trust me. You need to handle things there. You're the only one who can. You know what to do. And, Tom,"—he hesitated for a moment, then continued—"if you see Julie, tell her I'm okay." He hung up the phone before the deacon could ask any more questions. Now, the once distant sounds of sirens were getting louder.

Knowing Julie would worry when she didn't see him at Mass, and that the sirens would soon bring attention, he decided to leave a message on her voice mail, but just as he reached for the phone, his ears were pierced by the shrill sound of a siren. Then he heard it wane.

Figuring it was either the police or the paramedics, he parted the white curtains and peered through the kitchen window. The emblem of the Phoenix Bird, prominent on the front door, told him his call would have to wait.

A uniformed police officer got out of the cruiser and hastened up the sidewalk just as a second car came screeching to a halt. As the officer entered the foyer, Mike pointed to the room at the end of the hall. The second officer followed him as another siren sounded and waned.

A red ambulance was stopped in the middle of the street, directly in front of the house. The paramedics had arrived. Mike watched as they retrieved their equipment and rushed into the house. There were two of them; one male and one female. They sped past him as he once again pointed to where the body would be found. By now, the shrill sound of sirens piercing the air seemed to be coming from all directions. Though it was just seconds, Mike felt like he had been standing there for an eternity.

The first police officer came back and walked over to Mike while talking to someone through a handheld radio. "We have a DB," he said into the radio. "Need to block off Desert Oasis Drive from Fifty-Fifth." He paused a moment, then replied, "Ten four."

The look on the policeman's face was serious, but gentle, as he looked at Mike. He was just under six feet and looked to be around forty. "I'm Sergeant Jackson. Are you the one who found the body?"

"I did." Mike paused and asked, "He is dead then?"

"Yep. Looks like it. Tell me what happened."

Mike explained to him in detail why he was there and how he discovered the body.

"I'll need some information for the record. Name, address, date of birth and social security number," the cop said as he pulled a small notebook from his upper left pocket and handed it to Mike along with a pen.

Mike wrote the information on the pad and gave it and the pen back to the officer who said, "A homicide detective will be here shortly. He'll want to talk to you and get your statement. So please, don't go anywhere or touch anything."

"Homicide?" Mike asked. The word homicide caught him off guard.

"Routine. Don't be alarmed."

Just then the two paramedics came back up the hallway. The woman said, "The coroner has been called, the wagon is on its way."

All of a sudden Mike's legs felt wobbly. He could hardly stand, and he felt like his heart was pumping air so he went into the living room and sat down on the sofa. The moment he'd felt the priest's pulseless neck, he realized his pastor was dead. But her words seemed to reach out and stab him in the emotional bull's eye. As an insurance investigator, he had dealt with sudden death several times, but this one was too close to home.

As he sat on the sofa, Officer Jackson gave him a stern glare. Mike put his hands out in front of his face, palms out toward the cop and said, "Don't worry, I won't touch anything. I just need to sit down." The officer nodded in assent. Mike loosened his tie and thought, I need to get a message to Julie. But he knew it would have to wait.

He'd been sitting there about ten minutes when a man dressed in blue jeans, tennis shoes, and an Arizona Diamondbacks tee shirt came through the front door. The gold badge that hung over his belt told Mike this was the detective they were waiting for. Not at all like *Law and Order*, he thought as he watched him converse with Sergeant Jackson and then go down the hall to the bedroom.

Then, through the open front door, came two men. One carried a box, and on it was stenciled: Phoenix Crime Unit. The other toted a camera. They proceeded directly down the hall like they knew exactly where they were going.

About five minutes later the detective came back up the hall, and again conversed with the sergeant, who tore off a page from his notebook, handed it to him, and then pointed to Mike.

The detective nodded, walked into the room, extended his right hand and introduced himself. "Lieutenant Nick Greer, Phoenix PD."

"Michael Bradley." He stood up and returned his firm grip.

"You found the body?" He was direct, a quality Mike liked.

"I did."

The cop sat on the sofa and motioned for Mike to join him. The detective sat perfectly straight in his seat. His posture, combined with his six-foot-plus lanky frame reminded Mike of Gumby. He appeared to be in his mid- to late-thirties. His bushy mustache and close-cut beard seemed to bring attention to his thinning hairline. His brown eyes had a seriousness, but also a gentleness about them.

"Tell me what happened," he said as he produced a small tape recorder. Pushing a red button, he placed the black recorder on the sofa between them.

What happened to notepads? Mike thought.

The detective listened intently as Bradley repeated the events that led to his finding the body. Once he was sure Mike was completely finished, he asked, "Did you touch anything?"

"The arcadia door, interior doors, and maybe some of the furniture. I may have touched the dining room table. After I found the body . . . oh . . . I checked his neck to feel for a pulse. I don't know if I touched anything in the room. I was a little . . ." Mike paused. It was then that he saw the blood on his index and middle finger.

"That's okay, please continue," the detective said.

Holding up his handkerchief, he said, "When I realized he was dead, I used the phone to call you guys, but I used this."

The lieutenant nodded again. "Do you know any reason why Father . . ." He paused a moment as he reached into his pocket for the notepaper.

"Mignanelli." Mike said. "Father David Mignanelli. He's . . . was our pastor."

He continued questioning. "Do you know any reason why he would want to kill himself?"

"Not a clue," Mike shrugged. "Unless . . ."

Seriousness encaptured the detective's face. "Unless what?"

"I don't know, maybe the audit was too much for him, but I wouldn't think . . . nah." Bradley shook his head.

"Audit?"

"He was being investigated by the diocese. They were looking into how he managed funds, I guess."

"Hmmm," the lieutenant said as he stroked his hairy chin. "So, he was worried about an audit?"

"Didn't seem to be," Bradley replied. "Worried about it, that is."

The detective looked down the hall, then back at Mike, picked up the tape recorder and shut it off. "That's all I need for now." He stood and again extended his hand. As Mike shook it, the detective said in a tone of dismissal, "Thank you, Mr. Bradley. If I have any more questions, I'll call you."

Mike headed for the door and was almost through it when he heard the voice again. "Mr. Bradley."

He stopped and turned around. "Yes?"

The detective walked toward Mike. "Would you happen to know if the deceased was left or right handed?"

The deceased! Mike didn't care for the cop's impersonal description, and it showed in the tone of his voice as he answered, "I don't know."

"Thank you, sir. I'll call you if I need anything else." The response was emotionless.

* * *

Mike stepped outside and was startled by the large crowd of people that had formed.

Yellow tape with black letters—Police Line Do Not Cross—was strung around the entire perimeter of the property. He counted eight police cars, all parked in various places in the street. There were smoke and flames from the red flares on the street where it met Fifty-Fifth Avenue, a busy street on which cars sped up and down regularly. However, as one would expect, just about all of the cars slowed down to see what was happening, as curiosity did its duty.

The immensity of the crowd gave evidence that the service was now over. It seemed there were more people here than had been in the church.

News travels fast, Mike thought as he bent down and maneuvered his way under the yellow tape. He looked at his watch. Wow, he'd been here over two hours.

He kept hearing his name called. It seemed to come from all directions followed by: "What's happened? What's going on?" Finally he lifted his right hand to his head, pointed his index finger against his right temple, and jerked his thumb forward. Then, for added emphasis, he stuck his tongue out and let it hang over the left side of his mouth. The groans from the crowd told him they understood the gesture.

Through all the noise, he could hear his wife's voice. His eyes scanned the crowd and quickly found her. They rushed together and embraced.

"I thought something happened to you. You all right?" Julie asked. The redness in her eyes gave evidence that his wife had been crying.

"I'm okay, I guess. At least I'm a lot better than Father David."

A large van with a satellite link on its roof sat in the parking lot. From it, a reporter with a microphone in her hand rushed toward them. Behind her a man in blue jeans lugging a huge camera on his shoulder tried to keep pace.

"Sir, can you tell us what happened?" She almost attacked him as she tried to push the black microphone in Mike's face.

Seeing the distress on his wife's face, Mike grabbed her hand and said, "Let's get out of here." They hurried across the church parking lot to where Julie's car was parked. They were thankful the crowd was dense enough that the reporter couldn't follow. The Bradleys were glad to get away even though they could still hear her calling.

They were halfway across the lot when he caught sight of two priests getting out of a white Sedan. Mike immediately recognized one of them as a diocesan official he had met with a couple of weeks ago. That meeting led to the current investigation of Father David's activities.

"They sure got here quick."

"Who?"

"Those priests." Holding tightly onto Julie's hand, Mike motioned with his head. "Over there. They're from the diocese. The taller one is the bishop's numero uno. I don't know who the other one is."

They crossed the parking lot and Julie aimed her clicker at her car. As the doors unlocked, Mike slid into the passenger seat and said, "I'll pick up my car in the morning. I don't feel like driving. I just wanna go home."

"You okay?" He could hear the loving concern in her voice.

"I guess so," he said as the car's engine came to life. "Considering that it isn't every day I find my pastor with his brains blown out."

"Yuuuk," she groaned. "Did you have to put it that way? What happened, anyway?" She put the car in reverse and began backing from the parking spot.

"It looks like the bastard shot himself," Mike replied as the car began its forward movement.

"Oh God!" she exclaimed. "Was it the audit? God, I hope not."

"Who knows?"

"Did he leave a note?"

"Looks like it," he answered as she turned left onto Fifty-Fifth Avenue. "I accidentally bumped his mouse and the screen came alive. It said, 'I'm sorry.' He, or someone typed it."

Delicately, almost like she feared the answer, Julie asked, "What do you mean, or someone?"

"I don't know. I'm probably wrong, but . . ." He paused for a moment. "Something . . . something just doesn't seem right."

"Like what?"

"Well, you know what he is . . . or was like. As dictatorial and self-centered as he was, I . . . well, I guess I'm just a little shocked that he would kill himself. He's . . . was . . . so arrogant that . . . I don't know. I just can't see him quitting. He's not the type."

The remaining ride home was silent.

CHAPTER 2

Nick Greer walked back to the bedroom where the body was still slumped over the desk. The crime team was hard at work taking samples, measuring, and going about their routine. He always marveled at how they worked together like a finely tuned machine. Cameras would flash periodically as pictures were taken of the body and its surroundings. Little yellow, tent-shaped plastic cards with black numbers were scattered throughout the room, every angle accounted for. Nothing would be missed.

Nick had been on the Phoenix police force for twelve years. With a master's degree in criminology from Arizona State University, the FBI had offered him a position as a field agent upon graduation. Knowing life with that organization would involve many transfers, and none of them were likely to be here in Phoenix, he declined. Though a life with the FBI could take him to many places, his roots were here, and here he would stay. The thirty-six-year-old father of three had grown up in south Phoenix, and knew the turf as well as anyone ever could. Seven months ago he made lieutenant, a well-deserved promotion.

Roy Loomis had finished dusting for prints and was putting his brush away when he saw the detective standing to the right of the doorway with his arms folded, staring intensely at the laptop screen. The inquisitive look on his face aroused the CSI's curiosity.

"Something wrong there, Nick?" Roy asked as he closed his case and stood erect.

Roy was African American, about five-ten, with broad shoulders. He looked younger than his forty-seven years. His skin was smooth, without a wrinkle. If it weren't for the spots of gray on both temples, he could have easily passed for a man in his early thirties. He and Nick had been friends for several years. They had worked on numerous cases together. Both admired and respected the abilities of the other.

The detective continued to stare for a minute, then spoke, "Strange, mighty strange."

"What, Nick? What's so strange?" Roy asked.

"Look at his arms. It looks like he was hugging the computer."

"Okay, so?" Roy looked puzzled.

"Not natural." Nick pointed to the corpse as he stepped closer to it. "If he shot himself and fell forward, I could understand his right hand maybe ending up here." He pointed to the subject's right hand. "But his left hand the same way? With the gun still in it? Doesn't it seem strange to you? Not natural?"

"Possible," Roy replied. "Death didn't have to be instantaneous. A couple of seconds could make the difference, you know."

"Yeah . . . possible . . . yeah, maybe you're right. I guess it's okay." The detective stroked his chin, noting that nothing else seemed to have been touched, and there were no signs of forced entry or robbery. "Who would kill a priest anyway," he said. "Guess he was under some sort of scrutiny from the diocese. Maybe it was too much for him."

"Looks like a clean-cut case of suicide to me," Roy stated. "Seen 'nough of 'em to tell. Gonna finish up here and head back. These double shifts are murder." He looked up at the tall man and grinned. "Oops! I should know better than to use the M word around you."

Nick laughed and was about to comment when Sgt. Jackson walked in. "Excuse me, Detective."

"It's Lieutenant, what's up?"

"There are two priests outside. They say they're from the diocese of Phoenix, and they insist on speaking to the person in charge. That be you!"

"Tell them I'll be right out," he directed. "Go ahead and let them in, but make sure they don't touch anything. I'm not sure if they're done in there yet."

"Yes, sir," the sergeant agreed.

Roy walked over to the desk, picked up a plastic bag, and handed it to Nick. Inside the bag was the gun that had been in the priest's hand. It was covered with blood. The PPD sticker with Roy's initials next to the time and date were properly placed over the seal. Nick held the bag by the corner and looked at its contents. A .38 calibre Smith & Wesson. "You find any bull—?" He stopped himself in midsentence as Roy held up a smaller bag, also sealed with a PPD sticker. Nick could see that it held a small piece of lead.

"From the wall," Roy said as he pointed to a hole about halfway up the west wall of the room. "Went right through him!"

"Good job, Roy, as usual. Find anything out of the ordinary?" Nick asked.

"Naw, just the usual stuff for a scene like this. You know, normal shit. Blood, powder burns, entry, exit, note."

"What note?"

"Wrote it on the laptop. The 'puter was in hibernation, but when we turned it back on there it was, plain as can be. Said, I'M SORRY, big capital letters. I printed it out, see?" Roy held up a clear bag with the printed paper in it for his friend to see.

Loomis paused for a moment, grinned and said, "Looks like modern technology has even taken over suicides. RETURN . . . BANG . . . ESCAPE." Roy grinned wider. "A bit of computer humor there, don't ya know?"

"Funny, Roy, funny." Nick chuckled. "Sounds like you've been working too hard. By the way, if you decide to quit, don't try comedy." They both laughed.

"You about finished?" Nick asked.

"Yeah, think so."

"You got an extra pair of gloves? I might want to snoop around some more."

Roy unsnapped the metal latches on his case, reached in, and retrieved a pair of surgical gloves. He handed them to the detective. "Have at it, Sherlock. I'm outta here."

"Later!" Nick said over his shoulder as he walked over to the desk. He slid one of the tight-fitting gloves over his right hand, bent his lanky frame over the blood-stained desk, and carefully pressed the key marked: print screen. After a short delay, he heard the printer come alive as it answered the command. With his left hand, he carefully took the paper from the blood-splattered printer, folded it two times, and deposited it in his left rear pocket just as Sgt. Jackson came into the room.

"I'm sorry, Lieutenant," the man in blue said apologetically. "But those two priests are still waiting for you. I told them you were busy, but they insist—"

Greer cut the policeman short. "Okay! Okay! I'm on my way!" He threw his hands up, palms out as if in surrender.

The detective studied the two men as he approached them. The man on the left was about five feet ten, average build, with curly blond hair. He looked to be in his mid-forties. His face showed evidence of lost teenage battles with acne. His companion was about ten years his junior, slightly shorter, and about fifty pounds overweight. His hair was jet black, and contrasted a beard that had signs of early graying. Both were wearing the black and white collars of clergy.

The elder priest extended his hand to Nick. "Father Mike Kubic, Diocese of Phoenix." Nodding to the man on his left, he said, "Father John Frank, my associate."

Nick shook hands with the elder priest and then with the younger one. "Lieutenant Nick Greer, *City* of Phoenix." The emphasis he put on the word city appeared to go unnoticed. "What can I do for you gentlemen?"

The eldest one answered, "Can you tell us what's going on here?"

"The occupant of this house was found dead a couple of hours ago. I'm sorry," Nick said.

"May we see him?" Father Kubic asked.

"I'm not supposed . . ." He looked at the priest's face. Something told him it was all right.

"Oh, I guess it'll be okay." He nodded toward the room where the body rested. "I must ask you not to touch anything." The elder man nodded. "And let me warn you, Fathers, it's not a pretty sight in there."

Nick was surprised by the nonchalant mannerism of the older one. He thought it must be due to the large number of dead people these priests must have experienced in their lives.

"It's okay, we can handle it," Kubic said.

As they started down the hallway, Nick saw Roy Loomis and his crew coming toward him.

"We're done here," Roy said to Nick. "It's all yours. The wagon's on its way." Then he spied the two priests behind Nick and said in a slightly embarrassed tone, "Oops, sorry, Fathers."

The younger priest spoke for the first time, "It's all right." His voice was soft and pleasant.

Roy stepped around them and headed for the door. The trio continued to their destination.

Nick entered the room ahead of the two priests. "In here," he said, then stepped to the right. "Please remember not to touch anything. I'm not completely finished in here yet."

Both priests stopped. The elder one covered his mouth with his right hand. It looked like he was going to be sick; however, he breathed in deeply and quickly composed himself. He then walked over to the body, reached into the left pocket of his coat, and extracted a purple stole. Father Kubic reverently kissed the stole, placed it around his neck, crossed himself and began praying.

Nick studied Father Frank. He stood rigidly still, his face expressionless. He was surprised by the young priest's lack of emotion. This was one of their own, for Christ's sake! He also wondered how they had arrived so soon. Someone must have called them. Someone from the church. Looking to the younger one, he asked, "How did you guys get here so soon?"

"We came as soon as we got the call," he whispered, so as not to disturb his counterpart.

Nick asked, "Where did the call come from?"

The volume of his voice increased as he replied defensively, "We were called by the bishop. I guess someone called there."

Just then the elder priest looked up. The stern look on his face showed his irritation at their conversing during his prayer. He removed his stole, again kissed it, and returned it to his pocket, then looked at the detective. "When can we have the remains?"

"I don't know exactly. Probably a few days. The coroner's pretty backed up."

"Coroner? What's the coroner got to do with it?" Father Kubic asked.

"There's the autopsy and—"

The younger priest interrupted, "Autopsy? Why an autopsy? It's obviously a suicide!"

"Procedure. Normal procedure," the detective said defensively, mentally noting the emotion of the young cleric.

"Please excuse my associate, Lieutenant," the elder priest interjected. "It's just that we must send his body back to his family in Pennsylvania and would like to start the arrangements as soon as possible. I'm sure you understand."

"I understand your concern, Father; however, it's the coroner's call. You should have an answer in a few days, but it could take longer." Nick looked at the younger priest, then back to the elder before continuing, "You must talk to the coroner's office. I have no control there."

"Thank you, Lieutenant," said Kubic. "I'll do just that." As if on cue both priests turned, left the room, walked down the hallway, and exited the house through the front door. The detective stood and watched them as they left.

Nick decided to walk through the house. He went into the room and stood still for a few moments looking around and scanning it up and down with his eyes. Nothing seemed out of the ordinary. However, one of the first things this detective had learned was that "ordinary" could have many sides and meanings. What seemed ordinary in one situation could become the exact opposite in another. Nick considered ordinary the "fifth dimension" of criminology.

Other than the room with the dead body, the house was immaculate. Everything seemed to be in order except for the lone bottle of scotch on the dining room table. Chivas Regal. The man had taste, he thought.

He went into the kitchen. It, too, was tidy and clean. A coffee pot sat on the counter. The green light told him that it was still on. As he reached to shut it off, his eyes caught a small glass that had been partially obscured by the pot. It was about half full of a light brown liquid. He bent over the counter, and with his nose about an inch from the glass, he sniffed. Scotch. Probably from the bottle on the table, he thought.

The detective rushed out the front door and into the street. Most of the crowd had dispersed, except for a few curiosity seekers. Even the news crews were gone. The forensics van was just beginning to back from the space it occupied, so the detective called loudly, "Roy! Wait! Hold up a sec."

The van stopped. Nick watched the electric window lower and saw Roy Loomis peer out. The disturbance was evident on his face as he responded, "Whaaat?"

"Got something I want you to look at."

"What now?"

"I found a half-drunk glass of booze. I want you to check it out. Probably nothing, but you know me."

Roy smiled. "Yeah, I do. I know you can be a pain in the ass, too."

"You wouldn't have it any other way," Nick retorted.

The two men went back into the house. Nick watched as his friend prepared the glass and its contents for transport. "You might want to take that one, too." Nick pointed to the bottle that still sat on the dining table. "It should be the same stuff."

"Anything else?" Roy queried.

"Naw, that looks like it," Nick answered. "By the way, those two priests asked if you could expedite this one. They said something about shipping the body back east."

"Everybody wants it now," Loomis chided. "Roy, I need the tox report . . . now! Roy, I need the PM report . . . now! Roy, I need to wipe my ass . . . now!" He grinned. The detective laughed.

"Call me Monday morning," he said as he left the house. "Till then, leave me the hell alone!"

As Nick followed him out to the front yard he stopped, took a deep breath, held it in his lungs, and slowly exhaled. He looked at his watch: 8:02. Back to the station. Write a report. Make copies. That was the part he really hated. The events of the evening passed through his mind like a race car. Report . . . apparent suicide . . . priest . . . but something wasn't quite right. Something seemed a bit odd—but what?

CHAPTER 3

Julie pulled into the garage and parked the Prius in its usual resting place. They got out of the car, and the garage door emitted its normal grinding sound as it lowered to a stop behind them.

Julie followed close behind as her husband retrieved his key, unlocked the door that led from the garage into the house, and punched in the alarm code. Julie switched on the light and headed straight for the phone. She pressed the speaker button, and a loud fluttering dial tone alerted her that there were messages. Upon hearing the dial tone, Mike said, "Hurry! I gotta call the hospital. Mom is back in again."

She hung up the phone immediately and turned to her husband. "What happened? Her heart again?"

"Don't know. She had a spell, whatever that means." He was beginning to think that was some deep medical terminology for "whatever." "Aunt Teresa called just as I was going out the door. That's why I was so late."

"Hmm, wondered why you didn't come up before Mass." Julie had to be at the church about an hour early for choir practice. Usually the couple went together, but today a work project had held Mike up.

Sitting down at his desk, he pushed the on button and heard the laptop come to life. He pulled his chair closer to the desk just as Google came alive on the screen. Mike typed US AIR and called out to his wife, "Any new messages I'd want to know about?"

"Six calls. All about Father David."

She came up behind him and looked at the screen as the schedule popped up. Julie pointed to the 3:30 red eye. "Book it. I'll drive you."

"Three thirty a.m.? That's in the morning! Even God ain't up yet."

"But the pilots are, and you can sleep on the plane. When do you wanna come back?"

"Leave it open. Depends on how she is. Probably Tuesday, or maybe Wednesday. I'll call Doug and tell him what happened. He'll understand."

Doug Reeves and Mike Bradley were partners. They had opened their office together a little over five years ago. Arizona Insurance Investigators was doing well. They had contracts with several insurance companies. Mike's caseload was heavy, but it could all wait until his return. Doug would handle it.

Mike's mother had been in the hospital several times in the last few months. Enough that the phone number was committed to his memory. A female voice on the other end answered.

"Beaver County Medical Center."

Mike checked his watch. It was 9:47 in Pennsylvania. "I'm calling long distance from Arizona. I know it's late, but could you ring Mrs. Bradley's room, please? Marie Bradley. I'm her son, and I'm calling from Arizona," he reminded her.

"Room three ten, bed one," the pleasant voice said. "I'll ring it for you."

The phone rang, then rang again, and again. Finally, as he was about to hang up, he heard the sound of the phone being picked up. It sounded like it was dropped so he waited.

A frail voice said, "Haaalo." It was his mother's voice and her recognizable haaalo.

"Hi, Mom. What happened?'

"Hi, honey. I had another spell." Her voice was weak, and she spoke at a slower pace than normal.

"What do the doctors say happened to you, Mom?"

"I had a heart attack."

"How come you're not in intensive care?"

"I'm in the cardiac unit," she answered.

"But you should be . . . never mind. I made plane reservations. I'll be there tomorrow."

"You don't need to. I'll be all—"

"It's a done deal," he interrupted. "It's already on my credit card. I'll see you tomorrow."

"Okay. I'll be glad to see you. Bye." Then came the buzz of the dial tone as they were disconnected.

"I'm going to take a shower," he told Julie as he left for the bedroom.

The warm water felt relieving as it cascaded over his face. As his eyes cleared, he noticed there was blood on his fingers. Hope the bastard didn't have AIDS, he thought.

The rumors circulating throughout the parish about his pastor's lifestyle were what caused that unwelcomed thought to invade his mind. He felt guilty for feeling as he did; after all, this was a priest, but it was rumored that he and another pastor from across town were lovers. Mike didn't know if it was true or not and preferred not to believe it, even though the evidence had become more convincing as his affairs were being investigated.

Growing up in the Catholic Church taught him to put priests on a pedestal and to view them as kind, holy, righteous, and incapable of doing wrong. Mike struggled with his feelings. He felt Father David Mignanelli exemplified everything he thought a priest should not be. He viewed this priest as a hypocrite. These feelings fostered guilt in him for harboring such emotions for an ordained Catholic priest; however, these feelings were for the man only. He still respected the collar his pastor wore. He just didn't like the fact that he wore it.

As he toweled off, the events of the past few hours raced through his mind. Still picturing the lifeless body slumped over that desk and remembering how his arms were spread around the laptop, like he was hugging it, bothered him. Strange, he thought, strange.

Julie was already in bed. "I set the alarm for twelve thirty," she said. He crawled in next to her . . . wondering.

CHAPTER 4

Traces of gray ash left from burned out flares were all that remained from last night's incident as Lieutenant Greer turned onto Desert Oasis Drive. He brought the car to a stop directly in front of the house. A lone police car was parked across the street. He held his badge next to his face as he walked over to the cruiser. The patrolman nodded and rolled down his window as the detective approached. "Anybody been snooping around?"

The uniformed officer answered, "No, sir. Just some drivers by. Slowed down to look, but when they saw the car"—he reached out and tapped the Phoenix bird on the door—"they just kept on a goin'. Looky loos; ya know how they are."

"That's why you're here. You need a break?"

"Could use some coffee and maybe a restroom break," the policeman replied.

"Go ahead. I'll probably be here an hour or so."

"Don't mind if I do. You want me to bring you back something?"

"Naw, I'll be fine. Just don't be over an hour." He saw the smile on the young man's face as he raised the window and started the engine. He remembered his rookie year on the force and how he had hated this type of boring duty.

As the car rolled forward, Nick started toward the house. He followed the sidewalk to the front door, entered through the unlocked door, turned left, and proceeded down the hallway.

The air was stale, and he caught the smell of dried blood as he neared the room where the body had been the night before. He stood at the entrance of the room and looked around.

His head moved from side to side as he surveyed the scene.

It always seemed so much different after the body was removed. There was something eerie about a room, or a sidewalk, or an alley, or as in one case, a roof where a body had lain only a few hours before. That's one part of the job he felt he would never get used to. His eyes continued to scan the room, traveling up the west wall, across the ceiling, down the east wall and back to where the body had been. Nothing unusual here, he thought.

He pulled a pair of rubber gloves from his right rear pocket, slipped them over both hands, then walked to the blood-stained desk. A file drawer with a key in it was partially open. He scanned the labels on the files. As he searched through them, he found various types of correspondence, along with the cleric's personal checking statements. Finding nothing out of the ordinary, he closed the drawer and slid open the one directly above it. It contained various office items including a stapler, pens, and pencils. He closed the drawer, then opened the top drawer. It exhibited only his personal stationery and envelopes. The man was organized, Mike thought as he removed a sheet of stationery from the drawer. David R. Mignanelli, PC, was perfectly centered across the top. "How strange," he said out loud. "What happened to Reverend, or Father? Why PC?" He folded the paper, stowed it in his left rear pocket and closed the drawer. He tried to open the flat center drawer, but it wouldn't budge. Locked! He reached back down to the file drawer and retrieved the key. He slid it into the lock, turned it clockwise, and felt it turn. He opened the drawer and saw that it contained more pens, pencils, and blank notepads. To the right he saw a brown book. He picked it up and read the label: Professional Appointments. He opened it to yesterday's date. A diagonal line written in pencil had been drawn from 4:00 to 7:00. Along the line was written, Mass. Turning the page revealed the same type of line ran from 7:00 a.m. to 1:00 p.m. It also said Mass. He continued to thumb through the book finding that there were many entries. Some were full names, some were first names, and some were just initials. There also were several other places where the same type of diagonal line was drawn, but no notations were made. Some covered several hours, and some as little as a half hour. Strange, Nick thought. Deciding to take the book with him, he fished the letterhead paper from his back pocket and inserted it in the book.

He moved into the next room, which was obviously the dead priest's bedroom. It, too, was lavishly furnished and tidy. An oak entertainment center surrounding a plasma TV, a DVD, and a stereo system sat at one end of the room, opposite the bed. To the left, a four-drawer oak chest sat along the wall. He decided he would start there.

He began with the top drawer. It contained about twenty pairs of socks, neatly folded in half, not rolled inside each other as he would expect them to be. They were mostly black, with a couple pairs of white ones. The other side of the drawer contained about twenty white handkerchiefs and several of the little white collar tabs that clerics wear. Nick thought how they reminded him of little white tongue depressors. He closed the drawer and opened the one below it, finding only boxer shorts and tee shirts, all neatly folded, and each isolated to its own side of the drawer. Closing the drawer, he slid open the next one, finding only polo shirts in assorted colors. The bottom drawer netted three pair of blue jeans and two belts. He wondered why he was even doing this as he closed the drawer, uttering, "Nothing here."

He walked around the bed to the closet on the opposite wall. Opening one of the two sliding doors, Nick was again impressed by the neatness. Priestly black, brown, and blue shirts, along with several pairs of trousers, black, brown, and gray, hung like sentries from the long pole that spanned the length of the closet. Several pairs of shoes were lined up perfectly on the floor.

Seeing that the shelf above him supported several boxes, Nick retrieved each one and rummaged through it. He found pictures, letters, and what appeared to be normal memorabilia. "Nothing here," he again said out loud.

All that was left was a nightstand next to the bed. The top drawer wouldn't open. Must be stuck, he thought. Seeing a lock on it, he reached into the left front pocket of his jeans and retrieved a small pocketknife with which he quickly and skillfully opened the lock.

He stared for a moment, shocked by what he saw. He squinted his eyes in disbelief, then opened them again. Still there! Condoms!

He counted them. Four! "What the fuck is a priest doing with condoms? So much for celibacy," he remarked aloud as he closed the drawer.

His search of the rest of the interior rooms, including the living room, netted nothing out of the ordinary. He had the feeling he was missing something, but what?

The garage was next. He entered through the door that connected the kitchen to the garage. The smell of new rubber filled the enclosure. He stood still for a moment as he saw a new, sparkling, bright red Ford Mustang convertible. Seeing that the temporary tag was on the rear of the vehicle, he thought, A man doesn't buy a new car and then kill himself, not normally.

The top was down and the white seats stood tall against the crimson exterior. He thought, The priest business must be better than I thought. What happened to that poverty, chastity, and obedience stuff?

Deciding to start with the glove box, he opened it, and began removing its contents. Insurance card, owner's manual, map, handcuffs . . . handcuffs? And two more packs of condoms!

Returning the contents, Greer closed the glove box. He went around and opened the driver's door, reached down and pulled the trunk button. Going to the back of the car, he lifted the trunk lid. It was empty. He even lifted the mat, exposing the spare tire. Shrugging his lean shoulders, he closed the trunk. He'd had enough for today.

He returned to the kitchen the same way he had left it and went out the front door. The police car had returned and had assumed its same place as a sentry across the street. Nick shut the door behind him and waved at the patrolman as he headed for his own vehicle. He would wait until tomorrow to see what the coroner's people had to say, but something wasn't kosher.

Priest . . . condoms . . . computer . . . appointment book . . . handcuffs. What was this guy into?

What am I missing? he wondered.

CHAPTER 5

Mike Bradley pulled the rental car into the lot of the medical center, found an empty spot, parked, and walked about one hundred fifty feet to the entrance. Large gray letters above the door read: Beaver County Medical Center. The automatic doors slid open and he went through them, passed the information desk, then quickened his pace across the lobby floor to a set of elevators. He pushed the up button, and the door responded immediately. Entering the small cavern, he turned and pushed the button marked 3. Alone in the elevator, he felt the carrier rise and then slow to a stop. He wondered why it seemed to him as though the elevator went up past its destination and then came back down and if other people felt that way, too. The doors opened, and his eyes caught a sign on the tiled wall in front of him. An arrow pointing to the right below the words Cardiac Unit told him he was where he wanted to be. Following the hallway, he saw another sign that read, 301-320, with the arrow pointing to the right. Following the hallway, he came upon her room. A small plastic name holder to the left of the door read: Bradley, Marie.

She was lying in the bed asleep with a clear tube carrying life-giving oxygen running from around her ears to her nose. Her snow-white hair was brushed back against her pillow. It looked as though it had been brushed without lifting her head. It had been three months since Mike had seen his mother. She looked so frail lying there.

Being the only child, he knew it would be up to him to handle things. Her sister, Teresa, tried to help her, but she was in her eighties and couldn't do a lot. Marie would be ninety-one this year if she made it to her birthday, which was still several months away.

Her bed was on the windowed side of the room. Mike saw a large, green reclining chair nestled against the wall directly across from the foot of her bed. Its vinyl exterior squeaked as he sat in it. He would wait there for her to awaken.

About twenty minutes later, she opened her eyes. "Hello there," Mike said as he rose from the chair and went over to her. He bent down and kissed her on the forehead. "How ya feelin', Mom?"

She answered weakly, "Not so good. I had a heart attack. I think I'm going to die."

"Nonsense, you'll be fine. Besides, I'm not ready to be an orphan yet." A faint trace of a smile attempted to make its way to the corners of her wrinkled mouth.

"When does Dr. Olson come in?"

Seeing that she was trying to sit up, he pushed the button on her bed and raised her up a little. He heard the laboring sound of the motor as her upper body began to rise.

"That's enough," she said. He took his finger off the button. "The doctor just left. Didn't you see him?"

"No, Mom. I just got here about a half hour ago."

"What time is it?"

He checked his watch, then the clock above her bed. "It's five to seven."

She looked confused as she spoke, "I must have slept longer than I thought. He was here around four o'clock."

"What did he say?"

"He said I had a heart attack. The paramedics brought me here."

Mike didn't understand. If it really was a heart attack, why wasn't she in ICU? He would speak with her doctor tomorrow. Holding her hand, they talked for a while, mostly about family, friends, and memories until she dozed off. A few minutes later, a soft voice come through the speaker system, announcing that visiting hours were over.

Reaching into the cabinet beside her bed, Mike found her purse and removed her keys. He would need them to get into her apartment, where he would be staying. He lowered the bed. She was sleeping so soundly that even the movement and the noise didn't wake her. He kissed her on the cheek and said, "See ya in the morning."

He drove the rented Dodge up the steep grade that led to the parking lot outside of the three-story apartment building and parked in one of the empty spaces. It was a short distance to the double steel-framed doors at the entry. Pulling one of them open, he began to ascend the stairs. He never understood why the owners refused to install an elevator. What was once an old schoolhouse, had been converted into apartments for low income, mostly elderly. Marie Bradley had been the first resident in the building, something she liked to brag about. Perhaps that was the reason why he was never able to convince her to move to Arizona with him and Julie.

He reached the top of the stairs and walked directly to her apartment, unlocked the door, and went in. A walnut table sat to the left of the entry. Mike set his bag on it and stood there for a moment while his eyes scanned the room. Nothing had changed since his last visit. The room was spacious with a flowered sofa against the wall to the right. Both it and the matching chair that sat on an angle next to it had seen better days. He reminded himself to buy her new ones when she came home from the hospital. Across the room, a small table supporting a lamp and a telephone sat between two blue stuffed chairs. The four large windows that lined the wall behind the television still offered a breathtaking view of where the Beaver River flowed into the Ohio. It brought back childhood memories of summer regattas and Fourth of July fireworks shot into the night sky from barges on the river. There was a single bedroom and a bath off to the left and behind the table was a tiny but serviceable kitchen.

Sitting in one of the blue chairs, Mike reached over to the table beside it and pulled his cell phone from the case on his belt. Pushing speed dial one, he waited.

"Hello." It was Julie's voice.

"Hey. I made it."

"It's about time you called. I was worried."

"I'm sorry. The plane was fifty minutes late, and by the time I got to the rental car place they were almost closed. I went straight to the hospital. I just got back to the apartment."

"How is your mom?"

"She doesn't look good. Looks worn out. I'll see the doctor tomorrow. Should know more then."

"You okay?"

"Yeah, I'm okay. I just don't like seeing her that way. She was always so strong, and now it seems like if you touch her she'll crumble. I don't think she's going to make it this time."

Purposely changing the subject, he asked, "Are the kids okay?"

They had four daughters. Three were married and one was still at home.

"Guess so," she said.

"Okay, I'm gonna go get something to eat. The food on the plane was gross. Think I'll go to the Hot Dog Shoppe."

"Jerk!"

Mike laughed. They had moved to Phoenix in the early seventies, and one of the things they both missed about Beaver County, Pennsylvania, was that they could boast of the best chili dogs this side of the Mississippi at the Brighton Hot Dog Shoppe. Julie missed them as much as he did.

"Eat your heart out," she said.

"I'll think about you with each bite."

"Thanks!"

"You're welcome, I'm sure. Call ya tomorrow. Love you."

"I love you, too."

Returning the phone to its cradle, Mike followed his appetite to the Hot Dog Shoppe.

CHAPTER 6

The sign stenciled across the double doors read: Authorized Personnel Only.

It was 10:30 Monday morning when Nick pushed them open and went in. The smell caught his immediate attention. After all his years as a cop, the odor still made him uncomfortable. It smelled like a mixture of formaldehyde, ether, and stale beer. His friend Jack once told him, "It smells like a morgue."

Jack Konesky was the chief medical examiner. He had been there long before Nick joined the force. It was Jack who had been the examiner on his first case as a detective. Nick knew him to be a thorough and well-respected examiner. There was a rumor circulating that the county was trying to force him into retirement, a proposition he had no intention of accepting.

As the detective came in, he looked to the small desk that sat to the right of the entrance. As usual it was covered with papers and files. However today, sitting behind it was a young lady of Asian descent. He had never seen her before.

As he was about to pass the desk, the young lady looked up, cleared her throat, and said sternly, "Excuse me, sir. Can I help you with something?"

"Where's Jack?" Nick asked.

"Dr. Konesky is busy at the moment," she replied in a protective manner. As she stood up, she betrayed his location by looking to her left at room three. "Can I help you with something?"

"Nope," Nick said as he started toward the room where he knew Jack was working. By now she had moved out from behind the desk and stepped in front of her intruder.

She looked at him and said, "Excuse me, sir, authorized personnel only." She pointed to the sign on the door.

Nick looked at the backward red letters that barely showed through the frosted glass door.

"You can't go in there," she stated authoritatively.

Gutsy, he thought, as he reached his right hand into his rear pocket. "You must be new here, Miss . . . Miss . . ." Reaching his left hand across to the area above her breast pocket, he brushed her long, soft, black hair away from the identification tag that it obscured. He looked closely at the tag, squinted, and read aloud. "Sue . . . Kim."

He paused a moment, nodded his head in confidence, raised his right hand, and dangled his gold shield in front of her face and smiled. "This says I can!"

Not giving her a chance to react, he immediately turned and went into the room where he saw Jack with his back to him bent over a cadaver. Nick recognized the corpse from Saturday.

"How's he coming?" Greer asked.

"He's not. He's dead," came the answer from the man dressed in hospital green. "His coming days are over." He never looked up as he kept working.

Nick grinned. "Of course, he's dead. Isn't that required to earn your services?"

"Normally," the examiner answered, still concentrating on the task at hand. "Sometimes they say they're not, but by the time I get done with them, they're goners for sure."

Nick laughed. "You must really have been born for this job. You're the only guy I know who can find humor in a corpse."

"If I didn't," Jack replied, "I'd probably end up like this one, with a hole in my head. Heard he was a priest."

"Yup. St. Mike's, north Phoenix."

"They're all over my ass to hurry this one," Jack said. "What's with all the pressure? When I got here at six this morning, the phone was ringing off the wall. The mayor himself. Top priority! Do it now! What's the big hurry? I says. After all, he ain't goin' nowhere, I says. He says the bishop wants the body right away. I told him I did quality, not quantity. He says it's an obvious suicide. I says, who died and made him a medical examiner? It's a suicide when I say it's a suicide. What's he know anyway? He's a goddamn politician. He wouldn't know a suicide from a pastrami sandwich."

The detective laughed. "Well, Jack, which is it?"

"Huh?" The examiner looked up from his work for the first time since the detective came into the room. Nick could see the older man's forehead wrinkle between the protective mask he wore and the matching green cap that covered what had at one time been hair. "What do you mean?"

"Pastrami, or suicide?" Nick questioned. "Is it a pastrami sandwich, or is it suicide?"

"You don't see no bread around him, do ya?" he said with a grin. The corners of Nick's mouth curled up in a smile. "The guy killed himself." The examiner's tone was emphatic. He pointed to the corpse's left temple. "Powder burns . . . entry." He turned the head to expose the other side and pointed to a larger hole. "Exit. In, out." He held up a small plastic bag which held a bullet. Nick recognized it from two nights before. "Thirty-eight," Jack stated as he pointed to the bag that held the bullet. "Fits." The medical examiner rolled the plastic tightly around the bullet. He turned the head again and pretended he was going to stick it in the wound. "It fits. Wanna see?"

Nick shook his head and laughed. "No, I'll take your word that it fits, Jack."

"Ballistics say they match the gun," Konesky added.

"That was quick."

"Guess the mayor called them, too."

"Sounds like the bishop's got more power than us combined," Nick remarked.

"The mayor is Catholic, you know. He and O'Malley are buds. Rumor has it that if it wasn't for the bish, Murphy would still be a councilman." He took the white sheet from the foot of the table and pulled it over the head of the cadaver, covering the body completely. "Ahhh! Another satisfied customer!"

The detective asked, "Powder burns look okay?"

"Sure 'nuff. Paraffin test was positive on the left hand. Blood alcohol showed he had a couple of drinks. Everything else normal. Everything that we got time to do, that is. All consistent with suicide."

"Was he drunk?"

"Nope. Don't think he was even buzzed."

"Did you know about the position of his arms when we found him?"

"Saw the pix. Looked okay to me."

"He looked like he was hugging the computer screen," Nick stated. "You don't think that to be a little odd?"

"He could have collapsed a few seconds after the gun fired. Maybe as much as four or five seconds. The body can do funny things, you know. Ever wring a chicken's neck? There you are, holding its head in your hand and the body is just a floppin' away on the ground."

"So it is suicide?"

"Far as I'm concerned. That's the way it'll go down."

"Okay, you're the pro. Can you fax the report to my office?"

"I'll have the new one do it," Jack said as he nodded toward the young lady who was still at the desk.

"Thanks, Jack." Nick turned for the door. "Have a good one."

Nick heard Jack's voice behind him as he walked away. "I don't get good ones, only dead ones."

CHAPTER 7

Standing on the front porch of his aunt's home, Mike took a deep breath and allowed the fresh spring air to travel through his lungs. As he exhaled, he thought about how long it had been since he had experienced a western Pennsylvania spring and the new life it ushered in. It was now Wednesday afternoon. The funeral service had ended about an hour ago. It was small: mostly family, nieces, nephews, etc. At almost ninety-one, she had outlived most of her friends. Julie was relaxing on a glider. She said, as he joined her, "We should get one of these."

Everyone else was inside, and Mike was glad to be able to finally have a moment without a bunch of people around; not that he didn't like the people, or appreciate them, but he needed some time to relax without the hustle and bustle that had been constant since his mother's death.

Aunt Teresa was a blessing to them. She had a nice meal for the approximately thirty people who had attended the funeral. She was known for putting on nice feeds, as they called it, and loved for people to come to her house to eat. A more gracious hostess, there was not.

Awakened by the phone shortly after three o'clock Sunday morning, Mike had been informed by the hospital that his mother had suffered a massive coronary, and that he should come immediately. Unfortunately, she had passed away just a few minutes before his arrival.

The service was at St. Cecilia Catholic Church, where she had attended since before Mike was born. She was buried alongside his father in their crypt. He had preceded her there by twenty years.

"You okay?" Julie asked as Mike sat down next to her.

"Yeah," he replied as he took a bite of potato salad. "Just thinking about her and all the stuff that's gotta be done." He was not looking forward to the disposal of her property.

Julie picked up the newspaper from the seat next to her and began looking through it. "Her obituary came out nice."

"I haven't seen it. Let's see," he said as she handed him the paper.

"There, see?" Julie pointed to the write-up.

After carefully reading the article, Mike nodded. "Looks good. They even spelled all the names right." He handed the paper back to Julie.

She continued scanning the paper and suddenly shoved it in front of her husband's face, almost causing him to spill his plate. "Look at this!"

"Be careful!" Mike was annoyed, and it showed in his tone.

Julie pointed to the newspaper. "Look at this!" It was farther down and two columns over on the same page: Mignanelli, Reverend David Anthony.

Mike had been so wrapped up in the funeral that he had forgotten their ex-pastor was also from Beaver County. He put his plate on his lap as she handed him the paper.

"Died suddenly," he read the words out loud. "I'll say!" He read on: "Says here he's being buried tomorrow. He's laid out tonight at Frederick's Mortuary in Center Township."

"They got his body here pretty quick," Julie remarked.

"Yeah. Must have been on the red eye, or maybe on the plane with you." His eyes widened as he tried to give her an eerie look holding both hands next to his face and rocking his head and hands back and forth. "Maybe your bags were on top of his coffin in the cargo hold."

"Oh, you're gross!"

"Remember when my dad died while visiting us in Phoenix?" Not giving her a chance to answer, he kept going: "They flew his body back here. You remember? We were on the same plane then."

"Oh yeah, there should be some other way."

"What? UPS? Now there's an idea! I wonder how much would be left by the time it arrived. Can you see the driver trying to wheel a coffin up the sidewalk? What if there was no one there to sign for it? Would he take it next door? What would he say to the person next door? 'I have a package here for your neighbor. Could you see that he gets it? Oh, by the way, it's his grandfather! Sign here, please.' "

"I see you have your warped sense of humor back. I was just saying that . . . oh, never mind. You're impossible."

He smiled impishly at her. "Thank you for noticing. I work hard at it, you know."

She looked at her husband with a gentleness in her voice. "Do you think we should go?"

"Go where?"

"To the funeral home."

"We just came from there, remember? Why the hell would you want to go back?"

"Not that one." The gentleness had changed to irritation. "Frederick's. Father David. It would be nice for his family to see someone from his parish there, don't you think?"

"Why? They might think we liked him."

"Look, I didn't like him anymore than you did. I just thought it would be a nice gesture, that's all. After all . . ."

He caught the tone in her voice, the one that appeared when she was becoming irritated with him, so he took her hand and squeezed it lightly. "I'm only kidding, honey. Of course, we'll go. We'll go tonight."

She smiled. "You know where the funeral home is?"

"We'll find it." He got up from his seat and went inside the house.

Mike thanked Aunt Teresa for all she had done and excused himself and Julie, explaining that they were tired and they needed to make arrangements to dispose of his mother's belongings.

Upon hearing of their grandmother's death, the Bradley girls all wanted to come, but between their jobs, their own kids and airline fares, it was impossible, so only Julie had joined him. Her help would be essential in helping him handle the disposition of his mother's meager belongings.

"You come tonight for dinner?" Aunt Teresa asked.

"Appreciate it," Mike answered, "but we can't. Our pastor in Phoenix died. He's from over in Monaca. We're going to the funeral home there tonight."

"Oh, how nice," she said in that kind and gentle voice of hers. "You'll come tomorrow for lunch then?"

"Okay." He kissed her on the cheek. "Tomorrow. Lunch."

CHAPTER 8

The stairs to the funeral home were covered by a large, blue awning that seemed to be a fixture on all eastern funeral homes. Reaching the top of the stairs, they crossed a large porch to a set of double doors. The one on the right was opened by a middle-aged gentleman dressed in a suit and tie who said to them, "Welcome."

"Mignanelli?" Mike asked.

The attendant pointed at the hallway to his right and said in a soft voice, "Parlor A, the first door on your right."

Julie thanked him and they followed his directions. The door was open and to the right of it was a placard that read: Rev. David A. Mignanelli.

Her eyes caught sight of the guest book lying on a small stand to the right, just outside the door. Nodding toward it, she asked her husband, "Do you want to sign it?"

"Uhhh . . . I guess." He retrieved one of the two ballpoint pens that sat in a groove just above the book.

Julie watched him as he turned the pages. It looked to her like he was searching for something as he kept flipping the pages back and forth. Looking behind her, she was glad to see that no one was waiting for access to the book.

Finally she couldn't take it anymore. "What are you doing? What are you looking for?"

Mike looked into her eyes and summoned up the most innocent look he could. "I'm trying to find the right page."

"What do you mean?" She began to look inquisitively at the book, then looked up at him and pointed to the open page and said, "You can sign right there where all the other names are. See, right here." She pointed to the next unsigned line in the guest book.

"Uh uh." He shook his head in defiance. "No can do."

She looked puzzled. "Why not? What's wrong?"

"See what it says here?" Mike pointed to the italicized letters at the top of the page. "See, it says 'Family and Friends.' We ain't either of those!"

She glared at her husband with a look he knew so well and said in a whisper, "Someone is going to hear you."

"Your point?"

He could tell by the look in her eyes and her now pursed lips, that she was becoming agitated, so he shrugged his shoulders, picked up a pen and signed the book: Mr. and Mrs. Michael Bradley, Phoenix, Arizona.

Reaching for her hand, which she reluctantly took, they walked together into the room and followed an aisle between two rows of soft-seated folding chairs neatly arranged for space and comfort. Their dark gray fabric looked natural against the burgundy carpet upon which they sat. The tinting of the dual-colored walls made the whole room blend together; like the floor, walls, and chairs were all designed for each other. It was a peaceful setting complemented by paintings of children playing, flowing rivers, grassy fields, and snow-capped mountains, each strategically placed along the walls. They walked to the front of the room where their ex-pastor lay.

Numerous bouquets surrounded the copper-colored casket. The metal stand to the right that held Mass cards was completely full and overflowing. How ironic, Mike thought. He'd said so many Masses for the dead, now he's on the receiving end.

Mike leaned over and whispered in Julie's ear, "Whatever you do, do not say anything about me finding the body."

Julie nodded in agreement.

A lone picture sat on the top of the casket. It was a recent picture of him in his clerical collar. Completely surrounding it was a beautiful arrangement of red American Beauty roses. The golden paper ribbon that ran diagonally across it read: Loving Brother.

A sense of sadness come over Mike. Even though he didn't care much for the man, he was still a person who had loved and was loved. It was time to let go of the past.

Julie whispered, "Why is it closed?"

"There's a hole in his head, remember?"

She nodded. "Oh yeah."

Kneeling together they silently prayed, each with their own thoughts. Mike asked the Lord to look upon the good that he had done and to forgive him for any wrongdoings.

As they rose from the kneeler and began their trek toward the exit, they were approached by a man who appeared to be in his fifties. He stood just under six feet and looked to be about a hundred eighty or ninety pounds and sported a dark blue three-piece suit. His full head of wavy, jet-black hair was just beginning to gray. Extending his right hand to Mike and nodding politely to Julie, he said, "Anthony Mignanelli. I'm David's brother."

Through his glasses, Mike could see his red eyes that could only have been the result of tears.

"Mike Bradley." Nodding toward Julie he continued, "My wife, Julie."

"Pleased to meet you," he said graciously as he shook her hand. "Thank you for coming."

"We're from Phoenix," Julie answered before Mike could stop her. "He was our pastor."

"Oh my," Anthony exclaimed as his right hand sprung to cover his mouth in surprise. "You came all the way from Phoenix?"

Before Mike could tell him why they happened to be in town, Anthony turned and called out, "Dominic! Margaret! Come here, quick!" His words were directed toward a sofa to the left side of the room. A man and a woman immediately got up and came toward them. "I want you to meet someone." He continued as they approached, "This is Mr. and Mrs. Bradley. They were our brother's parishioners. They came all the way from Phoenix."

He looked back and forth between Julie and Mike. "This is my brother Dominic and my sister Margaret."

"Pleased to meet you," Mike said. "This is my wife, Julie."

"All the way from Phoenix," said Anthony, again. His chest stuck out like a proud peacock as he spoke the words.

Mike was about to tell him why they were in town, but before he could, Margaret spoke up.

"Thank you so much. We are honored you would come all this way. You must have loved him very much."

Mike looked at his wife. Her brown eyes silently spoke directly into his soul saying, "Don't you dare burst their bubble!"

"You knew our brother?"

Julie said, "Yes, we did, and we're sorry for your loss." Her husband remained silent.

Anthony escorted the couple around the room as he introduced them to several people. He made sure to tell each person that they were from his brother's parish in Phoenix. After all the introductions were over, Mike excused himself and escorted Julie back to the casket.

"I feel like a hypocrite," he stated.

"Shhh. Let them have their moment."

It was then that Mike heard a voice say, "I don't know how he could have done it. Not with his fingers like they were. No way. He couldn't even hold a pencil, let alone pull a trigger on a stupid gun!"

Startled, Mike looked up and saw that the words were spoken by David's sister, Margaret. He was about to dismiss the statement, but he allowed the inquisitive part of him to take control. He left Julie standing alone and walked over to Margaret. "Excuse me, ma'am. Could I speak with you a moment?"

Surprise captured her face and her voice as she answered, "Sure."

"Privately?"

She looked at the lady she had been talking with and excused herself as Mike's eyes scanned the room for a private spot. Seeing an empty sofa at the rear of the room and no one near it, he led her there and began the conversation, one he would never forget.

"Pardon me, I wasn't eavesdropping, but I couldn't help overhearing your conversation and what you said about your brother's fingers. What was wrong with them, if I may ask?"

She looked embarrassed, but answered as if it were common knowledge. "His arthritis!"

Puzzled by her statement, he questioned, "I don't understand?"

"Since you're from his parish, you probably heard how they say he died."

Nodding his head slightly, Bradley answered, "Yes." If she only knew, he thought.

"I just don't understand how he could have done what they say he did." She shook her head as she continued, "You didn't know about his arthritis?"

Mike shook his head. "No, ma'am."

"It was really bad in that hand, especially in his first two fingers. The pain to try to bend it was too much for him. He even had to learn to write with the other hand. That's why I think, and so do my brothers, that they're all wrong about him. It must have been some sort of accident or something. He just . . . he just . . . he couldn't have done it, that's all. He just couldn't have done it, Mr. Bradley. Our brother loved life. He loved being a priest."

Though tears were welling in her eyes, Mike continued to press, "You're positive about that?"

"Oh, yes, he loved . . ."

"I'm sorry, I mean are you positive about the arthritis?"

"Of course! Why would I make something like that up? Why do you ask?"

"I didn't mean that you did." He was now beginning to feel awkward. He'd left himself open, and this was not the time or the place to be interrogated by the family. All he wanted to do was escape.

Just then, Julie came over to them. Mike was thankful to see her. The timing could not have been better. My saving grace, he thought. "We must go," Mike stated. "It's been a long day for us. Again, please accept our condolences." Mike extended his hand and Margaret shook it, though it was obvious she wanted to continue their conversation.

"Thank you for coming," she said. "We'll see you at the funeral Mass tomorrow?"

"We'll see," he again lied, not wanting to tell her they would not be attending. He didn't want to open himself up to any more questions. All he wanted to do was get away. Taking Julie's hand, he led her out of the room as quickly as he could.

CHAPTER 9

The wipers moved in unison from right to left slowly, chasing the small beads of mist from the windshield of their rental car. KDKA radio was airing a commercial for a car dealer, and except for that and the sounds of the air whizzing by and the tires as they rolled along the road, the ride from the funeral home had been silent.

They were about halfway across the light blue painted bridge that spanned the Ohio River connecting the towns of Rochester and Monaca when Julie finally broke the silence.

"Okay, what's going on? You haven't said a word since we left the mortuary. Something happen in the funeral home?"

"You don't wanna know."

"Sure I do. Come on." She reached for his hand and took it tenderly in hers. "What's the matter?"

"Do you really wanna know? You ain't gonna like it!"

"What's wrong, Mike? Tell me."

The light turned yellow and then red as he slowed the car to a stop. He reached over and turned off the radio, looked into her eyes, and said, "What would you say if I told you Father David might not have killed himself?"

"What? What do you mean?" The tone in her voice said she wished she hadn't asked.

The light turned green, and he made the right turn onto Pinney Street to his mother's apartment building. "I have doubts it was suicide." He commenced explaining to her his conversation with Father David's sister. She listened intensely as he repeated what Margaret had said. He told her how sincere she seemed.

They were just pulling into the apartment building parking lot when he said, "We gotta get back to Phoenix. I gotta talk to the cops!"

The expression on her face said: don't get involved in this. Before she had a chance to speak, he said, "I told you, you wouldn't like it."

CHAPTER 10

The face of the female security guard was expressionless as Mike Bradley placed his loose change, keys, and cell phone in a small plastic bowl and passed through the security gate of the Phoenix police station. He was here to see Lieutenant Greer at 10:30 and was glad to avoid the early morning traffic.

Mike was tired. The night flight had been bumpy, and he got little sleep on the plane. As one who could normally sleep through a thunderstorm, his attempts at slumber were futile. He kept visioning the body dripping with blood and the priest's arms almost hugging the laptop. And the sincerity on Margaret's face wouldn't vacate his memory no matter how hard he tried to erase it. Whether or not she was correct about her brother's condition was yet to be known, but Mike Bradley was convinced that she believed it wholeheartedly.

Julie had called St. Cecilia's Church and donated her mother-in-law's furniture to their St. Vincent de Paul Society. They'd packed up some of the smaller items, mostly memorabilia, and sent them by UPS to Phoenix. There was nothing of any monetary value, just some sentimental items: pictures, records, and a clock Mike had bought her. They gave her food and dishes to one of her neighbors. Aunt Teresa had picked a couple of items she wanted and took them home with her.

After making a couple of quick stops to say good-bye to some friends and to Aunt Teresa, they had caught the night flight to Phoenix. It was a little after 4:00 a.m. when they'd landed, picked up the car that Julie had parked in a lot near the airport, and headed home.

After passing through the police station's metal detector, he was directed to a curved gray desk about thirty feet away. A uniformed male police officer stepped out from the desk and asked Mike for his driver's license which he produced. The officer looked at the picture on it, then back at Mike, and nodded. He wrote the numbers on a form attached to a clear plastic clipboard that he handed to Mike and pointed where to sign. A pen hung from the clipboard by a string. Mike took it and signed his name. The officer handed him a tag that read Visitor and as he clipped it to his shirt, the officer directed, "Take the elevator to the third floor, then make a right. It's the third door on the right."

Thanking him, Mike took the elevator to the third floor. When it stopped, the door opened, and he stepped out and as directed, turned right and followed the corridor to the third door on the right. A sign which read Homicide hung from the ceiling. The arrow pointed to the right. He entered through the open door and was immediately greeted.

"May I help you?" The voice came from behind a desk where sat a heavyset lady who looked to be in her early sixties. Black-rimmed glasses hung from a chain around her neck.

"Yes, please. I'm Michael Bradley. I'm here to see Lieutenant Greer."

She smiled. "Oh, yes. He is expecting you." She pushed three numbers into the telephone console on her desk and waited for a few moments, then said, "Mr. Bradley is here to see you."

She hung up the phone and pointed to a row of green chairs directly across from her and said, "Please have a seat."

Before he had a chance to sit, he saw the lanky lieutenant approach and extend his hand. As they shook hands, the detective said. "Thank you for coming. Would you like a cup of coffee?"

"No, thank you," Mike answered.

"Please come with me," he directed. Mike followed him across the hall to a small room. It contained only a small table and four chairs. "Have a seat," he said.

Bradley sat down and Greer took the seat directly across from him. The detective began the conversation.

"You say you have some information about the priest who shot himself last Saturday?"

"I sort of have some doubts that it was suicide," he answered.

The inquisitive look on the detective's face showed that Bradley had his attention. His eyes squinted as he sat up straight in his chair and asked, "Why do you say that?"

Mike explained in detail about his conversation with Margaret at the mortuary. Though his face was expressionless, the detective listened intently.

"How well did you know him?" the lieutenant asked.

"I guess as well as any of the regular parishioners. We're, my wife and I, active in several areas of the church, and we ran into him a lot. His staff knew him much better, though."

"Did he socialize with any of his congregation?"

"I don't think he socialized with any of his parishioners, except maybe if he thought it to be to his advantage." Mike wondered where he was going with the question.

"You didn't like him, did you?" His words were more of a statement than a question.

Surprised by the cop's perceptiveness, Mike responded, "Oh, he wasn't my idea of a perfect pastor. Why do you ask?"

"No reason. Just an observation." He continued, "Were you aware of his emotional state?"

"Huh?" Mike was puzzled by the question.

"Was he happy? Was he despondent? Did you notice any type of changes in his personality lately? Perhaps he had become withdrawn, maybe? You know, that kind of stuff."

"His personality sucked. That never changed," Mike stated emphatically. "He was mean to his staff, constantly threatening their jobs. He was rude and arrogant, and an intimidator and a poor example of a priest, if you ask me." The look of surprise on the policeman's face caused Mike to stop. He thought for a moment and said, "You know, I guess you're right. I didn't like the son of a bitch. He was a disgrace to the collar he wore."

"Did other people feel like that?"

"Oh yeah. I wasn't alone. He alienated a lot of people."

The detective leaned forward in his chair and said, "I understand he was under some kind of scrutiny by the bishop. Do you know anything about that?"

"There were some questions about his handling of money. The diocese was supposed to be doing a full-blown audit."

"Who accused him?"

"Oh, some of the parishioners. Someone got hold of a bunch of questionable canceled checks. But you should probably check with the bishop on that. He ordered the audit."

The policeman surprised Mike with his next question. "Do you think anyone disliked him enough to want him dead?"

"You mean would anyone in the parish want to kill him?" A feeling of defensiveness took control of him. He hadn't expected this type of questions, and it must have been obvious to the detective as Mike squinted and shook his head. "Nah. Egg his house? Maybe. Some kids supposedly did that. But kill him? No way! Besides, you don't kill someone for being an asshole, especially a priest, for God's sake."

"John Wesley Hardin shot and killed a man just because he snored too loud," he challenged.

"That was the Old West," Mike said defensively. "And legend. And the guy he shot was not a priest. He was some other outlaw."

"Mr. Bradley, you must think something, or you wouldn't have come down here today," the detective challenged.

"Look, you don't shoot a priest just for pissing off his parishioners. If so, half the priests in the diocese would be wearing bulletproof vests." He laughed and added, "And the bishop would have to wear two of them!"

A trace of amusement snuck through the detective's face as the corners of his mouth raised slightly as though he was attempting to stifle a smile.

"If you're asking me if I think he killed himself? I did, until I went to Pennsylvania. I did, until I talked with his sister. I did, until I saw the sincerity in her eyes. After all that, well, I . . . I . . . ." Pausing for a moment he continued, "I just don't know. That's why I'm here. That's your area of expertise. I just figured I should let you know what I heard, that's all."

Nick's lanky frame seemed to tower over Mike as he stood and said, "Thank you for coming, Mr. Bradley. I appreciate your input. Be assured I will look into this deeper now."

"Glad I could help," Mike answered. "Let me know if there's anything else I can do."

"There is one thing."

"What's that?"

"Could you get something for me? A list of the people he worked with regularly? Employees, current and past, and how about volunteers he worked closely with."

"Sure. I think I can, but why me? Isn't that the stuff you guys do?"

"Truthfully, Mr. Bradley, you'll draw less attention than I would, and I don't want to serve your church with a warrant if I don't have to."

Mike thought for a moment. "Makes sense to me. I'll get on it right away."

He left the building, took the freeway home, and mentally began creating the list.

CHAPTER 11

Nick Greer returned to his office and sat down at his gray metal desk. Picking up a pencil, he rolled his chair sideways and rested his right elbow on his desk. He sat there tapping the pencil on the rim of the paper cup of Pepsi that sat in the middle of his desk, pondering over this new information. After several minutes he sat up and reached to the corner of his desk for his Rolodex, and turned it to D. The card read: Diocese of Phoenix. Removing the phone from its cradle, he dialed.

A pleasant female voice answered, "The Roman Catholic Diocese of Phoenix."

"Good morning, ma'am," Nick responded. "This is Lieutenant Nick Greer, Phoenix Police Department. I'd like to make an appointment to see Bishop O'Malley."

"I'll put you through to his secretary," she responded.

He heard a click and then, "Bishop O'Malley's office. How can I help you?" Again, the voice was a pleasant one.

"Yes, ma'am, I'm Lieutenant Nick Greer, Phoenix PD. I need to see Bishop O'Malley as soon as possible. How soon can you arrange it?"

"May I ask what this is regarding, sir?" She was polite and professional.

"It's a police matter. I need to see him today, if possible."

"I'm sorry, Lieutenant, but the bishop is attending a conference in Baltimore. He'll be gone for a couple of weeks. Perhaps the vicar can help you?"

Nick thought for a moment and asked, "Could I see him today?"

"Please hold a moment while I check," she directed.

"Thank you," Nick replied. He tapped his pencil on the edge of his desk as he waited. After about three minutes, he heard the phone click.

"Father Denkens can see you at two o'clock this afternoon."

"That'll be fine. I'll be there at two. And thank you." Hanging up the phone, and leaning back in his chair, he raised both feet up and rested them on the corner of his desk. With the pencil still in it, he brought his hand to his face and cupped it around his chin. *I'm missing something*, he thought, *but what the hell is it?*

He stared at the pictures in the trifold frame on his desk. They sat just right of center next to the nameplate that bore his name. He thought of how his kids had changed since these photos were taken just a little over a year ago. It was time to get new ones, he thought. Sunday the kids would be with him. Maybe he'd take some pictures then. He would have to borrow a digital camera. Wondering who to ask, his concentration was broken by the sound of a loud voice.

"Hey Gumby! Wanna go to lunch?" The voice came from Sonny Madison, a good friend and fellow detective. They had worked on many cases together as partners until the caseloads got so large that the department split them up. It was Sonny who helped him through the early part of his separation. Sonny was one of the few people who could get away with calling him Gumby, a name Nick Greer despised.

"Whatcha got in mind?"

"Schlotzsky's?"

Nick asked with a grin, "You buyin'?"

"Yeah! My own. I'm still a lowly sergeant, you know."

"Right! Okay, you can drive," Nick said as he dropped his feet from their resting place on the desk. As he did, his hand hit the cup of Pepsi and toppled it over. The brown liquid spread rapidly across his desk. "Shit!" he said as he reactively set the cup upright. He quickly opened one of the desk drawers, removed some napkins, and began sopping up the liquid. He grabbed the cellular phone and carefully began wiping it off. "Damn! Now it'll be all sticky!"

Picking up his keys, he began wiping them off. Then suddenly, he held them out in front of his face and yelled, "That's it!" Everyone in the squad room looked at him.

"Huh?" Sonny said in puzzlement.

Nick was elated. "That's it! Keys! No fucking keys! Why no keys? Where are they?" His eyes widened as he looked at his friend and said, "I gotta take a rain check on lunch. Something just came up."

Sonny stood and watched as Nick picked up his phone and keys and hurried out the door.

Nick went straight to his car and drove the four blocks to the morgue. As he entered, he saw the young lady at the desk. He remembered her from Monday. "Is Jack here?"

"Dr. Konesky is at lunch," she said "And I am on my way out, too." The disturbance in her voice was obvious. Nick could easily tell, at least at this moment, he was not her favorite person. Remembering their meeting on Monday, and thinking he had been a little rough on her, he decided to try to use diplomacy as best he could. He hoped it would be enough.

"When will he be back?"

"An hour, maybe two," she answered reluctantly. "He said he had some errands to run."

His voice was gentle as he asked, "Can you help me with something?"

Nick could see the fire in her oval eyes as she said, "I told you, I'm on my way to lunch."

"Look, it's important. It won't take but a couple of minutes." He took care to deliver his words as humbly as he could. "I'd very much appreciate your help."

The tone in her voice remained defensive as she looked up at him and asked, "What is it?"

"The priest he examined on Monday? Mignanelli?"

"What about him?"

"I need to see the list of personal effects. Is it still here?"

Turning around to the desk behind her, and reaching into a stack of manila folders, she pulled one out. Handing it to Nick, she motioned for him to have a seat. "Here it is. It's already sealed, but you're a big bad cop. You know what to do."

He nodded appreciatively as he sat down behind the desk, opened the envelope and emptied its contents onto the desk in front of him. He retrieved the inventory list, carefully matching it with each item:

1 watch
1 gold hematite ring
1 gold ruby ring
1 gold chain with crucifix
2 contact lenses
1 brown wallet
1 white handkerchief
1 tee shirt
1 belt
1 pr. boxer shorts
1 pr. socks (black)

1 pr. shoes
cash $72
coin $1.04
1 cell phone

Nick shook his head as he dropped the list on the desk. No keys! Where the hell are his keys? Everybody has keys, he thought as he looked up and caught her staring at him. He had been so caught up in his work that he hadn't realized just how lovely she was. Her straight, long, black hair perfectly framed her thin oval face. One side of her hair hung back over her shoulder while the other covered her breast. Suddenly, they realized they were staring at each other. They both were embarrassed and Nick broke the silence. "About the other day. I might have come on a little strong."

"You think?" Her tone was gentle, but firm.

"Please accept my apology. I didn't mean to upset you."

"I guess it was my fault, too."

"No." Nick said. Standing up and reaching across the desk, he touched her lips with his fingertip. "It was me. I'll tell you what. Let me make it up to you. You have plans for lunch?"

"I was just going across the street to the deli," she replied.

Nick smiled gently. "How about if I join you? Better yet, my treat. It's the least I can do."

He could feel the tension between them ease slightly as she shyly gave a single nod and said, "Okay."

They left the building together and walked across the street to the deli where they talked about general things, family, work, etc. He discovered that she was twenty-eight, single, and was born in Okinawa but came to San Diego with her parents when she was eight. She had earned a degree from Stanford University.

Finding himself strangely attracted to her made him a little uncomfortable, because he had not been attracted to another woman in this way since he met his wife. He felt guilty, yet pleasantly adventurous. There was a tenderness about her that fascinated him in a mystical sort of way.

He told her about his impending divorce and his situation with his children. She seemed to understand. He asked her why she hadn't married.

"No time," she answered. "School, work, and my music take up most all of my time."

"Music? You sing?"

"No." She smiled. "I play. Cello."

He wondered how such a petite person could play a cello. She looked more like a flutist than a cellist. He said out loud, not intending to be heard, "A cello?"

She laughed lightly. "Yes! A cello. I play with The Phoenix Symphony."

He couldn't hide the surprise in his voice. "Wow! I'd like to hear you play sometime."

"You mean that?"

"Sure do."

"We're playing a benefit tonight. Would you like to come?"

"Well, sure. I'd love to."

She smiled. "Okay. Seven thirty tonight at Symphony Hall. Go to the north box office. There'll be a ticket there for you. You know where that is?"

"Sure. Symphony Hall. Seven thirty. North box office."

She looked down at the tiny watch on her wrist. "Oh my! I better get back. Dr. Konesky will have a cow!"

"Tell him you were with me," Nick said as he picked up the check, tossed two ones on the table and rose. "That'll shut him up. We go back a long way."

"It better be a lifetime."

He paid the check and asked, "Why do you say that?"

"Oh, nothing," she answered his question with an impish smile. She was thinking about the things she said about him after he left on Monday. She recalled how she had told her boss that this cop was the rudest, most arrogant person she had ever met and she hoped he never came around again. The examiner just smiled at her comment and continued his work.

CHAPTER 12

As they arrived at the door of the morgue, he said, "See you tonight, Sue Kim, the cello player."

Her brown eyes widened. "It's *cellist*!" she said emphatically. "See you tonight. And thanks for lunch."

He thought about her as he rode to the second floor. As the elevator door opened, his attention immediately returned to the tasks at hand. He walked straight down the hall to the familiar sign hanging from the ceiling: Forensics.

Roy Loomis was leaning back in his chair, eating a sandwich as Nick Greer walked in.

"Hey, guy. What's up?" Roy greeted his friend. "To what do I owe the pleasure? Or should I ask what the hell do you want?"

"Funny, Roy, funny," Nick answered. "Got a question for you."

"Didn't think it was a social visit. Ask away."

"That priest. Remember? Saturday?"

"Yeah," Roy answered as he took a bite of his sandwich. "What about him?"

"Did your team find any keys? Or do you remember seeing any?"

"Don't think so, but let me check." Loomis reached for a group of files standing upright in a holder on the corner of his desk. He thumbed through them and pulled one out. "Here ya go," he said. "Mignanelli. See for yourself."

Nick read through the file thoroughly, looking at each picture. There was no record of keys in the file, nor were there any in the pictures. He scratched his head. "Tell me, Roy, if a person had arthritis, say in this finger,"—Nick held up his right index finger to Roy— "could that prevent him from pulling the trigger on a gun?"

Roy wondered why he would ask this. "Depends. If the arthritis was severe enough, and the trigger pull was hard enough, it could cause a problem. Why?"

"Just a hunch." The detective looked at his watch: 1:40. I must have spent more time at lunch than I realized, he thought. He looked back at Roy and said, "Thanks, Roy. I gotta go."

The detective got into his car and drove about two miles down the street and pulled into the parking lot behind the beige-colored building that housed the diocesan offices. Walking around to the front of the building, he took the sidewalk to the front entrance.

This landmark was well over a hundred years old and the epitome of southwestern architecture. The two-level structure had a Mexican-tiled roof which set it apart from the other buildings that lined the streets of downtown Phoenix. The building consisted of four wings which came together to frame a beautiful courtyard. After many remodelings, this structure still stood proud against the new modern buildings that formed the Phoenix skyline.

He entered the building through a set of massive double doors and crossed the waiting room to the reception desk where a middle-aged Hispanic lady greeted him.

"Can I help you, sir?"

"Lieutenant Nick Greer, Phoenix PD." He displayed his badge to her. "I have an appointment to see Father Dickens."

"It's Father Denkens," she assertively corrected. "He's expecting you." She pointed to a door on Nick's right. "Go down the hall, take the first left. It's the third door on your left."

"Thank you," Nick said as he followed her direction and turned toward the door. A buzzer sounded as he approached the door. He opened it and followed the hall as she had directed until he saw a sign on a door that read: Rev. William R. Denkens, Vicar General.

Before he could decide whether to knock, or just walk in, the door opened. A man dressed in black and wearing the collar of clergy stood to the left, holding the door open.

"Lieutenant Greer?" The priest extended his hand and Nick shook it.

"Bill Denkens. Please have a seat." The vicar pointed to a set of stuffed red leather chairs facing a large oak desk. Nick sat down in the one on the right. The priest walked behind his desk and took his place in the matching red high-backed chair. "What is it I can do for you today?"

This priest looked to be about fifty with graying hair that was cut close and combed straight back. His ruddy complexion brought attention to bushy eyebrows in dire need of a trim.

The desktop was clear except for a telephone on the priest's left and a foot-high statue on the opposite corner. Nick thought back to his days growing up in a Catholic school and recognized it as The Sacred Heart. In the center was a yellow notepad and a pen. The matching credenza behind him was clear except for some neatly arranged books and three stacked black plastic in/out trays.

"I'm looking into the death of one of your colleagues," the detective began. "Father David Mignanelli. I have a few questions, if you don't mind."

The priest sat erect in his seat. "Excuse me, Lieutenant. But I don't understand. We all know that Father Mignanelli's death was a suicide." He almost whispered the words, as if he were telling a secret. "What could there possibly be to look into?"

The detective tried to make eye contact, but when he looked at him, the priest looked away. "Just some loose ends, Father. It's all routine stuff. Do you know anyone who would want to hurt him?"

A look of shock attacked the vicar's face. "No! Absolutely not! He was a good man and a good priest."

The demeanor of this priest did not intimidate the detective as he continued probing.

"How about his congregation? Were they happy with him?"

"Of course!" the priest answered as though his own dignity had been threatened. "Like I said, he was a good priest. He'll truly be missed." He nodded his assurance as he spoke.

"I understand your loyalty, Father, but I must tell you that I've heard differently," the detective said with certainty in his tone. The priest's mouth began to open as if to speak, but the cop continued with his challenge. "I understand he had come under some kind of scrutiny. What can you tell me about that?"

"Look, Lieutenant." It was obvious to Nick that he had struck a nerve. This tactic was one Nick was very good at. He found that when people speak purely from emotion they often tend to say things they would not normally say.

The vicar took a moment to compose himself before he continued, "Though we try, we cannot please all the people all the time. I'm sure you are aware of that." He looked at his interrogator as if seeking approval, but Nick didn't move or change his expression.

"There are over two thousand families at St. Mike's. One is bound to upset some of the people, especially those who are uncomfortable with change. As all new pastors do, Father Mignanelli made a few changes, and some people didn't adjust easily. It happens all the time."

"In what way did they react?"

"Oh, the usual, letters, phone calls. Some tried to rile up their friends. You know the type." Again the priest seemed to be looking for agreement, but Nick remained passive.

"We, here at the diocese, understand it. We expect a certain amount of complaints. We're used to dealing with it. It usually calms itself down after a couple of months. Like I said, we're used to it here. Like you would say, it's routine."

"So, you got letters from St. Michael's parishioners?"

"Some."

"How many?" Nick saw the look of disturbance on the cleric's face.

"Oh, I don't know. A few, I guess. About average." The priest's eyes seemed again to be focused beyond Nick.

Denkens was not being as cooperative as he could, so the detective kept on digging.

"How many are a few?"

"I don't know. Just a few!" The priest was clearly agitated.

"I assume they all come here?"

"Yes, of course."

"What do you do with them?"

"A lot are unsigned. We throw most of those out. The rest get read, filed, and acted upon if necessary."

"Acted upon? How so?"

"If there appears to be any merit to the complaint, we discuss it with the priest. We then counsel him."

"Did you counsel Father Mignanelli?"

"No."

"May I see them?"

"See what?" Father Denkens was puzzled by the question.

"The letters."

The look of shock on the priest's face told Nick he had again caught the man off guard.

"I . . . I . . . I don't know . . . uhm . . . I mean . . . well, they're confidential."

The vicar had been leaning back in his chair in a comfortable position, but suddenly he leaned forward, put both of his hands on the desk, and for the first time looked his guest in the eyes. "I don't see where it's any of your concern. That information is protected, but I'll check with the bishop when he returns. If he says okay, then—"

Nick cut him off. "Look, Father, I can be back here in less than an hour with a court order, but I don't think the bishop would want that, do you? You know . . . public record."

Nick knew it would not be easy to get a court order when the diocese was involved, but he was hoping the priest wasn't thinking that way. He also was aware that Bishop O'Malley had recently been dragged through the press due to his mishandling of several abuse cases and had not emerged as a hero. Nick assumed the bishop didn't want any more bad publicity and gambled that Father Denkens was concerned about that.

Dismay saturated the vicar's voice. "Well, I guess it would be all right." He hesitated for a moment, then stood up and said, "I'll get the files for you."

As he began to leave the room, the detective said, "Father, I'll also need to see his personnel file."

Anger flared up as the priest's face went from white to red. He looked at his visitor like he was going to say something, but then just nodded in displeasure and left the room.

Nick thought about his college boxing coach. He would say: "Ya gotta win the first round! Else it's all uphill from there." The detective knew he had won this first round.

From his seat, his eyes scanned the small office. Hanging on the left wall was a group photo that appeared to be the priest's graduation class. Next to it, a picture of him with the pope. The opposite wall supported a picture of an older couple, probably his parents, Nick thought. In the center of the wall, above the credenza behind the desk, hung several framed certificates of achievement, most of which were theological; however, one stood out. It was a master's degree in business administration from Syracuse University.

As the priest returned and took his seat behind the desk, Nick said, "I'm impressed."

Pointing to the diploma on the wall, he continued, "A master's degree. Syracuse. Good school. A long way from here, though. How'd you end up way out here?"

The priest smiled as he answered, "I'm from New York. Buffalo, actually. Came out here after the seminary. I was ordained here, you know."

Nick looked at the thick file folders the priest had placed on his desk. Father Denkens opened the top one and said, "Okay, Lieutenant. What would you like to know?"

"Are his medical records there, too?"

"No, his doctor would have them."

"Do you know who that is?"

The cleric began searching through the manila file for the information. Nick stood up, reached his arm across the desk, put his hand on the file, and said, "May I?" He pulled the files from the priest's grasp without waiting for an answer. Sitting back down, he put the files in his lap and began leafing through them searching for, he knew not what. He read some of the letters. He found Mignanelli's personal information. Pointing to the notepad still sitting on the vicar's desk, he asked, "May I?"

The priest handed him the pad, and the detective began taking notes as he thumbed through the folders. "Dr. Jerome Everett," he said aloud. "I've heard that name."

"Pardon me?" the priest queried.

"Oh, nothing," Nick replied. "Just talking out loud."

The vicar sat back in his chair and watched in uncomfortable silence as Nick sifted through the files page by page, stopping at times to scribble a note on the pad. It was clear the priest was disturbed by the policeman's actions, even though he tried to hide it.

Finally, Nick closed the second folder, ripped the pages he had written on from the pad, folded them in four, shoved them in his rear pocket, handed the pad and the files to the priest, stood up, shook his hand, and said, "Thank you, Father. I'll see myself out."

Denkens was silent as he watched the detective turn and leave. Immediately the priest grabbed the phone and dialed one zero. The voice on the other end answered, "Yes, Father."

"Get me the bishop, right away!"

"But he's in Balt—"

"Get him anyway!" the vicar shouted, and hung up the phone. He looked out the window to the flower garden below, nervously waiting for his boss to return his call.

As Nick backed out of the parking space, he thought, I'll bet he's calling the bishop right now.

CHAPTER 13

Mike Bradley hadn't seen his associate pastor since the tragedy and was concerned about his friend's welfare and peace of mind. He was a kind and gentle man and was easily intimidated, a trait that Father David had quickly recognized and used to his own advantage.

Father Roman was in his early sixties and had been a priest for over thirty years. He exhibited all the qualities Mike expected and was used to in a priest. There was an aura of spirituality about him.

A health problem had caused him to transfer to Phoenix from somewhere in North Carolina. No one knew what it was. Some said it was cancer, but Mike remembered him saying something about allergies, so he assumed that was the reason. This priest didn't like to talk about himself, much unlike his deceased superior who liked to bring attention to himself and his ailments, like the time he sprained his ankle. Apparently it was a bad sprain. He would hobble around in the back of the church on crutches. People would come up to him, and he would say, "Praaay for me." He relished the attention and didn't know that many of his parishioners were laughing at him behind his back.

Father Roman had been in the diocese for a little over three years now, the last two at St. Michael's. He was well liked and respected by the parishioners, young and old.

As Mike entered, Father Roman stood and embraced him. Feeling the pain that the priest struggled with in his heart, Mike held him for a moment, then sat down on the striped sofa that sat against the wall at a right angle to his desk. The priest sat down in a high-backed swivel chair and swirled it to face his guest. His snow-white hair glistened as the light from the window seemed to radiate from it. Through the silver-rimmed glasses that sat on a larger than average nose, Mike could see the eyes of a stress-laden man. His wrinkled face showed lines of worry, and his baggy eyes gave evidence of sleepless nights.

Rolling his chair from behind his desk, the priest extended his hands out, palms up, and reached across the small table that sat between them. Knowing this invitation to pray, Mike joined hands with him. He prayed for Mike's mother, Father David, St Michael's Parish, and for the strength to persevere. When he finished, he leaned back in his chair and sighed. Though he tried, he couldn't mask the pain in his heart.

"You okay?" Mike asked.

"Yeah. I guess so." Somehow his words seemed more of an attempt to convince himself than Mike, who could see that the priest wanted to appear in control. However, the lines in his face continued to betray him. This was a very sensitive man. Even though he didn't like Father David, and often feared him, he was obviously grieving. "I'm sorry about your mother," he said.

"Thank you. She's better off now."

"What can I do for you, Mike?"

"A couple of things, Father. First, I wanted to see how you were holding up, and if there's anything you need or anything Julie or I can do for you."

"I'm okay," he answered. "At least for now. The bishop makes new assignments in June. I guess we'll have to go on until then. I hear you found him?"

"Yeah, but we can talk about that some other time. Today, I wanted to see how you're doing. Are you gonna be able to handle the load yourself?"

"Won't be much different than before. We'll get a priest from the diocese, or one of the retirees to come and help with the Mass schedule. Most of the rest will be business as usual."

Mike knew the underlying truth in the priest's statement. His pastor had been, to say the least, derelict in his duties, passing them off onto Father Roman, or the deacons, or other staff members as much as possible. He refused to make sick calls or preside at some funerals and wouldn't work with the young people or the elderly. He delegated a lot of his own duties to his subordinates. It was common knowledge that if someone complained, he would threaten to fire them, thus creating a very stressful environment.

Both Mike and Julie had witnessed Father Roman's tears as the workload became more and more unbearable. "Can you hold on until June?"

"Have to." His voice cracked.

"If Julie or I can help, all you have to do is ask."

"Of course."

"The second thing I needed to discuss: I need to ask a favor."

He looked at his parishioner inquisitively. "Of course. What is it that you need?"

"Could you get me a list of everyone who works for the parish or the school? Name, address, and home phone?"

"I guess so, but what for?" His faced showed puzzlement.

Looking directly to his friend, Mike raised his eyebrows, rolled his eyes, and said, "Uhh . . . Christmas list? I believe in starting early."

The priest laughed, shook his head and asked, "How soon do you need it?"

Stroking his chin, Mike looked back at him, kind of puckered his face and said, "Uhh . . . Yesterday would be good."

"Hold on," Father Roman said as he rose and left the room.

About five minutes had passed when the priest came back carrying a large envelope and handed it to Mike, who asked, "Everybody on here? Staff, school, full and part time?"

"Think so," the priest nodded. "Christmas card list, eh? In March?"

Mike addressed his friend gently, "I can't tell you right now." This priest was under enough stress as it was, and Mike didn't want to alert him to the circumstances. "I'm just asking you to trust me. It's something I need. I promise not to abuse it."

The nod of the priest's head told Mike that he understood. They both stood up and embraced. Mike thanked him for his time and left.

He went directly to his office, which was about a mile north of the church, made a copy of the list and stuffed it into a large manila envelope. He wrote on the outside: Lt. Greer. On the other one he wrote: Christmas list. He put it in his briefcase. It was two forty-five. If he hurried, he might beat the traffic. He headed east on Thunderbird Road to Interstate 17, then south to downtown Phoenix.

CHAPTER 14

The directory sign read: Jerome Everett, MD, Suite 1-C. Nick followed the covered walkway to the suite, checking his watch as he entered. It was 10:27. His earlier phone call had favored him with a 10:30 appointment. He was surprised he was able to see him so easily on a Friday.

The office was smaller than Nick had anticipated. The reception area was only about ten by twelve. There were four chairs on each side and four against the front window. A stack of magazines sat on a small wooden table in the corner. Seeing that the waiting room was void of people on a Friday afternoon, he wondered why.

As he approached the front counter, he heard the grinding sound of the glass window as it slid partly open. From behind it came a female voice, "Can I help you?"

Nick reached into his pocket, retrieved his badge and dangled it through the opening just enough to be seen and said, "I'm Lieutenant Greer. I have an appointment with Dr. Everett at ten thirty."

The glass window slid all the way open, and a head popped through. The dishwater-blonde, freckled-faced lady replied, "Oh, yes. You're the cop who called this morning. The doctor is expecting you. He's just finishing up with some paperwork." The glass window slid shut, and a single door on the left side of the room opened. "Follow me." She led him past three examining rooms to a door at the end of the hallway. The sign on the door read: Jerome J. Everett, MD, PC.

She opened the door and said, "Please have a seat. The doctor will be with you shortly."

The office was modestly furnished. Nick's eyes scanned the walls that displayed two medical licenses, a diploma and a picture of a beautiful sailboat. He was about to get up to look at the boat when he heard a sound behind him. Turning he saw an elderly man enter the room. "You must be the policeman," he said as he extended his hand to his visitor.

Nick nodded and shook his hand. His grip was firm for a man of the doctor's years.

"Lieutenant Nick Greer, Phoenix PD. Thank you for seeing me on such short notice."

"No problem," the doctor answered. "As you can see, I'm not very busy. I'm retiring. I'm moving my patients to a colleague of mine. I'm just finishing up the last bit of paperwork. Today is my last day. When it's over, I'm officially retired!"

Jerome Everett had practiced medicine for almost fifty years and was well known in and around northwest Phoenix as the old-country-doctor type. He had even been known to make a house call when the situation called for it. He was in his mid-seventies and stood just under six feet tall. His snow-white hair provided the perfect background for his silver glasses upon which stuck out a small magnifying glass.

"What do you plan to do when you retire?" Nick asked.

The good doctor proudly pointed to the picture of the boat. "Going to San Diego. Gonna take 'er out. Yep, just me 'n Millie, that's the missus, you know. We've been waiting for this a long time. Gonna sail 'er down to the Baja and just relax for a month or two. Then, we'll see what happens from there."

"I wish you well and hope you both have a good time."

The doctor smiled. "I know you didn't come here to talk about my boat, Lieutenant. What is it I can do for you today?"

"You have, excuse me, had a patient by the name of David Mignanelli," Nick stated.

"Oh yes, the priest," the medic answered. "Killed himself, I understand. Terrible thing! Wouldn't have believed it. Real nice guy, you know."

Nick thought, You're the only one who seems to think so, then asked, "How long have you been his doctor?"

"Oh, let's see, about a year, I think. Ever since he came here, I guess." He scratched his chin as he continued, "I really wasn't taking on any new patients, but he was a patient of a colleague of mine up in Lake Havasu City. He asked me to look after him, so I did."

"What can you tell me about him?"

"The files are all packed up, but I'll tell you what I can remember. I guess doctor–patient confidentiality need not apply here. Besides, what can they do about it?"

"A couple of questions," the detective responded. "First of all, do you have any reason to think him to be despondent? Any reason he might take his own life?"

"Ya know, I was sure surprised to hear about him," the doctor answered. "He was always so happy and vibrant. I was totally shocked to hear he committed suicide."

"So there aren't any reasons you know of that would cause him to take his own life?"

"None that I can think of. But I'm a medical doctor, not a psychiatrist. I just deal with the physical parts."

"When was the last time you saw him?"

"About a month ago, I think. For his regular blood test."

"Blood test? Regular?" The detective was confused.

"Yes, he was worried about HIV."

"Why would he be worried about that?" Nick asked as he thought about the items he had found in the priest's nightstand and car.

"He said he had given last rights to an accident victim near his old parish in Lake Havasu. I guess they found out afterwards that the victim had AIDS. He said he was just being cautious."

"The results were negative, I assume," Nick said.

"Correct."

"You're sure? That might be a motive for suicide for a lot of people."

"Absolutely! Checked him every six weeks like clockwork. Each and every time the lab results were the same, negative. I told him he didn't need to keep on testing, but he insisted."

"What else can you tell me about him?"

"His general health was pretty good," the doctor answered. "He had a nasty case of arthritis, though. One of the worst cases I ever saw. He couldn't do much with his left hand. Couldn't bend his first two fingers, it hurt him so much. The thumb was bad, too."

"Doctor, could he have pulled the trigger on a gun?"

"Hmmm, don't know too much about guns. Did some hunting when I was young. Doubt it though. Not with the left hand, anyway. He couldn't even hold a pen. Fortunately for him, he was ambidextrous and could use the right just as well almost. Taught himself to write right-handed, he did."

"Thank you, Dr. Everett. I appreciate your help and your time."

The doctor smiled. "After today, time is gonna be all I have."

Nick stood and looked down at the elderly man sitting behind the desk. "One more thing. If you don't mind, I'd like to look at his file. Could you get it for me?"

"Well . . . I . . . I don't know . . . It's packed up . . ."

"It's okay, Doctor," Nick said in a comforting tone. "Doctor–patient privilege ends at death, and I prefer not to involve you with a warrant."

"It's beginning to sound like you don't accept it as a suicide," the doctor said. "Okay, I'll have Mariann dig it out and send it to your office, if that's okay? I won't have a use for it anyway, so you can keep it. What can they do? Shut down my practice?" He chuckled.

Nick smiled as he reached out and shook the doctor's hand. "Thank you so much for your time. You've been very helpful. I wish you and your wife a happy and long retirement."

"You're welcome, and thank you. I've been looking forward to this for a long time."

The detective turned toward the door, but stopped and turned back and said, almost as an afterthought, "One more thing, Doctor."

"Yes?"

"What did you know about his sexual appetite?"

"I thought being a priest meant he wasn't supposed to have one," the doctor answered. "But I think there was something going on that his bishop didn't know about."

"Why do you say that?"

Still in his chair, the doctor leaned forward and put both of his elbows on the desk. He cupped his right hand around his left, looked at his visitor and said, "Blood test? Every six weeks? Do you really think I bought that accident victim story? I might be old, but I'm not stupid."

Nick thanked the doctor again and left his office.

CHAPTER 15

The same lady who had greeted Mike earlier that morning greeted him again as he entered the homicide room. "Hello again, Mr. Bradley."

Impressed that she remembered his name, he smiled, and holding out the envelope in his hand, he said, "Hello again to you. I'd like to leave to this for Lieutenant Greer. Would you ask him to call me when he receives it, please?"

Just then, he heard the door behind him squeak. She looked past him, pointed toward the door and smiled. "You can tell him yourself." Turning around he saw that Nick Greer had just entered the room.

The detective looked surprised. "Hello there, Mr. Bradley. What can I do for you?"

"The list you asked for," Mike answered as he handed him the manila envelope.

"That was quick," he said as he took the envelope. "You got a minute?"

"Sure."

He motioned for Mike to follow him. This time they went to his desk. Nick took his place behind it and motioned for his visitor to sit in the gray chair next to it. Mike watched as the detective reached into his desk, pulled out a letter opener, and zipped open the envelope. Removing the contents, he began reading.

As Nick read over the papers, Mike's eyes scanned the room. He counted eight gray desks, each spaced as far apart as possible for the small room. Each contained a beige telephone and a computer, except for one that only had a phone on it. He was thinking how they compared to what was seen on television when his thoughts were interrupted.

"Quite a list," the lieutenant commented. "Lots of people."

"The church has a school," Mike informed him. "The list includes teachers, janitors, cafeteria workers, the whole nine yards."

"Good job. Can you tell me each person's position or duties?"

"Most of them, I think."

They went over the list and Mike dictated each person's duties as best he could while the detective made notes. When he was finished, he looked at his visitor and asked. "How well do you know these people?"

Thinking for a moment, he answered, "Some well, most casually, and some not at all. Why do you ask?"

Ignoring the question, the detective continued, "You've been at St. Michael's how long?"

"Don't know exactly. Over twenty years, I guess."

"Are you active in the church? Do the people know you?"

Squinting, he answered, "Uhh . . . a lot of them, I guess." Where is he going with this, he wondered? The answer came quickly.

"I want to ask you a favor."

"Go for it."

"Please understand, this is not our normal procedure, but how would you feel about accompanying me as I talk with some of these people?" The puzzled look on his guest's face prompted him to continue. "This being a church thing, and the deceased being their pastor, they might feel intimidated by me, you know, the badge and all. However, you're one of them. If you're there, some might be more comfortable. You just need to introduce me to them, and I'll take it from there. What do you think?"

"I guess so. I don't see any harm. When do you wanna start?"

"How about tomorrow? You decide who would be, excuse me, who would have been closest to him, who would know him the best, and we'll start there. Can you arrange that?"

"I guess so."

"Good. I'll call you in the morning." The detective nodded and Mike took that as a sign of dismissal.

As he worked his way through the Friday evening traffic, the events of the past few days controlled his thoughts. "Wow! A murder investigation! How exciting!" he said out loud. "I can't wait to tell Julie. Boy, is she going to be pissed."

CHAPTER 16

Lieutenant Nick Greer finished arranging the list of interviews in the order he felt the most comfortable with. He decided to begin with Father Roman, then the office staff consisting of the office manager, a receptionist, a secretary, and a liturgist. He had no idea what a liturgist did, but he figured he would soon find out. Then he wrote a note that said: check trigger pull.

Suddenly, he remembered the concert and Sue Kim. He looked at his watch. If he showered and changed in the police locker room, he would make it there on time. He stood to go but was interrupted by the ring of his cell phone. He picked it up from his desk and pushed the talk button. "Nick Greer," he answered.

"Hello, Nick." He immediately recognized the voice of his soon-to-be ex-wife. The tone of her voice told him he was not going to be happy with whatever it was she had to say. Thirteen years of marriage couldn't help but breed some familiarities.

"Yes, Cassie. How are the kids?"

"They're fine," she answered.

"Good. What time should I pick them up in the morning?"

"That's what I want to talk to you about." Nick knew what was coming.

"They're having such a great time here that we're gonna stay through Sunday. I'm sorry, but—"

"But shit!" The anger in his voice was perfectly clear as he interrupted her. "Goddammit! I only get them on weekends! I didn't have them last weekend. What are you trying to pull, Cassie?"

"I'm not trying to pull anything." Her voice suddenly became ice-cold and defensive.

"Yeah, right!" He heard the buzz of a dial tone as the phone disconnected on the other end. He brought the phone directly in front of his face and with fire in his eyes, yelled at it, "Bitch!" Everyone in the squad room heard him. As he looked up, they all looked back down and pretended to be busy.

His thoughts went back to when he and Cassie had met in college. Their romance, and subsequent marriage, had been a fairly smooth one. Until their separation, there had been barely a harsh word between them. Now he wondered how it had all happened. How could two people love each other so deeply one day, and go to battle against each other the next?

Knowing his job was becoming a stress on their relationship, he had promised her that he would take some time off. Though he'd been sincere in his intentions, he never followed through. Something always got in the way, usually another "special case." He should have realized the hidden consequences of her frequent remarks like: "Spend some time with me. I need you." The message became clear the day he came home early and caught her in their bed with another man.

It seemed like only yesterday. He had felt nauseous all morning so he had decided to go home and rest. He hadn't taken any sick time since he had been with the department, so he figured one day wouldn't hurt. Pulling into their driveway he had been surprised to see that Cassie's car was there. He wondered what she was doing home. The flu had been running rampant; maybe they both had it.

The nauseousness in his stomach was nothing compared to what he felt when he pushed open their bedroom door. He froze in his tracks! There she was, his wife, the woman he loved, sitting on top of her lover, gyrating like a machine. Her back was to Nick and her body blocked his view of her partner. He took several steps into the room. Now his view was no longer blocked. Her boss! Her fucking boss!

The man saw Nick and froze! Cassie turned her head and saw her husband standing there. Her mouth flew open, and her eyes widened as big as golf balls. She froze! The whole house was deathly silent. Many thoughts ran through his mind as he stood rigid. The first was to pull his Glock and blow them both away. Then he thought about his kids.

His fists tightened. He didn't speak. He just turned and left the house.

Nick Greer moved out of their home the next morning. He stayed at Sonny's house for a few days, then moved to a small motel with a kitchenette that he rented by the week. It was about a month later when she served him with divorce papers citing irreconcilable differences.

He asked himself, "What's that supposed to mean? Irreconcilable differences! Right! If a guy gets caught with another woman, it's adultery. She gets caught fucking her boss, and it's irreconcilable differences!"

At one time he had loved her so much, and now his life had been turned upside down.

CHAPTER 17

The note in the ticket envelope said: "Meet you here after the concert." It had been thirty minutes since the concert was over, and he asked himself how much longer he should wait? His question was answered as quickly as it was asked.

"Hi," Nick said as he saw her walk through the double doors.

She smiled. "Sorry it took so long." She reached for his hand.

"It's okay," he replied. "Where's your fiddle?"

She stopped dead in her tracks and abruptly pulled her hand from his. Her angst was obvious. "It's not a fiddle! It's a cello!"

The look on her face reminded him of their first meeting at the morgue. "Sorry," he said. "I didn't mean—"

She interrupted. "A fiddle is something you play at a barn dance! A cello is a delicate refined instrument. It takes grace, years of practice, and love of the instrument to do what I do. Don't ever call it a fiddle; that upsets me."

"Uhh, so I noticed. Sorry, I didn't mean to insult you."

Her face reddened with embarrassment. "It's okay," she said as she slipped her hand back into his. "I'm sorry, sometimes I get testy."

"Really?" Nick asked with a grin. "I hadn't noticed." He decided to hurriedly change the subject. "I feel like a drink. How about you?"

"Sure," she answered.

"Majors is right around the corner," he suggested.

"Sounds good to me," she replied.

Walking hand in hand, they crossed the foot bridge that spanned Washington Street from the plaza concourse and made their way to Majors. They were quickly seated and served. He was surprised that she ordered a beer. He expected her to order a fancy ladies' drink, maybe something with an umbrella in it. After all, she played a cello, not a fiddle. This chick is full of surprises, he thought.

They talked and listened to the band as it played a mixture of music. There were about a dozen couples on the dance floor, and as the tempo of the music slowed, she looked at the dance floor and then at her date. "Come on, dance with me."

Nick didn't like to dance. He was not very good at it, and he preferred to just watch; however, the inviting look in her eyes was irresistible. She was already up, reached out, and grabbed his hand, pulling him behind her to the dance floor.

As he held her, he looked out over the top of her head and wondered how they looked together. After all, he was at least a foot taller than her. But his attention quickly moved to her as she lay her head against his chest. He thought her head fit perfectly under his chin as the smell of her hair, mixed with her perfume, became intoxicating. They held each other close while moving slowly and gracefully to the music. She moved her head back and looked up into his eyes. As he looked at her, he found himself caught up in her beauty. Even in the dim light her eyes were captivating and inviting; her lips soft and sensuous. The song ended, but he continued to hold her. They stared into each other's eyes, and he felt a strong urge to kiss her, but the downbeat of the music broke their trance. "La Bamba"! The next thing Nick knew, the floor was full of people dancing. He took her hand to escort her from the floor, but she was already gyrating to the music.

They danced to a few more songs and then returned to their table. Nick looked at his watch. Almost midnight. They had literally danced the night away. He wondered if the time had passed as quickly for her as it had for him.

Seeing him looking at his watch, she glanced at hers. "It's late," she said. "It's been a long day."

I'll walk you to your car," Nick said.

She giggled. "It's a long walk. It's at my apartment."

"Huh?" Nick was puzzled.

"Carol Schmidt, she plays flute, lives in my complex. We take turns driving," she said. "You know the parking situation downtown at night. Tonight was her turn. That's why it took me so long after the concert. I had to take my cello to her car. Don't worry, I'll call a cab."

"Nonsense! I'll drive you home."

"You don't mind?"

"My pleasure!"

They got into his Ford Taurus. He turned the key, and the engine roared to life. "Where to?" he asked.

"Glendale and Thirty-Ninth Avenue," she answered.

CHAPTER 18

Nick steered the car into the Glendale Manor Apartments and followed her directions past the second building.

"Pull in here," she said, pointing to an empty space.

After stopping the car, he got out and opened the door for her. "Which apartment?"

Pointing up she said, "Two thirty-five, second floor, corner."

"I'll walk you up," he said as he took her hand.

They ascended the stairs to her floor, turned right, and walked to the end unit. He watched as she fished through her purse for her key and after finding it, slid it into the lock, turned it, and opened the door. Sue Kim turned to him. "Want some coffee?"

He nodded. "Sure."

"Come on in," she invited.

Nick followed her in and closed the door behind them. The living room was medium size. A small table with two chairs sat in the corner to the right in front of a small kitchen.

Laying her purse on the table, she disappeared into the kitchen where she measured two scoops of coffee and dropped them into a filter. Then she poured some water into the reservoir, pushed the brew button, and came back into the living room. Nodding in the direction of the sofa, she said, "Make yourself comfortable."

She removed the plastic clips that had held her hair behind her head for the last few hours, and her long, black hair fell and settled behind her back. "I need a quick shower. The coffee's brewing. I've got sugar. There's milk in the fridge. Sorry, no cream."

"That'll be fine," Nick said. "I prefer mine black."

"Okay, I won't be long." She looked around the room like she was searching for something. "There it is." She picked up the remote control hand unit from the table and tossed it to Nick. As he caught it, she pointed toward the television. "Here ya go. In case you get bored."

Nick looked in the direction she had pointed, then looked back at Sue Kim. She had disappeared from his sight.

Sitting down on the sofa, Nick looked around the room. The apartment was small but neat and tidy. There appeared to be a single bedroom located behind the wall he was facing.

The sofa exhibited a southwestern design and sat directly across from a matching loveseat. On the wall above it hung three framed posters of Arizona Diamondbacks baseball players.

Nick was curious so he got up from his seat and walked over to the posters. He was surprised to see that each poster had a personal note to Sue Kim and was autographed by each player. Wow, who is this girl, anyway? he thought as he returned to the sofa.

Along the left wall, a small entertainment center housed a stereo system, two speakers, a Blu-ray, and a medium-sized digital television. He was about to push the power button on the remote when Sue Kim walked back into the room.

She was brushing her hair and wearing a long white tee shirt that extended to her knees.

Nick always thought women wearing men's shirts were extremely sexy and this Nipponese beauty was no exception.

Again she disappeared into the kitchen and soon returned with a tray containing two steaming cups of coffee, a small cruet of milk, and some sugar packets. Placing the tray on the coffee table that sat in front of the sofa, she sat down beside her guest.

Nick pointed to the posters on the wall. "What's with the posters? I didn't know you were a baseball fan."

"I sure am!" The look on his face prompted, "You seem surprised."

He started to speak, "Well, uhh . . ."

"Is it because I work in a morgue?" She crossed her arms as she continued, "Is it because I play a cello? Or could it be because I'm a girrrrl?" She looked him in the eyes, and he could tell she was teasing him. "Actually, my friend Carol and I have season tickets."

"How'd you get the autographs? Are they real?"

"Oh, they're real all right. Every year we do a concert in conjunction with the Arizona Diamondbacks Charities. The owners know I'm a fan, and this is their way of saying thanks."

"You know the owners?"

"I've met them once or twice. A couple of them were sitting in front of you at the concert tonight and so were some of the players. You didn't see them?"

"Uhhh . . . Nooo."

"They were two rows in front of you. You're a cop. I thought cops were supposed to notice things."

"I was watching you."

She smiled, choosing to take his statement as a compliment.

"Amazing! Absolutely amazing," he said as he looked into her eyes.

"What do you mean?"

"Well, for a start, you work in a morgue, and you're a concert cellist. Then there's, well, I didn't picture you as a beer drinker."

Putting her hands on her hips, she responded, "And just what kind of drink did you think I would like?"

Taking care to pick his words, he answered, "Well, I don't know what I thought. I guess I thought a professional, accomplished musician would drink . . . well . . . Oh hell, I don't know, maybe a Harvey Cadillac, or something like that."

She laughed and looked up at him. "A Harvey what?"

"And then to see you are an avid baseball fan, well . . . you're full of surprises." He stopped speaking but continued looking at her. His eyes dropped to her breasts. Her hard, pointy nipples were trying their best to poke their way through the thin braless shirt, still a little damp from the shower. He looked into her eyes and said softly, "And you're, you're so beautiful."

He leaned down to her and gently pulled her to him. She offered no resistance as he kissed her. She reached her arms around his neck and pulled herself into his embrace.

They kissed again. Her lips were soft and warm and so inviting, like nothing he had ever experienced.

She took her arms from around his neck, pulled back, and stood up. He looked up at her wondering if he had done something wrong. The look on her face was sensuously inviting. She reached out her hand to him. He stood, took her hand, and followed her into her bedroom.

CHAPTER 19

Sue Kim set the tray down on the dresser. Light peeked its way through the slats of the window blinds as she partially opened them. Awakened as the light beamed across his face, Nick looked up and saw her with the tray in her hands. She bent down and kissed him as he sat up in the bed. "Good morning," she said as she lowered the tray to his lap.

"Wow!" He looked down at the two slices of ham, scrambled eggs, toast, orange juice, and coffee staring back at him invitingly. Taking a deep breath and allowing the aroma of the combination to permeate his olfactory system, he said, "Ahhh!, smells good. You didn't have to . . ."

"I know," she answered matter-of-factly, sitting down on the edge of the bed next to him. "I thought you might be a little hungry." Her face reddened as she continued, "Especially after last night."

Nick picked up the knife and fork from the tray. She watched him cut the ham into bite-sized pieces and devour it. "Uhmm . . . excellent! You can cook, too."

"Of course!"

Sensing disturbance in her voice, he said apologetically, "I'm sorry . . . I didn't mean . . . I mean . . ."

"You probably should shut up and eat while you're ahead," she said.

He held up the glass of orange juice like he was making a formal toast and said, "I'll drink to that."

Smiling and adorned in the same shirt she had worn last night, Sue Kim stood up. Nick watched her soft, long, black hair stream behind her as if being supported by a light wind as she turned and left the room.

Just as he finished eating, she came back into the room. He saw a clock on the nightstand next to him and reached for his own watch, and compared the time on it with that of the clock. "Shit! I slept too late. It's almost nine o'clock. I'm gonna be late."

She reached into the linen closet, chose a towel, and tossed it to Nick saying, "That's it. Go ahead, eat, and run." She pointed to the bathroom. "The shower is in there."

He started to toss the sheet off of himself but realized he was naked. She watched him as he slowly maneuvered to the edge of the bed with the corner of the sheet covering his privates.

"You're funny," she giggled.

"What's funny?"

Looking directly at his groin and back up again, Sue Kim said, "What's the matter, Mr. Bashful? You afraid I'll see your pee pee? Guess what, I already did. Remember last night?" She ran her tongue around her lips. "Remember?"

His face turned red as he grabbed the towel and wrapped it around his waist and stood up. "I'll take that shower. Care to join me?"

"Maybe. Maybe not," she said teasingly.

Nick adjusted the water valve until the temperature was to his liking, warm but not too hot. The water felt good as it sprayed over his face. Suddenly he heard the sound of the shower door sliding open, then sliding shut. He knew he had company. He reached out for her, pulled her into his arms, and passionately pressed his lips to hers. They were oblivious to the water that cascaded over them like a spring rain.

CHAPTER 20

It was almost noon Saturday, and they were at their third stop. They had already met with Dolores Gray and Rosemary Freese. Dolores was St Michael's office manager and Rosemary was the secretary. They found both women at home and eager to talk, but they were unable to glean anything from either of them that would help, at least nothing Mike Bradley didn't already know. The pair described their ex-pastor as a tyrant, and stated they had constantly felt threatened by him. Each spoke of their concern for the way he had handled the church's finances. When Nick asked them why they didn't question the priest about it, each woman stated her own fear of reprisal. Both had heard his threats to fire anyone who questioned him.

Pulling in front of Father Roman's residence, Nick stopped his car. They both got out and followed the sidewalk to the front door. The house sat next to that of the deceased pastor, and the yard was almost a mirror image of his. Even the roses were similar. The only difference was that the house was designed opposite of its next-door neighbor—therefore, the garage was on the left.

At Mike's request, Nick had made an appointment with the priest for noon. Feeling it would be more private, Father Roman asked to meet them at his home rather than at the church. As Mike reached for the doorbell, the door suddenly opened. Father Roman looked tense as he said, "Come in, gentlemen."

Mike introduced Nick to Father Roman. The priest shook his hand and led them to the living room. "Can I get you anything?" he asked. He motioned for his guests to have a seat. "Coffee? Soda? A glass of water?"

"Nothing for me," Mike replied.

"Me neither, Father, thank you," Nick followed.

The two sat down on a brown sofa that sat under a large window offering a generous view of the front yard and Desert Oasis Drive. Across from them was a sliding glass door that led to a rear patio. In the corner, next to a rocking chair that looked very old, perhaps an antique, was a small, round wooden table with a white cloth draped over it. On top of it was a Bible and a statue of the Virgin Mary. A rollaround stand housing a medium-sized television and a DVR player sat alone on the other side of the room.

Mike thought to himself how different this was from this priest's deceased boss's house. Two houses, identical in design, but certainly not in decorum.

The priest spoke first as he sat down in the rocking chair. "What can I do for you gentlemen today?"

Mike answered, "Father, Lieutenant Greer has some questions if you don't mind. It's mostly routine stuff, okay?"

"Yeah, I guess it's okay," he answered in a voice that exhibited a trace of fear.

The detective's tone was gentle. "Thank you, Father, for meeting with us like this, especially on such short notice. I know you are busy with all that has happened. First of all, please accept my condolences on the loss of your friend."

"Thank you." The priest seemed a bit more at ease.

The detective continued, "I understand Father Mignanelli had been here about a year. Is that correct?"

"Yes, that is correct. A year last month, I believe."

"Did you know him before he came here?" Nick asked.

"No, sir."

"Could you describe your relationship with him for me?"

"We . . . well . . . he was my pastor. He administered the church, and I was his associate."

The detective continued, "What about outside of the daily operation of the church?"

The priest looked puzzled. "I don't know what you mean."

"Did you go places together? Did you do things together? Were you close friends? I see you were neighbors."

Father Roman looked at Mike and then at Nick. He leaned forward in his chair as if telling a secret and said, "He was my pastor. I was obedient to him, but other than that, I didn't see him outside of the church. He went his way and I went mine. Things worked better that way."

"So, you didn't get along with him?"

The startled priest looked at Mike who easily read the question on the priest's face and said, "Go ahead, Padre. It's okay. Tell him . . . tell him all of it."

The priest looked away, then looked back at Nick, paused for a moment, crossed himself, and said, "Jesus, forgive me." Looking back to the detective, the cleric cleared his throat. "Okay. I didn't care for him. I found his administrative techniques to be, to say the least, questionable."

The detective questioned, "How so, Father?"

"He was not a nice man," the priest answered. "He showed no respect for people, especially his staff. They work hard, but he treated them like slaves. He overworked us all while he was out doing who knows what. And should anyone complain or question him? Look out! He would either threaten them with dismissal or disciplinary action, like poor Bob Flores. He's our liturgist and directs our choirs. You know, he's got a wife and six kids. Rarely a week went by that David didn't threaten to fire him."

"How did Mr. Flores react to these threats?" Nick asked.

"He was afraid for his job so he did what he was told."

"Did he hate him?"

"Hate him? That's a pretty strong word. He didn't like him, that's for sure. The truth is, none of us did. But hate him? I think not. But I can only speak for myself there."

"So you didn't hate him?"

"Did I hate the things he did? Did I hate the way he treated people? Sure. But did I hate the man? Our Lord taught us to love one another. He told us that even if a person wrongs you seventy times seven times, you must still forgive him and love him."

"You were afraid of him though, weren't you?" Nick challenged.

The startled priest immediately looked at Mike, who shrugged his shoulders and shook his head to show he had not betrayed his trust. A few weeks ago, the priest had told Julie and Mike that one time he felt he had been threatened physically by Father David, instilling fear in him. Both of them wondered how this cop knew.

The cleric asked with a certain tension in his voice, "How did you know?"

"Instinct, just instinct."

The priest said, "He told me that if I crossed him, I would be real sorry. He said he had friends in high places."

Nick asked, "What did he mean by high places?"

"At first I thought he was referring to the bishop's office. But lately, well, he kept reminding me that he was Italian. I just know I wouldn't want to meet him in the dark, you know? I know that isn't nice to say or feel. I struggled with it daily. But he scared me. He just scared me."

Seeing the tears welling up in his eyes, Mike got up and went over to him. "It's okay, Father." He wrapped his arm around the priest's shoulder and repeated, "It's okay. It's not your fault."

Mike looked at Nick. "Is there anything else? I think he's had enough for today."

"Just one more thing, if I may, Father," the detective said gently.

Father Roman looked at him, paused, then said, "Go ahead."

"Who all had keys to his residence?"

The priest thought for a moment. "I believe just him and maybe his housekeeper."

"Thank you, Father," Nick said as he stood up and extended his hand. They shook.

"You're welcome," Father Roman replied.

"We'll see our way out," Nick said as he headed for the door. He stopped and looked back at the priest. "By the way, would you know where he kept his keys? You know, car, house, church building?"

The priest thought for a moment and answered, "He always kept them on his belt as far as I know. Right here." He pointed to his side.

"Thank you again, Father," Nick said. "I appreciate your time. Have a nice day."

"See you tonight, Padre," Mike said as he followed the detective to the door.

"See you tonight, Mike."

They left, got into the detective's car, and drove away.

CHAPTER 21

Roger Korus had been St. Michael's school principal for seven years and was the next stop on the detective's list. He only lived a couple of miles from the church. They drove down Cactus Road to Sixty-Third Avenue; making a left into a middle-class subdivision. After continuing south for two blocks, Nick turned right and came to a stop in front of the corner house. A man was in the front yard pushing a lawn mower. Recognizing him, Mike pointed in his direction. "That's him. That's Mr. Korus."

Just as they got out the car, he looked up and saw them and with a puzzled look on his face, bent down, and killed the mower engine. He wondered why Mike Bradley would be coming to his house; after all, they barely knew each other, and Mike had never been to the Korus' home.

As they approached him, Mike said, "Hi, Roger. Sorry to disturb you on your day off, but we need to talk to you for a moment, if it's okay."

Hesitating, Korus looked at the stranger who had accompanied Bradley.

"Roger, this is Lieutenant Greer from the Phoenix PD," Mike said. Looking toward Nick, he continued, "Nick, this is Roger Korus." They shook hands, but the educator couldn't hide the tension in his face. "Roger is the principal at St. Michael's School."

"Yes, thank you, Mr. Bradley," Nick followed the lead. He looked at the educator and said, "I apologize for taking you away from your work; however, I would like to talk to you about your former pastor, Father Mignanelli."

The confused principal looked directly at Mike, who said gently, "It's okay, Roger. It's normal stuff. Won't take long."

Some of the tension seemed to depart from his face as he said, "Let's go around to the back patio. I'd rather sit in the shade."

He led them through a wooden gate and along a sidewalk that led to the rear yard. A covered patio spanned the length of the house, about fifty feet, and sitting in the center was a wooden picnic bench. Their host motioned for them to sit. Nick made certain to sit across from his host, and Mike sat on the end of the brown table and looked out into the yard.

The tiff grass was manicured to perfection and cut short like the green on a golf course. In the center of the yard was a swimming pool. Its sparkling blue water looked so inviting that Mike felt like jumping in with his clothes on. Surrounding the pool was a bed of small white stones that outlined its pear-shaped edges. In each corner of the yard stood two lofty palm trees from where he could hear the gentle coo of pigeons. The breeze felt good as it gently blew through. The temperature was in the mid-seventies, and there was not a cloud in the sky. What a beautiful Arizona morning, he thought.

The detective began, "Mr. Korus, how would you describe your relationship with the deceased?"

"Well, it's pretty simple, I guess," Roger replied. "He was the pastor of St. Michael's, and I am the school principal."

"I understand that, sir, but how would you describe your relationship with him on a personal level?"

The educator sat straight up in his seat, looked directly at Nick, and stated, "We had no personal relationship, only a professional one."

"You never had lunch together, or talked about other things like family or friends?"

"As I said, sir, our relationship was strictly professional. He ran the church. I run the school."

The detective prodded, "How did he treat you?"

"The same way he treated everyone else, I guess."

It was obvious the man was being evasive, but the detective persisted. "How was that?"

"He ran things. He gave orders. We followed them."

"Did the teachers like him?"

"Not particularly."

"Did you like him?"

"Not particularly," he conceded. It was apparent to the detective that he was becoming irritable.

"Why are you asking all this?"

"Just routine," Nick said.

"For a suicide?"

It was clear they were going nowhere so Mike decided to change the approach. Looking at Nick, he said, "Tell him. It's okay."

The educator peered out over the top of his glasses. Their black frames seemed to be an extension of his black hair from which some gray strands were beginning to make their appearance.

Seeing that the detective was irritated and that he was about to speak, Mike looked the principal in the eyes and said, "You won't say anything to anyone, will you, Roger?"

They both could see the confusion on Korus's face as he looked at each of them; first at his fellow parishioner, then at the detective. "Mum's the word," he said.

The detective's glaring look showed he was not happy with what Mike Bradley had just done, but he had no choice but to follow the lead. Looking at the man across the table, Nick leaned forward and said in almost a whisper, "I'm just checking to be sure it was suicide."

Roger's eyes got so wide they looked like ping-pong balls. His mouth flew open in surprise. "You mean he was—"

Nick stopped him before he could finish the sentence. "I didn't say that, Mr. Korus. Sometimes things don't line up quite right, and I need to put them into perspective. Don't be alarmed. And I must ask you not to say anything to any of your staff. I may want to speak to some of them, and I don't want any of them to have any preconceived ideas or notions. I'm looking for facts, and I don't want them to be clouded by rumors. Most of this is routine when there is a sudden death. Do you understand?"

"Oh my! Am I a suspect?"

The detective shook his head in wonder. "There are no suspects at this time. I'm just trying to find out if a crime has even been committed. Like I said, it's routine stuff, just normal procedure."

"You won't be talking to them at the school, will you?" the principal asked. "I don't want you to bother them there."

"I'll try not to, sir," he answered. "Now, I have just a couple more questions for you if we can continue." He didn't leave time for an answer. "First, did Father Mignanelli have any disagreements with anyone, or did he do anything that might have upset anyone you know of?"

"Just about everyone," Roger answered. "He cut all our salaries, you know."

"Why?"

"He circulated a memo to all church and school employees stating that our salaries were being cut." The principal was angry. "The more you made, the bigger the cut."

"Did he give a reason?"

Roger leaned forward and looked straight into Nick's eyes and said, "Yeah, he gave a reason all right. He said collections were down so he had to cut budgets. It was his own fault that collections were down. He drove so many parishioners away with his attitude that the church was going in the hole. But he found the money to refurnish his house. You asked me if people were angry? You bet!"

Mike was shocked to see this man so emotional. It looks like we struck a nerve, he thought.

The principal continued, "We're a parochial school. We don't receive the salaries that the secular educators do as it is. Half of my staff said they wouldn't be back next year. They're all dedicated teachers, some of the best there are, but they have bills to pay, too."

"Do you think anyone was mad enough to want to hurt him?"

Looking surprised by the question, Korus answered, "No, I think some kids egged his house, but that's about all. He thought one of the workers did it, but it was probably just neighborhood kids doing what kids do. The answer to something like that is to move on, and a lot of my staff will do exactly that, well, maybe not now."

"How about you?"

"I'd have stayed, even though my salary would have been cut."

"I assume that would be a rather large salary cut for you," Nick stated, then added what almost seemed an afterthought, "You'd have to hire new people, too. I'll betcha that's a real pain."

The principal sat up straight in his seat and proudly stated, "Did you know St Michael's was designated the number one parochial school in the state two years in a row? I've never had problems filling openings here. I may not get the experienced staff I have now, but we'd survive. As for me, my wife makes excellent money. There's no problem there."

"Wouldn't you have had trouble filling the positions?"

"Probably not. The new hires would be on lower salaries. That would probably have made him happy."

"I see," said the detective. "One more thing. Who is around the church on Saturday afternoons? Especially last Saturday."

Roger stroked his chin, thought for a moment and replied, "You never know. Whoever has stuff to do, I guess. Bill Jamison is the custodian; he's most always there. Only been around a couple of months. A weird kind of guy. You might want to ask him."

"Weird? Why do you say that?"

"Just weird. Gives me the willies."

Nick stood up, extended his hand, and said, "Thank you for your time, Mr. Korus."

The educator rose and the two men shook hands.

Roger turned to Mike who said, "Thanks, Roger, we'll see ourselves out."

The detective seemed unusually silent as they drove away in the direction of the church.

About halfway there Mike broke the silence, "Sorry about that."

"About what?" Nick questioned.

"About making you spill the beans to Roger. But I figured it would cause him to open up, and he did."

"I think it's okay," Nick said. "It caught me by surprise, though. The next time you think about doing something like that, warn me. It got us some info. I just hope he doesn't say anything to his staff."

"Don't worry. He won't. He's too much of a wimp!"

Nick laughed.

"So what's our next stop?"

"Let's see if the janitor is working today."

CHAPTER 22

Nick Greer and Mike Bradley entered St. Michael's church hall together. A man about six feet tall, thin, and in need of a shave, was busy arranging chairs and tables. His long, brown hair was pulled straight back and tied in a ponytail. A blue and white bandana stuck out under a dirty, red baseball cap. Mike wondered why he was stacking the chairs like that, then remembered that tomorrow was blood day. Once each quarter, United Blood Services was here for donations. Mike remembered his appointment was set for tomorrow morning.

"I don't know this guy. You're on your own with this one."

Nick nodded and led the way across the tiled floor. The man looked up and saw them, then dropped his head back down.

"Are you Mr. Jamison?" Nick asked.

Without looking up, he continued his work. "Who wants to know?"

Nick pulled his badge from his pocket, reached down, and shoved it in front of the man's face and said, "This wants to know!"

Seeing the badge, he stopped his work, and looked up at the cop. His eyes looked quickly at the back door, like they were seeking an escape route. Then he looked back down and continued with his work.

The detective nodded toward Mike and said, "You may know Mr. Bradley here?"

"Nope, can't say that I do," the custodian said. "I'm sort of new here. Ain't met everybody." He looked to Mike, nodded, and continued with his work.

The detective said, "I'm checking into the death of Father David Mignanelli. Do you mind answering a few questions?"

"I don't know nuthin' 'bout it," he answered as he continued his work. "I was here all day, working."

Keeping his focus on his work, he didn't look at the two men so they were unable to see the expression on his face; however, there was a tone of fear in his voice.

"How well did you know Father Mignanelli?" Nick asked.

"Only been here a couple months. Didn't know him well at all. He hired me to keep the place lookin' n' feelin' good. I do that, and I mind my own business."

The detective continued probing, "How did he treat you? Did you like him?"

"He was okay. Gave me a job."

"You were here last Saturday afternoon, then?"

Looking up from his work, he answered sharply, "I told you I was! Somebody shoved some tables in that closet over there and busted a sprinkler head." He pointed to a storage area under what was used as a stage. Mike knew tables and chairs were stored under there when not in use. "Musta been a inch of water in here. Took all day to sop up the mess."

"Did you hear or see anything unusual?"

"Nope. Can't say that I did." He scratched his left temple with his left hand, thought for a moment and said, " 'Cept."

"Except what?" Nick asked.

"Well, I did hear truck backfires. It had to a been a truck. Too loud fer a car." He put his hands over his ears as he continued, "Scared me. Made me drop my wrench."

"You said backfires? There were more than one?"

"Uhhh," the man stuttered and stopped his work. "No. I mean . . . Yeah, maybe."

The detective probed, "You said backfires. How many?"

Again Jamison was hesitant in his answer. "Couple."

"Exactly where were you when you heard the noise?"

"Right here, tightenin' up the new sprinkler head."

"What time was this?"

"Let's see . . . uhh . . . must a been . . . around three thirty."

Nick looked at Mike, then back at the custodian. "Are you sure it was a backfire? Could it have been something else, maybe gunshots?"

"Sounded like backfire to me. Hear 'em all the time. Busy street out there."

"One more thing," Nick said. "I assume you have pass keys?"

"Yep."

"To everything?"

"Nope, just to here, the school and the church."

"Thank you," the detective said. "I appreciate your help."

Mike followed Nick out of the building. As they stepped out onto the sidewalk, Nick looked at Mike. "I need a key to the pastor's house, pronto. Can you get it? It's not on our surveillance anymore, and I assume it's locked."

Bradley was puzzled. "I can try, but why?"

"I got a hunch. I want to look around one more time."

"For what?"

"I'm not sure. Maybe another bullet."

As Mike looked at Nick in puzzlement, he saw someone coming out of the office. He nudged Nick and said, "We just got lucky. There's Maria. She's his housekeeper. She'll probably have a key."

Mike called to her, "Maria! You got a minute?"

She had just stepped down onto the blacktopped parking lot when she heard him. She stepped back onto the sidewalk and walked toward the two men. She gave Mike a hug, and he asked, "You okay?"

"I just locked up after the restoration company. They cleaned up the mess, you know. I just can't bear to go back in there."

"I understand, Maria."

Maria was a Hispanic woman, a little over five feet and in her mid-fifties. She had short, black hair and dark brown eyes that bore evidence of recent tears.

"I heard you found him. I'm sure glad it was you instead of me." Feeling a tinge of embarrassment, she added, "I'm sorry. I didn't mean it that way. I didn't mean I was glad it was you. I'm just glad it wasn't me, that's all."

Mike Bradley said gently, "It's okay. I understand what you meant. Don't worry about it."

Putting his hands on her shoulders, he said, "Maria, I want you to meet someone. This is Lieutenant Nick Greer from the Phoenix PD. Nick, this is Maria Canez. Now don't be alarmed Maria, there's nothing to worry about. He's a friend of mine, and he needs to talk to you for a minute, okay?"

The little housekeeper looked up at the tall policeman, then back at Mike. "Okay, I guess it's okay."

"Can we go somewhere to talk?" Nick asked.

"We can go the office," she suggested.

Nick looked at Mike. "Is that wise?"

"I think it's okay. It's Saturday. Not a bunch of people hanging around." He looked at the gold badge dangling from the detective's belt and said, "You might want to hide that thing though."

He looked at Maria and asked, "Is anyone in there?"

"Just some new girl at the phone."

"We should have some privacy in the conference room," Mike stated.

They entered the office through the front door, and Mike led them to the conference room. They sat down at the end of a long table that sat directly centered in the large room. Straight-back chairs surrounded the table like perfectly placed sentinels. One end of the room had a large white board on the wall, and the other end contained a cabinet about four feet wide. On the top of the cabinet sat a cross and a closed Bible.

Mike again sat at the end, and Nick sat across the table from Maria with his back to the only window in the room. Mike put his hands on the table, and Maria reached for them as she looked across the table at the police officer. Mike cupped his hands around hers. He could feel her shaking as the detective began.

"Ma'am, I need to ask you some questions, is that okay?"

Mike felt the pressure on his hands as she squeezed them and nodded in assent. He was awed by the detective's gentleness.

"You were the de . . . Father Mignanelli's housekeeper?" He was about to say deceased, but thought better of it.

"Yes, yes, sir, I was."

"What was he like to work for?"

"He was strict," she answered. "But he was nice to me. He was very private though."

"How do you mean?"

"Well," she said as she looked down at the table, then looked back at Nick. "He was very particular about things. Like his clothes, for example, had to be folded just so, and he had to have space between everything that was on hangers."

The detective remembered how meticulous everything looked when he went through the priest's closets and drawers. "Did you get along with him okay?"

"Oh my, yes," she replied. "He used to talk about his family in Pennsylvania, and his ordination. He was proud of that, you know."

"I understand he was under some sort of scrutiny from the diocese, some sort of investigation? Do you know anything about that?"

She looked at Mike. He squeezed her hand lightly. She looked back at Nick and said, "I know he was upset. He said several times someone was out to get him, but they would never get away with it. He said they'd be sorry."

"They?" the detective questioned. "Do you know who he meant by they?"

"I don't know exactly. I guess some of the people in the parish who were trying to get rid of him." She looked directly at Mike. "They started some sort of petition."

"Do you know who they were?"

Maria again looked at Mike. He hoped her eyes didn't betray the fact that he was one of the parishioners behind the petition.

Looking at Nick, he said, "I'll tell you about it later."

The detective looked back to Maria. "Were you here last Saturday?"

"No, sir. I come in on Mondays, Wednesdays, and Fridays."

"Did he appear to you to be afraid of anyone? Did he ever say anything about anyone maybe wanting to hurt him?"

"Oh, heavens, no!"

"How about friends? Did he receive many visitors?"

Maria looked up at the ceiling for a moment as she pondered his question, then she looked back to Nick and said, "His friend, Father Blake, was there a lot for dinner. I cooked dinner for him on Wednesdays, you know." She smiled. "He liked my enchiladas."

"Anyone else?"

"There must have been, but I never met any of them," she answered.

"I'm sorry, ma'am, but I don't understand. Why do you say there must have been?"

"Almost every Monday his house was a mess. Lots of dirty dishes and empty bottles. There were often empty food containers like pizza boxes, KFC, Chinese, and lots more. He couldn't have possibly eaten all that food himself, so he must've had someone there."

"Bottles?" Nick questioned. "What kind of bottles?"

"Oh . . . I shouldn't say anymore," Maria said as she tightened her lips.

"It's okay, Maria," Mike said with as much comfort in his tone as he could muster up. "We need to know as much about him as possible. Were they liquor bottles?"

She nodded and said shyly, "Lots of them." She looked down at the table again as if she was ashamed of what she was telling them.

The detective continued his questioning. "Was it like that every Monday?"

"Almost." She giggled and her face reddened. "I think he was a party animal."

Nick smiled and leaned back in the chair, laced his hands behind his head and looked up toward the ceiling. He was reminded of the items he found in the priest's nightstand and in his car. He leaned forward and placed his hands on the table. "Mrs. Canez, do you know where he kept his keys?"

"He either had them on him, like that." She pointed to Mike's keys hanging from his belt. "Or they were in his bedroom on the nightstand."

Nick's tone again was gentle. "Mrs. Canez, we're having trouble locating his keys. They weren't in his personal effects, and I couldn't find them anywhere in the house or in his car. I'd really like to find them."

She shrugged her tiny shoulders and shook her head.

Satisfied with her answer, the detective nodded. "One more thing, ma'am. I need to go back into the house. Would you care to let us in? Or would you rather let us borrow the key?"

Maria looked at Mike as if asking his approval. He nodded. She stood and said, "Would you excuse me for a moment?"

After she left the room, Mike asked Nick, "Would you mind if I asked her a couple of questions?"

"Be my guest," he answered. "But first I have one for you."

A look of puzzlement came to Mike Bradley's face. "Go ahead."

"Why didn't you tell me you were one of the ones trying to get rid of him?" It was easy to tell by the tone of his voice that he was upset.

Mike's answer was interrupted by a rustling sound coming from behind the detective, who sprang to his feet and rushed to the large window and quickly parted the slats of the mini-blind.

Bradley watched as the detective peered out the window, looking from side to side, covering all angles. "What was that about?" Mike asked.

"I'm not sure," he answered. "But I think someone was interested in our conversation. I saw something there, but it's gone now."

Just then Maria returned holding a bright shiny silver key in her right hand. She handed it to Mike along with a small folded piece of paper. "I can't bear to go back in there right now. Just bring the key back when you're finished. I called Father Roman, and he said it's okay."

Nick turned his attention from the window back to Maria. "Where is the key kept?"

"In the key box," she stated. "There are extras of all the keys in there."

"Where is the key box?"

"In the copier room."

"Who has access to this key box?"

"The secretaries, the office people, the staff, and I guess . . . I guess anyone."

Mike interjected, "The box is normally open. Anyone can sign out a key if they need it. I've picked up the hall key several times, but I had no clue his house key was there."

"Do they have to be signed out?" Nick asked.

"Supposed to be, but most of us just take them," Mike answered.

"So anyone could get in his house?"

"Oh no! No way," Maria said. "They'd have to have the alarm code. Only Father David and I have that. He changed it as soon as he moved in. He wouldn't let anyone have it but me."

"Thank you, Mrs. Canez," Nick said. "You've been a big help."

"Maria," Mike said, "there's something I'm curious about. I understand that delivery trucks of some sort have been seen in front of the house on several occasions. Do you know anything about them?"

"I guess he couldn't make up his mind on what he liked," she answered. "He was very picky, you know. He'd get some new stuff delivered . . . nice stuff. The next thing you know, it would be gone and something else would be there."

"Maria, What kind of stuff?" Bradley probed.

"Oh, you know, furniture, TVs, stereos, computers, even refrigerators. One day they'd come, a week or two later they were gone, and another one came." She lifted both of her hands about shoulder height, shrugged and whispered like a little child telling a secret, "Did you know he had three different big plasma TVs this year?"

"Didn't you think that to be a little unusual?"

She folded her hands across her chest, pursed her lips tightly, and said, "None of my business!"

Mike chuckled, gave her a hug, and said, "Thanks, Maria. I'll bring the key back when we're done."

They left the room and exited the building the way they came in. As they started down the sidewalk, Nick suddenly turned left and walked on the grass. He stopped in front of the conference room window and squatted down to the ground. He appeared to be looking at something in the dirt. Then he stood and walked back over to where Mike was standing.

"What's up?" Bradley asked.

"Your janitor has been busy spying on us," the detective answered.

"You sure? How do you know it was him?"

"Footprint." He pointed toward the window. "I'll bet if you were to walk through the hall over there, you'll find a certain janitor with a muddy right boot."

Accepting the challenge, Mike said, "Wait here." He turned before Nick could stop him and taking care to hide his true intentions, walked into the hall through the front entrance and out through the side door. He knew people were constantly cutting through there, so no attention should come to him. He could hear clanging and bumping that told him tables and chairs were still being stacked. Nodding to the custodian as he passed, Mike saw that the lieutenant was right. There was mud on his right boot.

The detective was waiting for him on the sidewalk. "Sure glad I didn't bet you," said Bradley. "How did you know?"

"Beside you and me, he seems to be the only male on the premises, and I ain't never met a woman who wore a size-twelve boot, nor do I wanna!"

They both laughed as they began the walk across the parking lot to the priest's house.

About halfway there, Nick saw the folded paper that Maria had put in Mike's hand. "What's on the paper?" he asked.

"The alarm code, what else?"

"Thought so."

CHAPTER 23

Detective Lieutenant Nick Greer and Mike Bradley followed the sidewalk to the front door of Father David Mignanelli's residence, retracing their steps of a week ago. The roses were still blooming just as they were on that fateful night. Mike thought about all that had happened in the last week. If he hadn't experienced it himself, he wouldn't have thought it possible. Handing the key to the cop, he watched him shove it into the lock and heard the slapping sound of the dead bolt as he turned the key.

The alarm beeped as it came to life, and he looked at the tiny piece of paper that Maria had given him and punched in the numbers, four . . . two . . . five . . . seven. The detective was already heading down the hall when the beeping ceased. Mike followed him to the room where he had discovered the body only a week before and watched as the detective stood in the center of the room, with his hands on his hips. There was an eerie silence as Greer meticulously surveyed the room, not missing an angle.

Mike was amazed at how clean the room was. The carpet and drapes looked spotless. The desk and chair were as clean as new, and there was barely a trace of the red splatters of blood that had dotted the wall. A little painting and no one would ever know. The only thing missing was the computer. Where was it? Maybe the cops have it, he thought.

As an insurance investigator, Mike dealt regularly with restoration companies. This one was good. He made a mental note to find out who they were when he looked up and saw the detective standing along the west wall with his index finger over a small hole about three feet above the floor. "Was that where the bullet went?" Mike asked.

"One of them," he answered. "We pulled a thirty-eight slug out of here last week."

"Mike was momentarily stunned by his statement. "What do you mean by 'one of them'?"

"I got a hunch," he answered as he pointed to the desk. "You know those little colored push-type pins you use on corkboard?"

"Yeah . . ."

"See if you can find a couple, or something similar in there, maybe a thumbtack. I'll be right back."

Mike opened the middle drawer of the desk and seeing a black plastic organizer, found a small supply of multi-colored push-pins. He took out two and laid them on the desk.

Nick returned with a ball of string he had retrieved from his car. Mike pointed to the pins on the desk. Nick nodded and walked over to the desk, looked at it, then at the floor. Dropping to his knees beside the desk, the detective slowly began running his fingers over the carpet, feeling the fiber and probing. Then he stood up and went to the right side of the desk, pushed on it, moving it about six inches to the left placing the legs of the desk in the indentations of the carpet. Even after a thorough cleaning, the marks from where the desk had been, though barely visible, were still in the carpet.

The detective looked at Mike and said as he rolled a chair to the desk, "You're about his height. Sit down in the chair."

"Do I have to? You know what happened to the last guy who sat in this chair," Mike said as he sat down and pulled the chair up to the desk.

Greer ignored the comment. "Now, sit up perfectly straight," he directed.

As Mike sat erect, the detective took the string, put one end on the right side of Mike's head, slightly above and in front of Mike's ear, and said, "Hold this here and don't move."

Holding the string to his head with his right index finger, he watched out of the corner of his eye as the detective stretched the string to the empty bullet hole and anchored it with one of the pins. Nick stood back, looked at the string, and said, "Notice anything?"

"You told me to be still. I can't move my head. How the hell can I see anything?"

"Okay, hold on." Nick laughed and took the end of the string at Mike's head and held it there steady in the air. "Okay, go ahead and get up."

The policeman's steady hand never wavered as Mike got up and stood back and looked at the string. Holding both of his hands out in front of him waist-high and palms out, he shrugged his shoulders. "Ookaaaaay?"

"Look at the trajectory. See anything strange?"

He shrugged again.

"The hole in the wall is twelve to fourteen inches lower than the exit wound. Now, if a person is going to shoot himself in the head, odds are he would sit up straight, almost at attention. If he did so, and if he held the gun in a normal manner"—he pointed his right index finger to his head to demonstrate—"the bullet's trajectory should be slightly upward a few degrees, or at best straight."

"So what does that mean?"

"Maybe nothing, and maybe something," he said as he began looking around the room.

Directly next to the room's entrance was a small closet. Nick went over to it and opened the door. Inside were some clothes hanging from a rod that spanned the closet. There were two windbreakers, two light coats and a heavier one. He ran his hands up and down each piece of clothing feeling the cloth. He noticed one had a small hole in it. He put his finger into the hole, and then quickly slid everything to the left.

"Voila!" he exclaimed. "Take a look at this." He pointed to a small hole in the back wall of the closet and pulled a small jackknife from his trousers pocket, then began probing the hole. He retrieved a tiny flashlight from his key chain and shined it into the hole. "Son of a bitch!"

"What's wrong?" Bradley asked.

He handed the flashlight to Mike and pointed to the hole. "Take a look and tell me what you see."

Mike aimed the light into the opening and said, "I see a hole. I guess a bullet hole?"

Nick smiled. "It's obviously a bullet hole. It's the same size as the one over there." He pointed to the adjoining wall. "See this?" he continued as he took the jacket down and showed Mike the hole. "Same height as the hole. I'll bet forensics will find powder residue on it, too."

"What happened to the bullet?"

"Good question. The crime scene techs missed it, and I'm sorry to say, so did I. It looks like someone dug it out of the wall. The door must have been open, see, no hole. The perp knew the bullet would make a hole wherever it went, so he figured he'd hide it as best he could, hoping we'd miss it. We did! This guy knows how to cover his tracks."

"That's why the janitor said he heard two backfires," Bradley stated more than asked.

"Exactly. That's why we came back here. When he stumbled about how many times he heard a backfire, I figured it must be some coincidence or else there were two shots. One of the first things I learned on this job is there are no coincidences. So it made me think, there must have been two gunshots. So where was the other bullet?

"Here's my theory," he said as he walked over to the chair. "Your pastor was sitting here." He pointed to the chair. "His back was to the door. He was using the computer, and music was playing so he didn't hear anyone come in. The perp sneaks in and shoots him in the left temple. Now, the perp would have been standing up. That would explain the downward trajectory of the bullet." He pointed to the hole in the west wall. "Now this perp was no dummy. He knew the first thing we would look for was GSR, gunshot residue, on the victim's hand, so he put the gun in the dead man's hand and fired again, this time into the closet. He replaced one of the bullets in the gun so it would look like only one shot was fired. Then he dug the bullet out of the closet wall and split."

"No hole in the door," Bradley remarked.

"Maybe it was already open. Maybe the perp opened it," the detective responded.

"That part isn't important. What's important is this: I'm sure your pastor didn't kill himself, and whoever did it knew what he was doing."

"You mean a professional?"

"I don't want to go that far. It's a little sloppy for a pro. But I don't think it was random. Whoever did it had a well-thought-out plan though, and knew the victim was left-handed."

They got back into Nick's car. Mike was just about to ask what the next stop was when Nick pulled back into St. Michael's parking lot, stopped the car, jammed it into park, but didn't shut off the engine. The detective looked directly at his passenger and said, "Why didn't you tell me you were involved in the petition to remove your pastor?"

Temporarily stunned by the sternness in his voice, Mike replied, "Umm . . . I didn't consider it relevant, and, besides, you never asked."

"Let me decide what's relevant," the detective lectured. "I expect you to tell me anything and everything you think of, no matter how relevant you think it might be. Now, what else haven't you told me?"

Mike's voice betrayed his feeling of defensiveness. "What else do you want to know?"

"Exactly what was your part in the petition?"

"First of all, it wasn't a petition," he answered. "We sent a letter to every registered St. Michael's parishioner. It simply said there were some questionable discrepancies in the church's finances. There were approximately twenty thousand unaccounted for dollars. The letter stated we had copies of cancelled checks available for anyone who wanted to see them. It said clearly that we were not, at this time, accusing our pastor of anything. However, he had been asked several times to explain where the money went, and to this date, has refused to cooperate. We even listed the checks, who they were made out to, and how much each one was written for."

"Who were they written to?" Nick asked.

"Let's see. Audio City, Best Buy, Sears, Fry's Electronics, Marshall's TV & Stereo, Spencer's, and various other appliance, electronics or furniture stores.

"Nick, something wasn't right. Christmas was coming, and that brings lots of dollars into the church. We were concerned that the money be properly allocated, so we told the people what their options were. That's all. We were careful not to tell them not to give."

"The options being?"

"They could give as usual, of course," Mike replied. "Or they could designate their money to go to a particular place like St. Vincent de Paul, the school, the teens, the choir, or a specific ministry. If you do so it was "supposed" to go there. Personally, I wasn't sure it would. We also told them they had the option to hold back the funds until the bishop did something about the situation."

"What were the results?" the detective questioned.

"A home run! The collection was less than half of what it normally was. Father David lied about it, but a friend of mine on the finance committee told me the truth. After that, the regular collections got worse and worse. Father David was sly. He tried to cover it up by publishing the income statements monthly, instead of weekly. I guess he thought it would look like more to the people, or something like that."

"How many people were involved in it?"

"It started out with just a handful," Mike answered. "But it grew fast. Most of the church and school employees didn't sign, because they were afraid of being fired. But they worked behind the scenes getting copies of checks, mailing lists, or spreading the word as to when and where the letter would be available for signing. Some of the employees wanted to sign, but I told them not to. I didn't want them to get fired, and, besides, we had enough signers. We had over a hundred signatures on the letter, and most of them were well known, high-profile parishioners."

Focusing on Mike's reference to, 'I', the detective asked: "*Exactly* what was your part in all of it?"

Mike looked at Nick. He felt like the proverbial cookie jar lid had just been slammed shut with his fingers in it, so he decided the whole truth was probably the best.

"Well, let's see." He hesitated for a moment. "I drafted the letter. I was the first to sign it, and . . . oh yeah . . . I funded it, you know, mail, stamps. Other than that, I guess I didn't have much to do with it."

The detective's eyes widened as he shook his head. " 'Other than that'?"

"Sorry," Mike said. "Look, here's the deal. People, I mean hundreds, had sent letters to the bishop's office about Father David. The answer, if there was one at all, was the same to everyone: 'Talk to Father Mignanelli about it.' Nick, that was the problem. He refused to discuss it with anyone. He told them it was none of their business. I wrote three letters, myself. The first one outlined what was happening here. The answer was, 'Talk to Father Mignanelli about it.' I had already tried that before I ever wrote to the bishop and guess what? . . . The prick threw me out of his fucking office!"

Mike's disturbance was obvious. He saw the look on the detective's face and realized he had been, he guessed, borderline yelling. He took a breath and calmed down before continuing.

"In the second letter, I told the bishop I'd been thrown out when I tried to discuss the situation with Father David, and guess what his answer was."

The detective nodded. "Let me guess . . . Go talk to Father Mignanelli about it?"

"Bingo! So I sent a third letter asking for a meeting with the bishop. I never received a response. The bishop didn't seem to care that people were leaving St. Michael's in herds. I guess he figured they'd go to a neighboring parish. Oh, by the way, the answers weren't even from the bishop, but from one of his lackeys, a Father Denkens."

Nick remembered his own meeting with Father Denkens. Now he understood why the vicar had been so defensive.

"So why the letter? What did you expect it to accomplish?"

"It got O'Malley's attention," Mike answered. "One thing for sure about this bishop, money talks. I figured if we could choke off the money supply, then maybe, just maybe, he might respond. And guess what? He did. It worked."

"In what way?" Nick questioned.

"The bishop ordered a full-blown audit of the church's finances. He also appointed a committee to interview some of St. Michael's employees and parishioners about how he interacted with people and about his personality."

"Were all employees interviewed?"

"Don't know. I know the ones who worked close to him were."

"Were you interviewed?"

"Yep."

"And what did you tell them?"

"The truth. I told them in a very diplomatic manner—after all, these were priests and one was a nun—that he was an arrogant pompous ass."

Nick grinned. "Anything else I should know?"

"Not that I can think of. But I want you to understand something."

"What's that?"

"We had several meetings about this. Sometimes over a hundred people were there. Some wanted to take it to the media. They even mentioned *20/20* and *Dateline*. I didn't want my church dragged through the media. The bishop was taking enough shots about his cover-ups of pedophiles, you know what I mean. This was the last shot, and it worked."

"How so?"

"We got a call from the bishop's office. They wanted to talk. Three of us attended a meeting at the diocesan office: Roseanne Rush, Les

Barrella and me. We met with Father Denkens. I guess the bishop was too busy for us peons."

The detective asked, "What happened at the meeting?"

"We explained all that had transpired at St. Michael's since Father David took over. Father Denkens was still protective of his priest, but open for input. He even asked what would happen if the audit was clean. Would things be better at St. Michael's? We knew things would never be right as long as he was there. He'd alienated too many people. It was like a cancer that needed removal. Our church was a very spiritual community until he took over. He needed to be replaced by someone who could resurrect the passion and the spirituality that was once alive at St. Michael's."

"How did Father Denkens react to that?"

"Still protective of his priest, but he promised to seriously look into the situation. The next thing you know, there are people from the diocese here, and you know the rest.

"By the way," Mike added, "rumor had it that he was out, that he was being transferred."

"Where did you hear that?"

"One of the employees here used to work at the diocese. She still has contacts there. She told me a little over a week ago that he was being moved."

"Do you trust her information?"

"Absolutely!" Mike affirmed, wondering why the detective didn't ask for her name. He decided not to volunteer it.

Nick shut off the engine and said, "Let's go talk to Mr. Dirty Boots."

All the chairs were neatly stacked on top of the long brown tables. The room was quiet, and there were no signs of human life. The silence was broken by the sound of running water. Knowing where it was coming from, Mike motioned for Nick to follow him down the hallway. As they came to the first door on the left, they saw the custodian filling a bucket with water from a short black hose. Brooms and mops sat in the corner. A dank, musty smell came from the mops that never seemed to dry out. Shelves littered with cans and bottles of cleaning materials hung on the left wall.

"Mr. Jamison," the detective began. "I have a couple more questions for you."

Jamison continued working. "I already told ya all I know," he said without trying to hide his irritation.

"I just need to clear up a couple of things," the cop said as the custodian shut off the water and reached for a mop. "What time did you hear the truck backfiring?"

"Like I said. 'Round three thirty."

The detective continued, "*Around* three thirty. Can you narrow it down anymore? Maybe a little before or a little after?"

"Nope," Jamison replied. "Look, I gotta git this floor mopped."

Nick looked down at the janitor's boots. They were both clean. Traces of water told the detective that the man had just rinsed them off, probably with the hose he still had in his hand.

"Have you been in here all afternoon?" the detective questioned.

"Yup. Never left the building."

"Thank you for your time," Nick said.

As they walked across the parking lot, Mike questioned the detective. "Did you see his shoes?"

"Yep."

Surprised by such a short answer he probed, "Why didn't you ask him about them?"

"It wouldn't have done any good."

"Why not?"

"He just would have lied."

CHAPTER 24

It was almost 3:30 when Mike arrived home. They'd worked through lunch, so he thought he'd make a sandwich, sit for a while and unwind before showering and heading for the church. Reaching up to the car's sun visor, he pressed the button for the garage door opener. The door rose and he brought the car to a stop inside. He got out of the car, pushed the button on the wall, and heard the familiar grinding of the garage door as it made its way to the cement floor.

Julie was dressed for church and was heating something on the stove. "How was your day?" Mike asked.

"Lonely," she answered. "You were gone all day. You didn't even bother to call."

"Sorry. We just kept going all day. We didn't even stop for lunch. I'm hungry!"

"It wouldn't hurt you to miss a few lunches," she said. "You had a bunch of calls. It looks like you and that cop friend of yours are causing quite an uproar."

"What do you mean?"

Julie handed him a list with names and phone numbers on it. "See for yourself."

He looked at the list. Dolores Gray, Rosemary Freese, Roger Korus and Roseanne Rush. "Shit!" he exclaimed as he wadded up the paper and tossed it into the trash can. Mike knew very well what they wanted, but he asked Julie anyway. She said Rosemary, Dolores and Roger all called about the meetings today, and she didn't know what Roseanne wanted. Her message had been left on voice mail.

Roseanne was the church busybody, though she considered herself the information center. Most likely she had called to find out what was going on. Mike thought about calling her, but decided to let it wait. He wasn't in the mood to deal with anyone now.

"I'm not going to Mass tonight," he stated emphatically.

"Why not?"

"I don't want them bugging me. I don't want to deal with it. Not tonight! They're just going to ask a bunch of questions I can't answer anyway."

"Oh, I see," Julie said. He could feel the fire heating up. "So you're going to leave me to deal with them. Do you think for one minute they'll believe me when I tell them I don't know anything, even though I don't?"

"Okay! Fine! I'll go. But I'm gonna sit in the back." He thought for a moment and added, "I know what I want for my birthday."

She wondered what all of a sudden brought that on. "What?"

"An unlisted phone number!"

CHAPTER 25

It was 7:50 Monday morning when Nick Greer drove into the police parking lot. All during the drive this morning, his thoughts were on Sue Kim. Saturday evening they went to dinner and to a movie, then went to his townhouse where they spent the night.

He thought about how lovely she was and how natural it seemed when they made love. He'd known no one like her before. She could be subservient and timid, and she could be feisty and bold. He'd only met her a little more than a week ago but feelings already were beginning to take root in him. He wondered if he was falling in love. No, not this quickly, but was he really certain?

As he entered the homicide room, he instinctively reached to his left and plucked his messages from the small slot above his name. His attention went to the first one. In large capital letters was written: CAPTAIN MENDOZA, IMMEDIATELY!

The door was closed. The black letters on the frosted glass door looked almost three-dimensional: Agapito Mendoza, Captain. He knocked on the door and heard the voice from inside say, "Come in."

Nick opened the door. "You wanted to see me, Pete?"

Not looking up from the file he was studying, he answered, "Yeah, Nick, have a seat."

The captain's office was small but well organized. A five-foot wooden desk sat in the center of the room just far enough away from the rear wall to comfortably accommodate the large brown leather swivel chair in which its occupant sat. There were pictures and credentials hung on the wall behind him surrounding the department insignia of the Phoenix Bird and the motto: To Protect and to Serve.

The large bookshelf on the wall to Nick's left held mostly department instruction and training manuals. There were two brown leather chairs facing the captain's desk. Nick had sat there many times before, mostly to discuss cases and sometimes just to talk.

Pete Mendoza was in his early fifties. His wavy hair was losing its battle to stay black, but other than that, he appeared younger than his years. Regular workouts kept him in good physical condition. They had worked together previously on several cases and shared a mutual respect for each other. When Pete was promoted to captain and assigned to the homicide division, Nick was elated.

"What's up? Your note said immediately." The lieutenant sat down in one of the two chairs that sat in front of his captain's desk.

The captain picked up a note from the left side of his desk, leaned back in his chair and studied it for a brief moment. "You're working a case involving the death of a priest. A Father David Mignanelli." His words were more a statement of fact than a question.

Nick nodded.

"What's the deal with it? Why isn't it closed? It isn't like you to waste so much time on a suicide. Isn't your caseload big enough? I can fix that, you know."

Shocked at what he just heard from his boss and friend, Nick answered, "You know better than that, Pete. If it was a suicide, I would have signed off on it by now."

"What do you mean . . . if?"

The lieutenant looked directly at his boss. "I'm not so sure it was suicide."

"Come on, Nick, it's so obvious. Besides, who would kill a priest anyway?"

"That's what I intend to find out. And it's not as obvious as you may think."

The detective explained to his boss what he had found in the rooms, especially the second bullet hole.

"Do you have a suspect?" Mendoza asked.

"I'm working on it."

"Motive?"

"Uhhh . . . not yet," he admitted.

The captain looked straight into his detective's face. "I think you should close this one out."

"Is that an order, boss?"

"Let's just call it a strong suggestion."

The detective was stunned, and anger began to take root inside him. "Why? You all of a sudden don't think I know what the hell I'm doing?"

The captain now found himself on the defensive. "Look, Lieutenant." It had been a long time since this captain addressed his friend by rank. "You have a large caseload, and you're wasting time on a suicide! You need to move on."

Nick leaned forward. "Who put you up to this, Pete?"

"What do you mean?" Greer felt the disturbance in his captain's voice.

"Pete, you've never gotten involved like this in any of my cases. Why now? Who's pushing you?"

The captain stood up, walked to the window, and peered out for several seconds, then turned, and sat back down. Looking at his friend, he said, "Off the record?"

The lieutenant nodded.

"Upstairs thinks we have more important things to do than waste man-hours on what they insist is an obvious suicide."

"Upstairs? Upstairs? You tell those idiots I'll handle my cases as I see fit."

The captain looked at his subordinate and said sternly, "Lieutenant, this isn't just from the brass."

The look in Mendoza's eyes told Nick his boss was dead serious. "This isn't just from upstairs." Nick said. "It's from the mayor, isn't it?"

He waited for a denial. None came. The anger continued rising inside him like a volcano ready to spew hot lava. "You can tell Murphy, I'll close the case when I'm convinced it was a suicide or when I find the perp. And you can tell him if he doesn't like it, he can go into his fancy private office, and shove it up his fat ass!"

Greer got up to leave, stopped, turned back to his boss, and said, "And his buddy the bishop can join him!"

He didn't hear his boss comment as he left. "That's what I thought you'd say, sort of."

Nick returned to his desk. This was the first time he had ever had a disagreement of this magnitude with Pete Mendoza. He sat down at his desk and pondered over what had just occurred. Did he overreact? Should he go back and apologize? Thinking it over for a moment, he decided the answer to both was no.

Picking up the messages on his desk and seeing that one was from Sue Kim, he smiled. It was from Thursday. He'd seen her since then so he wadded it up, reached under his desk, and dropped it in the trash can. The next one was from Cassie. Surprised to see that it didn't say ex-wife as it usually did, but that it actually said Cassie, he murmured out loud. "She wants something." He decided he would call her later.

He spent the rest of the day reviewing the Mignanelli file. He never left his desk as he studied it page by page carefully reviewing the reports, paying special attention to the angle of the bullet's entry and exit. They supported his theory. Convinced that the priest didn't kill himself, he couldn't abandon this case now. But who would have done such a thing? And why? I gotta find his keys, he thought as he looked over his notes. I gotta find his keys!

Removing a pen and a yellow pad from the center drawer of his desk, he began making notes: Check trigger pull.

Then he added: Possibles. Jamison. Korus.

He stroked his chin for a moment, and then added another name to the list: Bradley.

CHAPTER 26

Nick decided he should call Cassie. The message on his desk revealed that the area code was 928. Recognizing the number as belonging to Cassie's parents in Prescott, he said aloud, "Why the hell is she still in Prescott?" He checked the date written on the pink message form. It was today at 7:40 a.m. He dialed the number and listened as it rang; two rings, three, four and five. Just as he was about to hang up a voice came from the other end.

"Metzlers' residence."

He recognized the voice on the other end. It was Cassie's father. "Hello, Rod."

"Nick, my boy. How are you?"

Rod Metzler was in his late sixties and was well known in Phoenix and Prescott. He was a real estate developer who had projects throughout the state. He and his wife of forty-five years had moved to Prescott five years ago to "get out of the heat," they said.

Nick and Rod had gotten along well since the first day they met. The Metzlers raised two daughters, and Rod considered Nick the son he never had. He was not happy with the marriage breakup; however, he was a loyal father and took his daughter's side.

"I'm fine," Nick answered. "Cassie left a message. Can I speak to her?"

"She's not here. She's at the school."

"School? What school?" Nick asked.

"She's registering the kids," the elder answered.

"Registering them? For what?"

"School, of course," Rod answered. "I thought you knew."

There was a momentary silence, then Nick Greer was seized by anger. "Knew what? What school?"

"Cassie said it was okay with you," Metzler said with a tone of surprise in his voice.

"*What* is supposed to be okay with me?"

"Cassie and the kids are moving in with us. We have lots of room and—"

"Like hell they are!" Nick yelled as his anger reached its boiling point. "No fucking way!"

"Nick," Metzler said calmly but firmly, "you don't need to use that kind of language with me. It's a good move for the kids. There's much less crime here and there's no pollution either. Good for Kelli's allergies, you know."

Nick retorted sharply with ice in his tone, "You have your daughter call my cell phone the moment she returns!"

"I'll give her the message," Metzler answered.

Nick slammed the phone down on its cradle so hard that it was heard throughout the room. Looking up, he saw several people staring at him.

When they saw him look up they went about their routines, except for Sonny Madison who was standing directly in front of Nick's desk listening to it all. "Let me guess," he said, "Uhhh . . . Cassie! What did she do this time?"

"She's trying to keep the kids away from me. She's moved up north."

"Whoa! Whatever caused that?" Sonny asked.

Nick knew the concern in his friend's voice was legitimate as he sat down and rubbed his fingers against his forehead in a massaging motion. "Probably her mother. The bitch has been trying to suck her in ever since they moved to Prescott."

"Can she do that?" Sonny questioned.

"I don't know. Probably. The custody papers say she can't take them out of state without my permission. The last time I checked, Prescott was still in Arizona. I guess I'll have to call my lawyer."

He checked his watch. It was ten after five. He'd have to wait until tomorrow.

CHAPTER 27

As Nick Greer took the elevator back to his office, he ran the events of the past days through his mind. It was Tuesday morning. He had already been to the evidence room and checked the trigger pull on what he was now convinced was the murder weapon. It was a hard pull: six to seven pounds. There was no doubt in his mind now. The priest's death was not a suicide. Now . . . how to prove it. With no strong suspects and no motive and the brass on him to drop the case, he had a tough job ahead of him, he thought as he entered the squad room. But he was a tough cop, and determined to solve this case.

There were two messages waiting for him. One from Sue Kim that said, "Lunch?" The other was from Cassie. He'd answer that one first.

Going directly to his desk, Nick sat down and dialed the number on the message. Again, it was her parents in Prescott. "I told her to call my cell," he said to himself in a whisper. The phone was answered after the third ring. He recognized the voice of his estranged wife as she answered, "Metzlers."

"Cassie, what the hell do you think you're doing?" Nick said without hesitation.

"Whatever do you mean?" She tried to sound as innocent as she could.

"You are *not* moving my kids to Prescott! Do you understand? I won't allow it!" His tone was as challenging as it had ever been with her.

"Well, guess what," she chided. "I already have, and I started them in school today, so you'll just have to get used to it. I'm staying here! I have custody, you know."

Now he truly wished he had not so willingly given her custody. Knowing the demands of his job, he had agreed not to ask for joint custody. He had settled for every other weekend and certain holidays. As his emotions began to seize him, he said, "That's not fair. How am I supposed to see them? You're two hours away!"

"You know where we are," she answered. "You know how to get here. And it's only an hour and a half!"

He could feel his emotional temperature rising. "You're not going to get away with this, Cassie. The custody agreement says I get them every other weekend."

"That's fine," she answered. "Come and get them. Just have them back on time. Like I said, you know where we are."

Nick tried to hold his anger in as he responded, "Cassie, why are you doing this? I've given you everything you asked for in the divorce agreement. I didn't fight you on child support, health care, or anything else. All I want to do is see my kids; after all, I am their father. Think about them. For Christ sake, for once in your life think about someone else instead of yourself!" He wished he could reach out and grab the last several words and shove them back into his mouth and swallow them.

Her icy response could have frozen water. "That's exactly what I'm doing. It's a lot better for them here. There is less crime and—"

"That's your mother's bullshit!" Nick interrupted. "She's been trying to get you up there ever since the day they moved. That's not you talking. It's her, and I am not going to accept it."

Her voice was lower and firm as she responded, "Accept it, Nick. As Dad would say, it's a done deal."

"We'll see how done it is! I'll see what my lawyer has to say about it," he threatened.

"Do what you must, but read the custody agreement!"

Nick heard the sound of the dial tone as she hung up. Shaking his head, he hung up the handset and immediately began searching through his cell phone and found the number he was looking for. After only one ring there was an answer: "Law offices."

He recognized the voice of his lawyer's secretary. "Paul Wesley, please. This is Nick Greer."

"I'm sorry, Mr. Greer, but Mr. Wesley is out of the office. He's on vacation."

"I need to talk to him right away, Lori," Nick replied. "Can you reach him, please?"

"Mr. Wesley is on a cruise. It's a second honeymoon. Only in a matter of life and death would I even try to reach him," she answered.

Nick thought for a moment. He knew that Wesley was a one-man law office, so there was no one else to answer his question.

Lori asked, "Is there something I can help you with, Mr. Greer?"

"My ex-wife moved herself and the kids to Prescott," he said in a slightly raised tone. "Can she do that? Can you stop her?"

"I'm sorry, Mr. Greer. I wish I could," she answered sympatheti-cally. "But I'll see that Mr. Wesley gets your message first thing when he returns. He is due back in the office next Monday."

"Thank you." He hung up the phone. What a way to start the fucking day, he thought.

The rest of the day was spent studying the case, going over notes, and on the computer. Nick pulled background checks on all of St. Michael's staff and anyone on the suspect list, including Mike Brad-ley. All were clean except for Bill Jamison. His rap sheet showed three arrests for petty theft, but only one conviction for which he spent six months in Phoenix's infamous tent city. He'd been released four months ago, and subsequently was employed at St Michael's. Greer wondered why the priest would hire him? He didn't seem the type to hire a felon, but maybe he wanted to give him a second chance. Maybe he had more of a heart than some people thought.

He decided to run a check on Mignanelli. As he expected, the priest's background was clean; however, there was a civil suit of some sort six years ago that had been settled out of court. The records had been sealed, but Nick did find a co-defendant. The name, Blake Beyers, sounded familiar to the detective. Then he remembered his conversa-tion with Mignanelli's housekeeper. She had mentioned a Father Blake.

The detective checked the diocesan website and found that Fa-ther Blake Beyers was the pastor at St. John's in Scottsdale. He decided to go see the priest. It was getting late, and he had a date with Sue Kim. Tomorrow would work.

* * *

He picked up Sue Kim at six thirty. They decided on Applebee's for dinner. She could tell that he was pre-occupied all evening and when they were driving back to her place, she asked, "You okay?"

"Uhh . . . yeah. Why do you ask?"

"You seem like you're somewhere else tonight. Something on your mind?"

"Personal. Nothing you can help with."

"I can listen," she said.

Nick explained his phone conversation with Cassie. Sue Kim seemed very concerned and receptive to his situation. It was so easy to talk to her. Even though there wasn't anything she could do, he found comfort in just holding her hand and was moved by the sincere compassion she exhibited. He had only met her a little over a week ago, but felt like he had known her all his life.

CHAPTER 28

As Nick Greer pulled into the parking lot of St John's Church, he immediately noticed the contrast between the two churches. St. Michael's was nice, but it was easy to see that this one was in a more upscale community. Killing the motor, he got out of the car and walked toward the parish office. Passing three vehicles parked in a row, he saw that the space reserved for "Pastor" was empty. He'd considered phoning first, but decided against it due to his previous experience with those at the diocesan offices. Besides, he always got better information when the person had no time to prepare.

He was impressed by the beauty of the grounds and the perfectly placed array of flowers and plants as he followed the short sidewalk to the entry. A yellow-on-green sign that read "Parish Office" with an arrow pointing to the left was surrounded by a lantana plant. The bushy green leaves and bright yellow flowers made the sign look as if it was part of the plant. He entered the building through one of two large doors and was greeted by a picture of the pope and one of the bishop, just as at St. Michael's. However, this one lacked the pictures of the pastor's ordination.

He was about halfway across the small lobby when he heard, "Good morning. Can I help you, sir?" The receptionist appeared to be in her fifties. Her auburn hair was short and looked like it had just been trimmed.

"Yes, ma'am," Nick answered as he retrieved his badge from his pocket and held it for her to see. "I'm Lieutenant Nick Greer from the Phoenix PD. I would like to speak with Father Beyers, please."

An uncomfortable look descended upon her as she looked at the badge and answered, "I'm sorry, sir, but Father Beyers is not here."

The detective queried, "When do you expect him?"

She appeared more uncomfortable as she looked at Nick. "Uhh, I don't know."

"What time is he due in today?

She hesitated. "We don't expect him today. He's on sabbatical, I guess."

"On sabbatical? When should he return? Do you know where he is taking this sabbatical? Is there a way to reach him?" The detective fired all the questions at once.

She was becoming more flustered, but managed to compose herself. "I really don't know, sir. No one here does, not even our associate. He got a call from the diocese that Father Beyers was taking some time off, and they would send some temporary help. I assume it was because of the death of his friend."

"Father David Mignanelli?"

She nodded. "Yes, sir. They had been close friends for many years."

"Who received the call?"

"Father Brett, our associate pastor."

"I would like to speak with him."

Just then the door next to the receptionist opened and from behind it came a voice: "Yes, sir. Please come into my office." A young man dressed in the normal black priestly garb was standing at the door. He smiled and offered his hand. "Father Brett Masters."

Nick shook his hand. "Lieutenant Nick Greer, Phoenix PD."

"Please follow me," the young priest said as he led his visitor into an office, closed the the door, and gestured for Nick to have a seat. He picked up the phone, pressed a button, and said, "Gaby, please hold my calls." After a brief pause, he answered, "Yes, that's correct, thank you," and hung up the phone.

His office looked very professional. The oak desk sitting in the center of the room looked fairly new, and behind Nick was a bookcase full of books and papers. The room appeared a little unorganized but much more elaborate than that of St. Michael's. This priest was in his early to mid-twenties, about five-six, with brown wavy hair. "Can I offer you anything? A bottle of water, maybe?" His pleasant demeanor was welcoming.

"No, thank you," Nick answered. "I just have a few questions."

"Yes, I heard you speaking with our receptionist," he answered. "Actually, there is not much more I can tell you. I received a call from the diocese stating that Father Blake was going to take some time off, and they would let me know what arrangements would be made. That's about it."

"When did you get the call?"

"Let's see . . . it must have been . . . a week ago Monday . . . around noon."

"Who phoned you?"

"Father Denkens. He's the—"

"Yes, I know who he is," the detective interrupted. "Did he say where he was going or why?"

"No, sir. I assume it was due to the death of his friend, another priest—"

Again Nick cut him short. "Father Mignanelli. Yes, I know. Did you know him?"

"I only met him once. You see, I was just recently ordained." He sat up straight and smiled. "This is my first assignment. I never really talked with him."

Nick stroked his chin and asked, "What was their relationship?"

"I understand they were friends for a long time. I think they both came from back east somewhere." He looked inquisitively at the detective. "May I ask why you want to know?"

"I'm investigating the death of Father Mignanelli—"

This time the priest interrupted. "Investigating? What do you mean? I thought he took his own life."

Choosing his words carefully so as not to alert the priest to his suspicions, the detective responded, "Anytime a death is sudden and unnatural, even when self-inflicted, we have to check it out. It's just part of the job. We have to find out what we can about the vic, excuse me, deceased. It's all routine. Nothing for you to be concerned about."

The young priest seemed to relax and leaned back in his chair.

The detective continued, "You really have no idea where your pastor is or how to reach him?"

"No, sir. I do not. I got all my information from the diocese. If they know more, they aren't telling me."

"When was the last time you saw him or spoke with him?"

"Uhhh . . . Friday. The Friday before he went . . ."

The hesitation and the tone of his voice told the detective that he may have stumbled onto something and remembering his own Catholic upbringing, he asked, "What about Saturday night, the weekend before you got the call? You do have a Saturday night Mass, don't you?"

"Yes, at five o'clock. I celebrated that one."

"Was your pastor around?"

"Uh . . . no. He usually greets people after Mass, but he didn't come, now that you mention it."

"Didn't you find that unusual?"

"No, not really. He usually greets people at all the Masses, whether he celebrates or not, but there have been times when he didn't, so I figured he was busy."

The detective bombarded the priest with questions. "How about Sunday? Didn't he say Mass? Which ones? Did you see him then? Did you talk to him?"

The young associate was becoming uncomfortable with all the questions and began to squirm in his seat. "Lieutenant, I'm sorry, but there's nothing else I can tell you. If you have any more questions, I would appreciate it if you would direct them to the diocese."

The young priest was flustered and Nick felt sorry for him, so he decided not to push him anymore. Besides, he knew how to get the rest of the answers. "I think I'll do just that. Thank you for your help. I'll see myself out."

* * *

The lieutenant got into his car and drove straight to the beige stucco building that housed the diocesan offices, and, just as before, he parked his car and walked around to the front of the building. He was greeted by the same lady he met on Friday as he crossed the main lobby.

"Father Denkens is in his office. He is expecting you." She buzzed him through.

Hmmm, Nick thought as he traversed down the hall to the priest's office. Knowing that the new priest had warned his boss, he thought the kid didn't waste any time. He'll fit in well.

This time the door was already open, and Father Denkens sat behind his desk. The vicar motioned for him to take a seat. Before he could speak, the priest said, "Lieutenant, I would appreciate it if you would stop harassing our staff."

His demanding tone irked Nick, who tried to speak but was unable to as the priest kept talking. "We have been cooperative with you and with your department, but for some reason you won't accept the fact that Father Mignanelli took his own life. We here have accepted that and so should you. You had no right to go to Scottsdale and harass Father Masters. He is a new priest. This is his first assignment, and he has no idea how things work here. Your boss told you to leave it alone. Don't you—"

"Where is Father Beyers?" Nick interrupted in a loud voice.

"Huh? Wha . . . ?" The priest could see the intenseness in Nick's eyes.

"I asked you a question. I expect a straight answer. I'm tired of the bullshit you're trying to hand out.

"How will *your* boss react if I arrest you right here, right now for obstructing a police investigation?" The detective took his handcuffs from his belt, held them up and shook them.

A look of terror struck the face of the cleric. "That won't be necessary."

"Fine!" Nick stated. He put the handcuffs back on his belt and bent his lanky frame over the vicar's desk. "I want answers, and I want them now! Where is Beyers, and how can I talk with him?"

"I don't know." His voice shook as he spoke.

"That's it!" Nick said as he again pulled his handcuffs from his belt and headed around the desk to the priest. "You're under arr—"

"Please, Lieutenant. I'm not lying. I don't know! No one knows! Not even the bishop!"

Nick stopped. He looked in the eyes of the priest and saw the truth in them along with fear. *He really has no idea where Beyers is? Wow!* he thought.

The detective sat back down, looked at the priest, and said, "I'm listening."

"He's gone. No one knows where he is. Saturday, we received a phone call saying he would be gone for a while, nothing more."

"Which Saturday was that?"

"Uhhh . . . a week ago," the priest stammered.

"The same day as the death of Father Mignanelli?"

The cleric appeared more nervous than ever as he answered, "Uh . . . yesss."

"And you have had no contact with him since?"

"None."

"Have you checked his residence?"

"Yes, we have. No one answered the door. We tried twice."

"What's the address?" Nick questioned.

The priest replied nervously, "6767 East Yucca Street, in Scottsdale."

"The bishop? Has he heard from him?" Nick continued.

"No. No one has heard from him, at least not that I know of."

"You're sure it was he who called? Did you recognize his voice?"

"Uhhh, I assume so. I didn't take the call, but who else could it have been?"

"Who did?"

"Did what?"

"Who took the call?" The detective knew he had the man where he wanted him.

"Mike. I mean Father Kubic."

The detective's mind traveled back to that Saturday evening, and his meeting with the two priests. He again wondered how they had arrived so soon. "Why him?" Nick asked.

"He was the vicar on call. He'd be the one to report such things to, especially when the bishop or I are not available."

"How can I speak with him?"

The priest reached for his phone, and punched in a number. "Mike? . . . Can you come in here a minute? . . . Yes, it's important."

The phone had just been hung up when the door opened, and Nick recognized the priest who entered. The cleric had a disturbed look on his face.

"Lieutenant Greer, this is—"

Nick didn't give him time to end the sentence. "Yes, Father Kubic and I have met."

"Lieutenant," the priest said as he extended his hand to Nick. "It's nice to see you again."

"Mike, the lieutenant has some questions—"

Again the priest was unable to finish his words as the detective cut him short. "You spoke with Father Beyers a week ago last Saturday, the same night we met?"

"Yes."

"Well, what did he say?"

"It was on my voice mail. He said something had happened and that he would be gone for a while. He said he would explain later and to get someone to cover his weekend."

"And?"

"And what?" The priest shrugged. His face showed that he was confused by the question.

"That was the whole message? He didn't explain why he was leaving you in a lurch? Are you telling me that he just took off with no notice, no warning? That he just, poof, vanished? I'd think he would give you a reason of some sort."

Father Kubic answered, "Yes, unusually sudden and unexpected."

"What time was this?"

"I'm not sure what time he called. I was taking a nap and had my phone shut off. I took a shower, and then I remembered to turn it on somewhere around four o'clock, I guess."

The detective pushed, "Didn't the message say what time it came in?"

"I didn't pay attention. Sorry, that's all I know."

"Do you have the phone with you? Can I hear the message?"

"Sorry, I erased it."

"Are you sure it was him?" The priest looked at Nick with a questioning look on his face as the detective pressed on, "Did you recognize his voice? Are you absolutely positive it was Father Beyers?"

The priest's face flushed. Nick knew he had opened a door of doubt in the man's mind. "Uhhh . . . yeah. It sounded like him. Who else would it be? Why would you ask such a question?"

"I'm a cop. That's what I do. I ask questions."

"You'll have to excuse me, Lieutenant, but I have someone in my office so I must . . ."

Father Kubic turned and headed out the door. The detective called out to him, "Why didn't you tell me?"

The priest stopped and turned around. "Tell you what?"

"Last week at the deceased Father's home, why didn't you tell me about Father Beyers?"

Kubic's face reddened, making his blondish-brown hair look almost white. Greer knew he had struck a vein. "I didn't see the relevance, nor do I now!"

"You've got a dead priest, and his friend has gone AWOL. You don't see relevance?"

"No, I don't," Kubic responded as he turned and left the room.

As soon as the vicar left, Nick stood up, looked at Father Denkens and said, "Thank you, Father, I'll see my way out." He headed for the door and stopped. He turned back to the priest, looked him straight in the eyes, and asked sternly, "How did you know what my boss told me?"

"I . . . well . . . I . . . uhh," the priest stuttered.

I'll deal with that later, he thought, as he turned and left the room.

As he drove back to the precinct, he went over the details of the day in his mind. His instinct told him that Father Kubic knew more than he was letting on. He thought about adding him as a possible to his suspect list, even though he was a priest. He said to himself out loud, "I gotta find Beyers! I gotta find Beyers!"

Just as he pulled his car into the police parking lot, he remembered that the housekeeper had mentioned a condo that the deceased shared with Father Blake. He thought, I'll start there.

Feeling hungry, Nick thought about calling Sue Kim. Perhaps they could have lunch together. He looked at his watch. It was a quarter to one, and Sue Kim would already be gone. She would probably be on her way back by now. He wanted to tell her why he took her home right after dinner last night, left her off, and went to his condo. Somehow he knew she understood, and that it wasn't necessary to tell her he had needed some alone time to sort things out about Cassie, the kids and Prescott. What Sue Kim didn't know was that she was part of this, a big part. He'd known her for only a short time, but he was quickly developing feelings for her. He wanted to spend every moment he could with her.

As long as he had known Cassie, whom he thought he had loved dearly, he had never felt this way about her. He searched both his mind and his heart for answers to no avail. Tonight sleep would evade him and so would the answers he was searching for.

CHAPTER 29

Nick Greer sat outside of his townhouse on the small enclosed patio, just off the kitchen. He enjoyed the quiet solitude. When in need of relaxation, he found himself there usually stretched out in his chaise lounge listening to his iPod. Somehow, here, the troubles of the world could not disturb the serenity this place provided. It was like his own emotional fortress that couldn't be penetrated by the cares and woes of the outside world. It was this tranquil feeling that first attracted him to the home.

It was 6:15 Thursday and a beautiful Arizona morning. The light breeze felt good as he watched the morning sun as it gently greeted the earth while slowly rising over the eastern mountains to begin the new day. Sitting at a small round table in the corner of the patio, sipping on a cup of coffee and reading the morning paper, he knew he still had time for a second cup before heading out.

As he thumbed through the paper he was suddenly struck by a headline:

Longtime Phoenix Physician Dies

Dr. Jerome Everett of Phoenix passed away suddenly at his home Wednesday morning. According to a family spokesperson, the longtime Phoenix resident and family physician died suddenly. Services pending.

Nick's heart skipped a beat as he remembered his meeting with the kind doctor just this past week. How sad it was to think that this man would never again set sail and experience his lifelong dream.

There's something wrong with life, he thought. You work all your life with the expectation of relaxing someday and enjoying what life you have left, just to have it snatched away from you before you have the chance . . . well . . . it's just not fair, that's all, it's just not fair.

CHAPTER 30

Nick Greer fired up his computer, and logged on with his password: Cassie1. Many times since their estrangement he had thought about changing his password, but never did. "I'll change it the next time," he would say each time he logged on. Now is the time, he decided. Nick tried to think of something that wouldn't remind him of her, but nothing came to him so he typed in MORGUE1. "Password accepted" appeared on the screen. "Works for me," he said, grinning.

The detective searched the Maricopa County property records under Mignanelli. Nothing. He tried Beyers and found a property in east Phoenix for a Blake M. Beyers that had been sold to BMK Enterprises, LLC a little over a year ago. It was a condo in an upscale community.

Accessing the Arizona Corporation Commission website, the detective typed in BMK Enterprises. He found that it was a company formed three years ago. The statutory agent was David A. Mignanelli and the members were listed as Blake Beyers and—he looked again just to be sure—Michael J. Kubic. Reaching into his pocket for a pen and taking a notepad from his desk, he scribbled down the address and immediately picked up the phone and dialed the office of Judge Cavallo.

"Judge Cavallo's office." He recognized the voice on the other end.

"Hi, Cindy. Nick Greer."

"How are things in the world of homicide?" Her perky voice was pleasant.

"People are still killing each other," he answered.

The detective explained the circumstances and his need for a warrant. She informed him it would be ready in about thirty minutes. "Perfect," he said, then added, "Cindy, I need you to add another address."

"What is that?"

He retrieved his notebook and said, "6767 East Yucca Street, in Scottsdale."

* * *

Nick rang the doorbell and knocked twice to no avail, then called out, "Police! Anybody in there?" The two uniformed Scottsdale police officers who had met him there just looked at each other as they watched him feel around the door jamb. He saw a small white gnome sitting in the corner to the left of the door and lifted it. "Life is good," he said, as he removed the key hidden under it and unlocked the door. The alarm company had been notified and had disabled the alarm so he entered the missing priest's home and the two uniforms followed.

After having seen the home of Father Mignanelli, he expected to see a nice place. The home of the dead priest had been elaborate, but this one was breathtaking.

The two Scottsdale officers were in awe over what they saw. Nick heard one remark to the other, "Should a been a priest when I had the chance."

The other officer said, "Yeah, but don't forget, no pussy."

"Yeah, I guess everything has its price," his partner responded.

The remark reminded the detective of the condoms he found at Father Mignanelli's house. He thought about making a comment, but decided to keep quiet.

There were two flat-screen plasma TVs, one in the living room and one in the priest's bedroom. The furniture was very high-end throughout the home. The living room was set up similar to that of Father Mignanelli's, with the giant TV surrounded by a cherry entertainment system that housed a stereo system, at least a couple hundred CDs and DVDs. Like his friend, there was track lighting hanging from the ceiling and expensive lamps and accessories. There were paintings strategically placed on the walls throughout the house. Nick knew enough about art to know that they were original paintings, though he didn't recognize the artists. He counted six.

Their inspection found no sign of the occupant, nor were there any signs of a struggle. Everything appeared to be in order. They were not able to perform a thorough search because of the restrictions on the warrant, allowing a welfare check with entry only if there was no answer at the door.

One thing caught Nick's attention. All of the rooms were well furnished and decorated, except, as in Mignanelli's home, one room looked dreary and had a lone futon in the middle of it.

They checked the garage. It was empty and since the warrant didn't allow for more, they left. Nick thanked the Scottsdale officers for their help, then checked the occupant's mailbox and found that no mail had been picked up for several days.

Lieutenant Greer waited as the police squad car pulled next to him in front of the BMK condo and two police officers got out. He knew them both and explained their purpose there. Like the Scottsdale warrant, it was a welfare check only, unless there was probable cause for more. It was an upscale condominium community of about a hundred and fifty units. Each unit was two levels with the living area on the ground floor, and the floor above spanned out over a double-car garage. After ringing the doorbell three times and calling out, Nick knocked hard on the door and to his surprise, it opened. He entered first, and the two uniformed officers followed.

As was the Scottsdale home, the condo was elaborately furnished; however, the first thing the detective saw was what looked like spots of dried blood on the carpet. Entering the living room, the detective reached to his side and drew his Glock as broken glass and an overturned cocktail table caught his eye. The two uniforms followed his lead and with their guns drawn they split up and searched the condo. After the last "clear" was called they holstered their weapons. Though unsure that a crime had been committed, the detective still called for a crime scene unit.

He walked through the rest of the condo and didn't find anything out of the ordinary. That is, what had become ordinary for this case. It mirrored the Scottsdale home with expensive paintings on the walls, plasma TVs, plush furnishings, and a dark dreary room with a futon in the center.

Nick left the two policemen inside the condo and went into the garage. It was empty. He had only half-expected to find Father Blake's car there. It's presence would have added credibility to a theory of abduction, making searching the condo, should it be challenged, more agreeable to a judge.

His ears caught the ring of his cell phone. He pulled it from his belt. "Nick Greer."

"Where are you and what the hell are you doing?" Nick recognized the voice of his captain.

"I'm on a case. I'm working. What am I always doing, Pete?"

"I want you back here, pronto."

"I'm kind of busy, probably a couple of hours."

"You find a DB?"

"No."

"Then get it on back here. We got problems."

"Okay, I'll get there as soon as I can," he said, and returned his phone to his belt.

The lieutenant instructed the officers to guard the unit until the crime team got there.

CHAPTER 31

Nick entered the squad room and headed straight for Mendoza's office. The door was open and he went in. Pete Mendoza was sitting behind his desk. The look on his face was a mixture of anger and concern. He pointed to a chair and said, "Sit!"

The captain placed his elbows on the desk, folded his hands together as if in prayer and rested his chin on them. He took a deep breath, then exhaled.

"Lieutenant, yesterday we spoke about the Mignanelli case, and I thought it was clearly understood that it would go down as a suicide. Today I am informed that you've caused another ruckus within the diocese."

"The diocese causes its own ruckus. I just stirred it up a little." He leaned forward to continue his defense, but the captain held up his index finger through his still-folded hands and glared at him with fire in his eyes.

"Let me finish, Lieutenant." Nick leaned back in the chair.

"I had two calls from the chief this morning," Mendoza said. "He wants to know why my men don't listen to me. He wants your badge and my ass. Explain why I shouldn't give him at least one of them. Now, before you do, remember what I said; explain it to me."

Seeing that his boss was looking for a way to save him, not to chastise him, but also knowing that he was serious, Nick thought for a moment and said confidently, "That priest was murdered. If not murdered, someone helped him. He did not act alone. I'm sure of it. And the diocese knows more than they are telling us. I'm not sure there isn't some type of involvement there."

The sincerity in Nick's voice intrigued the captain. "How sure are you? You know the power this bishop has with the mayor. Your badge, and maybe mine could be at stake here!"

The lieutenant explained what had transpired up until now. Pete Mendoza knew his detective's abilities. He was the best investigator on the squad and had a natural instinct which you don't find very often. Mendoza recognized Greer's determination and knew that if Nick was convinced it was not a suicide, then he was probably right. But could he prove it? How long would it take? There was no motive and a flimsy list of suspects. Both of their careers could be affected by the decision Captain Mendoza was about to make.

Pete thought for a moment with his hands still folded, but the index fingers now together and pointing at Nick. "One week! You got one week. Bring me something. Anything. An arrest would be nice. If you have nothing more by then, you will close the case. And, for Christ's sake, stay away from the diocese. Another call from them and we'll both be gone. You got that? Agreed?"

"I'll find something," Nick stated as he looked into the worried face of his captain. "I'll figure it out." He was aware of the trust that his boss and friend had just placed in him. He had a week to make it worth it. Two careers depended on it.

"You're not going to figure it out in here talking to me. Get to work, Lieutenant!"

CHAPTER 32

For some unknown reason, the death of Dr. Everett seemed to stay on Nick's mind. Work all your life for a goal, reach out to touch it and die before you get to experience it. What a rotten hand life dealt him. Maybe it was his own fault. Maybe he should have retired earlier.

Nick had Sue Kim copy the coroner's preliminary report for him. As he read the cause of death—cardiac infarction—he remembered he had not yet received the file on Father Mignanelli. He decided to phone his office, perhaps he could find out where it went. His call was answered by a recording that said all records and patients had been referred to a Dr. Epstein, and gave his phone number. Nick phoned and after pressing several numbers, as prompted by the recording, he decided to press 0.

"Canyon State Medical Center," was the response.

"Oh great. A live person," Nick responded.

"How can I help you, sir?" The direct response was impersonal and businesslike, so much different than his first call to Dr Everett.

"I'm Lieutenant Greer, Phoenix PD. I need to speak to the person in charge of your medical records, expressly those of the late Dr. Everett."

"Let me transfer you," was the response.

He heard the phone click and then: "This is Marge. How can I help you?"

"Lieutenant Nick Greer, Phoenix PD. I'm looking for the medical file on a recently deceased patient of Dr. Everett. How would I go about obtaining it?"

"All medical records are confidential. I'm sure you are aware that I can't give out any information without a court order," she replied. "And besides, Dr Everett's files are all in boxes. We haven't been able to assimilate them yet."

"Ma'am," Nick replied, "I'm perfectly aware of doctor-patient privilege and that it stops at death, and this patient is dead. I'll be there in an hour. Please have it ready. Mignanelli! David! Reverend!"

"I'm sorry." Her tone was defensive and argumentative. "But I can't do that without the doctor's permission, and he is very busy today."

"Ma'am, I believe you said your name was Marge? We can do this two ways. You can get the file for me, or I can bring a crew with a warrant and we'll find it ourselves. I'm sure your patients will be impressed by a bunch of cops going through your office, especially when we may not be real tidy in how we go about it."

"I'll have the file ready for you when you get here." The coldness in her voice could have frozen water.

"Thank you," Nick said. "Mignanelli. David." By the time he finished, he could already hear the humming of the dial tone.

The detective left the squad room and took the elevator down to the ground floor. He got into his car and drove north on the Black Canyon Freeway to the Bell Road exit and turned west. It was eleven o'clock when he turned into the upscale condominium-style office complex. He parked his car in a vacant space across from the medical center. He got out of his vehicle and walked to the door that read:

Canyon State Medical Center, LLC

James Elliott, DO
Kathryn Berger, DPM
Paul Prentiss, MD
David Epstein, PC
Barbara Pettitte, MD

The waiting room was larger than Dr. Everett's whole office. There were at least forty rose-colored chairs neatly arranged in rows and along the walls. About one third of them were filled. There was a large U-shaped counter in the far right side of the room. The rose-colored counter top was a perfect match for the chairs.

Four females sat at various places behind the counter; each seemed to be busy. Nick walked to the counter and stood there for about a minute. No one noticed him until he loudly cleared his throat.

A young lady said, "I'll be with you in a moment. Please sign in." She didn't look up as she spoke, but laid a clipboard on the counter in front of him.

The lieutenant took his badge, clipped it to the clipboard, and set it in front of her. Her eyes widened as she saw the badge, and she finally looked up at him.

"I'm Lieutenant Greer. I'm here to see Marge." He pulled his badge from the clipboard.

"Oh yes, sir, she's expecting you." She stood and walked through a door to what appeared to be the back office. In about thirty seconds, a door on the left side of the room opened and he heard: "Mr. Greer?" A lady, about forty, a little heavyset, with short black hair was holding the door open as if he were a patient. "Please follow me."

He followed her down a hallway, about thirty feet. The sign on the door said: Private. She opened it and invited him in. It was small, but it was easy to see that it was a busy office. In the center of the desk, at the front, sat a desk plate that read: M. Hatcher, Office Manager.

The windowless office had four filing cabinets on the left wall. A laptop computer sat in the middle of the desk and next to it was a small yellow notepad. The rest of the desk was riddled with stacks of files and papers that almost covered the phone sitting on the far left.

"Please have a seat, Officer," she began.

"It's Lieutenant. Greer. Nick Greer," he stated as he showed her his gold shield.

"My mistake, Lieutenant, my apologies." Her gracious demeanor was in total contrast with her attitude on the phone. Nick wondered why the change. He was about to find out.

"Let me get to the point, Lieutenant. You asked for the file for a David Migelli?"

"Mignanelli," Nick corrected.

"That's right, thank you. I hate to tell you this, but I cannot supply it for you."

"I thought we discussed this on the phone. You know—"

"I understand," she interrupted. "I would give it to you if we had it, but we don't. You see, there seems to be some records missing, and that is one of them."

"Missing? Why missing?"

"It seems a whole box, all Ms, never made it here." She seemed sincere in her answer. "After your phone call, I had one of the girls look for the file. She informed me about ten minutes ago that it was not there. She's back there as we speak looking through the other boxes to see if they were mismarked. Let me call her."

"I'd rather speak to her in person, if you don't mind."

"Sure, follow me." She stood, exited the room and led him down a hallway. They passed two rooms to a third, which was open, and they went in.

Cardboard file boxes were stacked haphazardly all over the room, and a young lady who appeared to Nick to be a teenager was busy going through them. Her face emitted frustration as she looked up and saw her boss and Nick standing there.

"Any luck yet, Brittany?" Marge questioned.

She shook her head and her brown hair fell over her eyes. As she brushed it back, Nick noticed the ring over her left eye, and one through her left nostril.

"No. I can't find them. M–A to M–E are there, but M–I and so on are not. All the boxes are labeled right. They must have forgotten a box."

"Thank you, Brittany," Marge replied. "You can go to lunch now if you want."

"Thanks," she replied as she got up and left the room.

"I don't know what to tell you, Lieutenant. It looks like we never got them. That makes it hard for us, because those were patient records we are responsible for. I fear it will come down on me because I signed for them. I haven't told the doctor yet. He's been busy with patients. I'm going to call the service that delivered them. I shouldn't have signed without counting them. I just assumed . . ."

"Service?" Nick questioned. "What service?"

"Statewide Courier. They sent them over in a van."

"Do you have the receipt?"

"Yes, it's still on my desk. They just came yesterday."

"Would you get it for me?"

"Be right back." She left the room.

Nick began counting the boxes. Sixty-two. He had just finished counting when Marge returned and handed him a small yellow paper. Across the top was printed Statewide Courier Service. In the body of the paper, handwritten, it showed Dr. Everett's office address as pickup and this medical center as delivery, sixty-two boxes, exactly what Nick had counted.

"Well, ma'am, I have good news and bad news." She looked at him inquisitively.

"Good new, it's not your fault. Bad news, one box is definitely missing."

The detective could see the relief on the lady's face. Then she said, "I still have the number for his daughter. I can call her."

"Daughter?" Nick asked.

"Yes, Dr. Everett's daughter, Mariann. She was his office manager. She sent the files here. She arranged it all. I'll call her. I have her home number, or her cell, I think."

"Why don't you just give me her number, and I'll call her," Nick directed.

"Okay," she responded. "It's in my office."

They went back into her office. She typed something into her laptop and scribbled a name and number on the yellow pad, ripped it off, and handed it to the detective. "I think that's her cell phone number. If you find the records, can I have them, please?"

"I guess so, but I'll keep the priest's file," the detective answered.

"Priest?"

"Yeah, he was a priest."

"I saw something on the news a few days ago about a priest who shot himself. Is that what this is all about?"

"Thanks for your help. I'll be in touch." Without answering her question, the detective turned and left.

Nick started his car, backed out of the parking spot, and headed back to the station. He was halfway down the freeway when he pulled his Android from its holder on his belt, retrieved the phone number, entered it in his phone, and pressed send.

"This is Mariann."

"Ma'am, my name is Lieutenant Nick Greer with the Phoenix PD. I'm sorry to bother you, but I knew your father, Dr. Everett. First of all, I'm sorry for your loss."

"Thank you," she replied. "What do you want?" He could tell by the tone of her voice that she was disturbed by his call.

"I have an urgent matter I need to talk with you about. It won't take long, but I need to see you right away if possible."

"What's it about? Can we do this on the phone? I'm very busy. I have a funeral to arrange and a business to close." Her tone was harsher and firm.

"I don't want to discuss it on the phone. I promise not to take any more of your time than necessary. I understand your situation, and I respect it. Please know that I wouldn't ask during this critical time for you, if it wasn't extremely important."

"Aren't you that cop who came to see my dad the last day we were open?"

"Yes, ma'am, I am."

"Okay, I guess. I'm on my way to the office now to check a couple of things. I'll be there in about ten minutes."

"Thank you," Nick said as he laid the phone on the seat beside him, made a right at the next exit, and drove to the deceased doctor's office wondering what it was she had to check on.

Just as he pulled his car into one of the empty space in front of Dr. Everett's office, a vehicle pulled up next to him. He recognized the driver and realized that the doctor's office manager and his daughter were one and the same. The detective nodded to her as she got out of her car, walked to the front door, and unlocked it. Nick reached for his badge, but Mariann said, "You don't have to do that. I remember you. What did you want to see me about?" Her tone was not as harsh, but it was still edgy.

"First of all," Nick said, "May I say again, I'm sorry for your loss. I only met the doctor, your dad, once, but he seemed like a very nice man."

"Thank you. He was." Her reddened and swollen eyes showed she had been crying. "How did you get my cell phone number?"

"From Dr. Epstein's office."

"Oh, yes. He is taking over my dad's patients, at least most of them."

"That's what I wanted to talk to you about. I understand you sent all your records to Dr. Epstein. Is that correct?"

"Yes." Her hair fell over her eyes as she nodded her head.

"There seems to be some missing. Do you know why?"

Mariann looked puzzled as she brushed the hair back from her eyes. "Uhh . . . no. I packed them all myself. What's missing?"

"Apparently some of the Ms."

"So that explains it," she said. Her eyes opened wide, and there was a sense of new discovery in her voice.

"Explains what?"

"Three days ago I when I got here, I found the back door open. It had been pried open. I didn't know why. Nothing was missing. I thought maybe it was someone looking for drugs, and since there weren't any here, they left. I looked around the office and nothing was missing as far as I could tell. That's why I came back today, to be sure they fixed the door. Mom and I are going to sell the building, and I wanted it to be right."

"You didn't notice any boxes missing?" the detective questioned.

"Now that you mention it, the boxes were piled nice and straight when I left them. But when I returned, they were crooked, and two had fallen on the floor. I thought whoever broke in had bumped them or something. I never thought, I mean, why would anyone want a bunch of medical files anyway?"

"That's what I am trying to figure out. Do you remember which ones were on the floor?"

"Yeah, it was MO and NA. I picked them up and put them back on the pile."

"Are you sure nothing else was disturbed?"

"Like I said, everything else was just as I left it."

"Do you remember how many boxes there were?"

"Let's see," she said as she cupped her hand around her freckled chin. I stacked them as high as I could, six high. There were ten stacks. That makes sixty. And there were two, no, three on the last row. That would make sixty-three."

"When you found them on the floor, what did you do?"

"I picked them up and put them back on the pile."

"How many were there then? Did you notice how many?"

"Now that you mention it, when I put them back, that pile was short. I never realized that until now." Her face turned red. "I should have seen that. I'm sorry."

"Don't worry about it," he replied in a comforting voice. "You've been through a lot, and it's an easy thing to miss. Thank you for your help. I appreciate it.

"By the way, what about the alarm?" he added. "You do have an alarm, don't you? Didn't it go off?"

"Uhh. I had it disabled the day before this all happened. I didn't think there was a need since there was nothing here but boxes. Sorry, if I'd have known—"

"It's okay," Nick interrupted. He figured she was going through enough, and he didn't need to add guilt to her emotions. "If you have an extra key I can borrow, it would help. I promise to return it."

"What for?"

"Gonna send someone to check for prints and stuff."

She commented more than questioned, "All for a stupid box of records?" Mariann then locked the door from the outside, turned and headed toward her car, tossing the key over her shoulder.

As Nick swiftly reached out his left hand and caught the key in the air, she said, "Keep it. I got another one."

He stowed it in his front pocket. "Sure," he answered as he watched her get into her car and drive away.

He returned to the station and arranged for someone to check the doctor's office for prints, even though he knew the effort would be fruitless.

CHAPTER 33

The cool spring air blew past him through the open windows as he sped along I-17 and took the Cordes Junction exit through Mayer and Dewey toward Prescott. He relished the peacefulness as the road wound its way through scenic rocky cliffs. The tops of the Bradshaw Mountains glistened as the morning sun kissed their peaks. Even though he hadn't been to church for years, he was reminded that there is a God.

This was the first time he made this trip without Cassie and the kids in the car. The solitude gave him time to reflect on the happenings of the last few days. He was anxious to see the kids. He didn't know where he would take them or what they would do, but he would get a room at Bucky's and go with the flow. This weekend was for his girls. Whatever they wanted, he would do.

He'd informed Cassie, through her father, that he would be there around noon. Rod agreed to tell his daughter and said he would see that she had the kids available for him. Nick was confident Rod Metzler would keep his word.

Last night as Nick had been stuffing some clothes and toiletries into a bag for his weekend trip, he began to reflect back to his youth growing up in the Catholic Church. The last time he had packed a bag like this was for his Confirmation retreat. It was at a camp that the diocese of Phoenix owned in the mountains about a half hour out of Prescott. As Nick reminisced, he remembered that one of the cabins was set apart from the others and when he asked his youth leader what it was for, he was told it was a special cabin they called the bishop's cabin. The leader told him the priests would stay there when they came to the camp, and they sometimes just used it as a getaway when they wanted to be alone. The thought of the missing priest had come to his mind. He was about to dismiss the idea, but then thought he'd be up there anyway so it wouldn't kill him to check it out. Looking it up on the Internet, he found that it was still there. *I know it's a long shot, but what the hell. I'll leave a couple of hours early,* he thought.

He decided to check out the cabin at the camp first, just to get that out of the way, and the rest of the weekend was for the kids. He followed Gurley Street, then turned onto Copper Basin Road and followed it to the camp. He remembered it surprisingly well, and with the help of his GPS, he found it easily.

He came to a sign that read: Welcome to Sacred Heart Camp. He crossed a small bridge that spanned a clear running creek and followed the dirt road up a steep hill to the top where he caught sight of the cabins. Seeing a lone cabin set away from the main camp, he recognized it as that special cabin in his memory. Not really expecting to find anything there, Nick was surprised when he saw a white Chevy Camaro parked on the brown dirt in front of the cabin. He pulled up beside it, put the Ford in park, turned the key and waited as the engine became silent.

The frame redwood cabin sat on a raised block foundation with three wooden steps leading up to a small wooden porch. The smell of the statuesque ponderosa pines that surrounded the structure on three sides was welcoming to his city boy senses. He thought for a moment about how he should approach the cabin. He placed his left hand on the hood of the Camaro. Cold and wet. The misty dew told him that the car had probably been there at least overnight. The wooden steps squeaked under his feet as he ascended onto the porch. He stood still for a moment. Except for the sound of flowing water lapping against the rocks of a nearby stream and birds chirping their morning songs, it was quiet and peaceful. He understood why the Metzlers liked it up here.

Breaking his trance, Nick thought it was odd that all the windows and doors were closed and the curtains were drawn as if no one was there. It's such a beautiful day, he thought. The windows and doors should be open so the fresh mountain air would earn its due.

He decided to continue with caution as he raised his right hand and rapped four times on the door. He waited about a minute and rapped again, this time a little harder. He called out, "Anyone in there?" Again there was no response. "I'm Nick Greer. I'm a Phoenix police officer. I'm looking for Father Blake Beyers. If you're in there, I need to speak with you. Please open the door."

Nick waited and was pondering his next move when he saw the curtain in the window next to the door part slightly and then immediately close. He waited, expecting the door to open. Nothing. "Father Beyers. I'm not going to hurt you. I'm here to help." Retrieving his badge, he tapped it several times against the window in the exact spot he had seen the curtain part. "Look, here is my badge. See? I'm a police officer. I'm here to help you." He continued holding the gold badge against the pane, then tapped it against the glass two more times until he saw the curtain part and a face looking carefully at the badge.

Then the curtain closed. He waited a few seconds. What to do next? If the occupant didn't open the door, Nick had no reason to use forced entry. He had no local authority, and he didn't want to go into Prescott for help from their police because it would make him late picking up the kids. Cassie would make the most of that.

Suddenly he heard the sound of the door lock opening. "Come in, but stand back. I'm armed," came a voice from inside.

Nick instinctively reached for his Glock when he remembered, knowing that he would be with the kids today, that he had stowed it and his backup in the trunk of his car before leaving Phoenix. His first thought was to go to his car and get it, but he knew if he did, the priest might lock the door. He doubted he was really armed, anyway, so he opened the door and entered the cabin with his arms in the air and his badge in one hand.

A man, about five-ten, approximately one hundred sixty pounds, stood with his back against the far wall of the small room. He was holding a baseball bat above the right side of his head. It was plain that this man was thoroughly frightened. Nick almost laughed out loud when he saw the man had a reversed grip on the bat; the left hand was on top of the right. Were he to swing it, he had more chance of breaking his own wrist than actually hurting anyone.

"Father Beyers? Are you Father Blake Beyers?" Nick queried.

The man's face was white as he stammered, "Who wants to know and why?"

Nick no longer could hold back his amusement. He shook his head and let out a light chuckle. "I told you. I'm from the Phoenix PD." He pushed his badge out in front of himself as he boldly walked toward the man. "I just want to ask you some questions about Father Mignanelli." He pointed to the bat and said, "And put that thing down before you hurt yourself!"

As the man looked into Nick's eyes, the detective could see the fear mixed with relief as he lowered the bat. Nick took the bat from his hand and put it in the corner of the small room. "Sit. We need to talk." He pointed to the sofa and chair sitting in the front of the room. "Are you Father Blake Beyers?"

The man nodded as he sat down in one of two high-back chairs. Their flowered pattern matched the sofa upon which Nick sat. An old, brown coffee table thoroughly needing refinishing sat between them on a dark brown oval carpet. The rest of the floor was covered with vinyl tile, some of which were loose. The only lamp in the room was on a small maple table placed between the two chairs. A Bible laid next to the lamp. It was obvious that décor was not important in this rustic setting.

"I really wouldn't have hurt you," the priest said as he pointed to the bat leaning against the wall in the corner.

It was all Nick could do to keep a straight face as he remembered how the man had held the bat. "It wasn't me I was worried about, Father. You are Father Blake Beyers, are you not?"

"I am he."

"I assume you are aware of the passing of Father David Mignanelli?"

The priest squirmed slightly in his chair and nodded.

"First of all, please accept my sympathies for the loss of your friend."

"Thank you," the priest answered.

"Exactly what was your relationship with the decea . . . Father Mignanelli?"

"We were both priests and friends."

"Friends? What does that mean exactly? How well did you know him?"

He nervously answered, "Uhh . . . We were both priests in the diocese. We attended meetings and sometimes shared a meal together."

Nick looked into the priest's eyes and shook his head. "Look, Father, I know you had more than a casual relationship with him. I came all the way up here from Phoenix, because I'm looking into his death. I don't have time for a runaround. I know you were friends before you came here. I know you share business interests, and I know you know more about his death than I do, and I know you're afraid of someone or something. Now tell me what's going on. Why are you here and who are you hiding from?"

The priest's face turned white when he heard Nick's words. "Hiding? Why . . . uhh . . . I'm not hiding. I'm here because I'm in mourning."

"Father, I'm not buying this at all. Why would you be defending yourself with a bat? There are no ax murderers in these woods. Whether or not you're in mourning, you are hiding. Tell me, who are you hiding from and why."

"There's nothing to tell you. I thought you might be a burglar, that's all. I just want to be left alone. Hey, how did you know I was here anyway? I didn't tell anyone where I was going except Puzzleman, and I know he wouldn't tell."

"Puzzleman? Who's Puzzleman?"

"Uhhm . . . just another priest."

"Who? Who is this Puzzleman? What is his real name?" The detective looked into the eyes of his emissary. He could see the fear but continued, "Listen to my words carefully! First, lying to a police officer is a criminal offense. If you lie to me, I *will* arrest you. I have a job to do, and your collar will not stop me from doing it. Second, it's plain you're in trouble of some sort. I can help you. I can protect you. But you've got to be forthright with me. Now, tell me what is going on. All of it! Starting with who the hell is this Puzzleman?"

"Mike. Mike Kubic. He's a fellow priest," he surrendered.

"Yes, I know who he is. Why do you call him Puzzleman?"

"Oh. He loves puzzles. He is the best I have ever seen at crosswords and such. Remember the Rubik's Cube? He was a whiz at it. Rubik, Kubic, get it?"

"I never thought of priests using nicknames for each other."

"Oh, a few of us have nicknames for each other. Like Father Frank. We call him Tuck. I guess it's because he looks like the Robin Hood character; you know, short and heavy. He doesn't mind the nickname."

"Anyone else?"

The priest hesitated and looked away. "No. That's all."

The detective knew he was lying but decided not to press the issue at this time. "Do you really think Father Mignanelli killed himself?"

The priest looked stunned as he seemed to ponder his answer. "Why would you ask such a thing? I just know what I was told. He shot himself. That's it."

"Why?" The detective could see that the priest was mentally searching for reasons the questions were asked and for adequate answers.

"I don't know."

"Yes, you do," Nick challenged and fired a salvo at him. "You were his friend, maybe his best friend, maybe lovers. You've known him for years. You were from the same town in Pennsylvania. You got him to come out here. If there was a problem serious enough to cause him to take his own life, you'd know about it. What was it? Did it have anything to do with the audit?" Though he was guessing at most of his statements, the lack of rebuttal and the look on the priest's face told him he was on the right track. He looked directly into the man's eyes and added. "Yeah, you're right. I did my homework. Now, give, Father!"

"The audit was bothering him . . . yeah . . . that was it . . . I'm sure of it."

"Father, I'm not playing this game with you. You and I both know he didn't kill himself. You know who did, or at least you have an idea who did, and you're scared. Are they after you, too? Is that why you're here? If I found you here, how soon do you think it will be before they do?"

Again the priest's face turned white. He emitted a sigh of surrender. He didn't know that it was luck Nick knew about the camp and that he hadn't really expected to find anyone here. The detective had him, at least for now.

Beyers shook his head. "I don't want to go to jail."

Nick was surprised at the response. He didn't know whether to read him his rights. If he did, he would have to arrest him and take him in.

He looked at his watch. It was after ten, and he hadn't procured a room yet. He needed to pick up the kids by noon or Cassie might pull something.

"Father, I need you to answer one question, and it must be the honest-to-God truth, okay?"

He looked into the priest's eyes and saw the earnestness in his answer. "Yes, I promise."

"Did you have anything to do with the death of David Mignanelli?"

The priest put both feet flat on the floor, leaned toward Nick, looked him in the eyes and said, "No, sir, I did not."

The detective saw and heard truth in the priest's response. "Okay, Father, I believe you, but I need to know everything. We can do this two ways. I don't want to put you in jail, but if we continue this here and now I may have to read you your rights. That means I'll have to arrest you. I don't think you want that and neither do I, so I'll make you a deal. If you promise me, I mean swear on that Bible over there"— he pointed to the Bible on the table next to the priest—"that you will come to the precinct first thing Monday, I'll talk to the assistant district attorney about immunity for you. As long as you weren't complicit, you shouldn't have anything to worry about. I can't speak for your bishop, only for the city of Phoenix. Is that okay? Do we have a deal?"

"Thank you, Lieutenant. I'll be there. I promise. First thing Monday. I'll be there at ten o'clock. I promise, okay?"

"See you at ten." The detective rose and turned toward the door. I hope I'm doing the right thing, he thought.

He stopped and turned around to the priest. "There's an odd thing about this case. The de . . . Father Mignanelli's car was in his garage, but there were no keys. No house keys or keys to the church either. No keys at all. Everybody has keys. Do you have any idea what could have happened to them?"

"I didn't know they were missing. He always had them with him or at the house."

Nick decided to let this subject ride until tomorrow. This guy knew more and another day wouldn't matter. He'd get it out of him Monday at the precinct. Right now he just wanted to see his girls.

As Nick stepped down from the last wooden step into the moist green grass, he called over his shoulder, "By the way, you guys got a name for the bishop?"

"Napoleon."

CHAPTER 34

It was now eleven o'clock Monday morning. The priest had promised to be here by ten. Nick figured he'd get a warrant. He'd need one for Prescott, too, since Beyers was probably still hiding. Damn! I really thought he'd show, he thought.

Nick had spent the morning working on the computer looking for any information to help with the case and making notes for the interview. He got a verbal agreement for immunity from Shelley Kisler, an ADA he trusted. She had already called twice this morning and was not happy that the subject was late.

Nick thought about the weekend. It had gone well. He'd made it to the Metzlers in time and Cassie stayed out of the way. Saturday he took his daughters to see *Spiderman*, and they had spent most of Sunday at the mall. He'd bought them some clothes and CDs and they were happy. He had gotten home shortly after eight p.m., opened his mail, called Sue Kim, drank a beer, took a shower, and went to bed.

His thoughts were interrupted by the buzz of the phone. He reached out and retrieved it from its cradle. "Greer."

He recognized Rosa the receptionist's voice on the other end as she said, "ADA Kisler again. Line two."

He looked at his watch: 11:08. He punched in the second button on the phone and said, "Hi, Shelley. No show yet. Beginning to think he won't."

"Sounds like it to me, too. If he shows, let me know. I'm about to renege on our agreement. Nothing personal, but you know how it goes. This guy is beginning to piss me off."

"Yeah, me, too." He put the phone back in its cradle, got up from his desk, and went to the back of the room to his captain's office.

Pete Mendoza was on the phone as Nick entered his office. The captain gestured for him to sit down as he continued his conversation. "Yes, sir. I'll handle it. No problem." He hung up the phone and looked at Nick. He was silent, waiting for Nick to speak.

"Pete, I wanted to give you a heads-up. I'm going after a warrant for a priest. Thought you should know. I'll explain—"

"Let me guess," Mendoza interrupted. "Beyers. Father Blake Beyers."

The detective was only slightly surprised. "Sounds like the chief called again."

"Nope!"

"Mayor?"

"Yep. Murphy himself! Seems like one of my detectives went cleeeear up to Prescott to harass another priest." He leaned forward and looked at Nick. "You wouldn't know who that certain detective would be, would you? Since we agreed you wouldn't cause any more trouble with the bishop's people, I'm sure it wasn't you!"

The captain looked into Nick's eyes. "It appears you spooked him so bad he lost control of his car, went into a ravine, and now he's in St Joe's Hospital."

"Who?" Greer asked.

"Who what?" Mendoza responded.

"Who is at St. Joe's? The mayor?"

"The priest! Beyers!"

"What?"

"If that ain't enough, the bishop called Murphy from Baltimore raising holy hell! Murphy wants me and the chief in his office pronto!"

"Son of a bitch!" Nick exclaimed. "You gotta be fucking kidding me. No wonder he didn't show."

"What? Who didn't show? Where? When?" The captain was puzzled.

"Beyers! Here! This morning! Pete, we gotta impound his car!"

"Whaaaat? Didn't you hear me? The mayor is pissed! The chief is pissed! I'm gonna get my ass reamed!" He reached his right hand down behind him as if to cover his backside.

"Okay, Pete. Here's what's going on." Nick gave his captain the complete account of his meeting with the priest and his promise to come in this morning. "I shouldn't have left him. I should've brought him in myself."

The stunned captain put both elbows on his desk and closed his eyes. He rubbed his forehead in a circular motion with the fingertips of both hands, took a deep breath, and let it out as he tried to bring all this new information into focus. He then turned both hands forward with the palms out and said, "Okay. Looks like we got cause. Get the fucking car impounded and checked out. We both better hope you're right. Right now, I sure as hell ain't the mayor's favorite person. And you, I don't want to even think about it."

Nick began to get up, but the captain had already risen and was walking past him as he said, "Get Madison to help you. Tell him I said to drop whatever he's doing. We need to make this top priority!"

"Where you going, Pete?" Nick asked, talking to the captain's back as he went through the doorway.

"I'm gonna pick up some KY and go see the chief."

Nick sat still for a few moments as he gathered his thoughts before he got up and exited Captain Mendoza's office. As he crossed the squad room floor to the front, he saw Rosa ending a phone call and said, "Can you get Sonny for me? I need him to come in right away. Captain's orders."

"He's on his way. Just hung up. Captain sure seemed in a hurry. 'Get Maddox in here now,' he said. 'Tell him TFP,' he said. Never even stopped. I said, 'What do I tell him?' 'See Greer,' he said."

She looked at him with a caring look in her eyes. "Everything okay, Lieutenant? I ain't never seen the captain quite like that before. Do you know where he went? And what's TFP?"

Nick turned, headed back to his desk, and answered over his shoulder. "He went to earn his pension." He didn't answer her last question. He didn't want to tell her that it meant top fucking priority.

Nick immediately made a phone call and found that the priest's car had been towed to Harris Auto Body in Black Canyon City. He arranged for it to be picked up and taken to the police impound yard. He then called forensics to examine it when it arrived. The lady who answered told him that they were already aware of it and would be waiting for it. "The chief's office called about five minutes ago," she said. "Top priority. We'll have techs standing by."

"Thanks," Nick said as he hung up the phone. Good. Pete was successful with the chief, he thought. He then picked up the phone and called for search warrants for all of Beyers' and BMK properties.

He was about to call Shelley Kisler when Sonny came in. "What's all the hoopla about?"

"Do me a favor," Nick said as he took a pen and scribbled some notes on a yellow pad, ripped the paper from the pad, and handed it to Sonny. "Pick up these warrants and call me when you have 'em. I'll explain later."

Nick grabbed his keys from the corner of his desk and headed toward the door.

"Where ya goin'?" Sonny asked.

"St Joe's Hospital."

CHAPTER 35

As he arrived at St. Joseph's Hospital, he passed the statue of St. Joseph, and it reminded him of happier days. His and Cassie's kids were born here. He remembered how happy they'd been then and wondered how things could've changed so fast.

Pulling the Ford Taurus into a parking spot labeled "Police," he killed the engine and followed the sidewalk to a large set of doors and then straight to the hospitality desk. Pulling his gold shield from his belt, he held it up and said, "Beyers, Blake, please."

The white-haired volunteer behind the desk looked over her glasses as she pushed some buttons on her computer and responded, "Third floor ICU, room seven. It's—"

"I know where it is, thank you," he interrupted and headed straight for the elevator. He pushed the up button, and the door immediately opened like it was waiting for him. He entered the elevator, pressed three, and felt the elevator ascend. The doors slid open, and he exited to the left and followed the passageway to the Intensive Care Unit.

The sign to the left side of the double doors read: Authorized Personnel Only. Push for Admittance. Pushing the intercom on the wall to the right brought a response through the speaker. "Can I help you?"

"Phoenix police," he responded. A buzzer sounded and both doors swung open. Nick went through them and followed the hallway to room seven.

Even though his head was wrapped with white bandages, the detective immediately recognized the man he met on the mountaintop just two days before. His head was bandaged from above the eyebrows, and his face was covered with lacerations; a large one next to his left eye had been sutured. His right leg was elevated and in traction; both hands were bandaged and an IV ran into his left arm.

A nurse was busy adjusting a machine that was recording his vitals. She looked up at Nick through black-rimmed glasses and said, "Can I help you?"

Displaying his badge, he said, "I'm Lieutenant Greer from the Phoenix PD." He looked at the patient and asked, "How is he doing?"

"He was comatose but he's sleeping now," she answered. "Lucky to be alive. The doctors removed his spleen and repaired some internal bleeding. Car accident, I'm told."

"When can I speak to him?" Nick asked.

"Like I said, he's sleeping now but when he wakes, I think it would be all right. His vitals are looking good. We'll have to see what the doctor says though."

"I understand." He handed her his card. "Please call my cell the moment he wakes up. It's very important."

"Okay." She took his card and dropped it her right front pocket.

Nick turned and left the hospital wondering if he should place a guard at the priest's door.

He had just fired up the engine and reached to the car's center console to put it in reverse when his cell phone rang. The caller ID said: St Joseph's Hospital.

"Lieutenant Greer," he answered.

"This is Amy from ICU. Mr. Beyers is awake, and the doctor said it's okay for you to see him."

"Thank you," he said as he shut off the engine and returned to the hospital.

The priest's bed had been cranked up, and he was partially sitting up. Amy was tending to him when Nick entered the room. He asked, "How is he?"

"In and out. He just dozed off again," she answered.

"Can we wake him?"

"I don't think that's . . ." She didn't finish the sentence as her patient began to stir.

Nick watched as the priest opened his blackened eyes. Amy took a cup, poured water into it from a green plastic pitcher, bent a straw, and placed it between his lips. He took a small sip and shook his head slightly. It was obvious the man was in pain.

"Father Beyers. Do you remember me? I'm Lieutenant Greer."

The priest slowly nodded.

"Can you tell me what happened? I know you were in an accident. Do you remember what happened?"

The priest took a small breath. "Brakes. Brakes. Didn't work." He managed to get the words out in a little more than a whisper before he closed his eyes.

"He's asleep again," the young nurse stated. "He'll be in and out for the next few hours. He's had quite a shock to his system." She looked up at Nick and asked, "Did you call him Father? Is he a priest?"

The detective nodded as he turned to leave. "Sure is."

He returned to the precinct, checked messages, none. Funny Sue Kim hadn't called, he thought. Maybe she's pissed because I didn't go over last night. I'll call her. He reached for his cell phone, but he caught sight of a stack of warrants on his desk. His eyes scanned the room but he didn't see Sonny. He wondered where he was. He decided he should report his findings to his captain. Maybe Pete would know where Sonny was.

Captain Mendoza was reviewing some papers and looked up as Nick sat down.

"Whatcha got for me?"

"Thanks for getting the ball rolling with the chief, Pete."

The captain was all business. "What good news do you have for me?" The look on his face was intense.

"I talked to Beyers. He was pretty much out of it, but he managed to say, 'Brakes. Brakes. Didn't work,' before he dropped off."

The captain said, "The car should be in soon. Forensics is to get on it immediately. That's the first thing they'll check."

"I'm wondering if we should put someone at the hospital," Nick stated.

Mendoza let out a breath and said, "I don't know. Let's see what else shakes. The bishop is raising holy hell with Murphy, and Murphy is all over the chief but the chief is a good man. He's with us on this now. But you better be right or the proverbial egg on his face will spill right on *this* desk." He lifted both arms, extended his index fingers, and pointed straight down to his gray desk.

"I'm right, Pete. I know it! That priest was murdered. Whoever did it tried to take Beyers out, too."

"Any ideas yet? Motive?"

Nick slowly shook his head. "Not a fucking clue! But somehow, someone in the diocese is either involved or knows who is. We gotta wait till Beyers is coherent enough to really talk. He knows what's going on, and he's scared shitless! I'll bet he'll talk. We might need to protect him, though."

"I'll need more than that to put a guard on him," the captain stated. "You get Sonny out of the shitter and get to work. The bishop is cutting his trip short and coming back. Things may not be so easy once he gets here."

"Easy? Easy? What's easy about this whole thing?" Nick said as he stood up to leave. "How much harder can it get?"

"The bish ain't here yet!" Mendoza answered.

CHAPTER 36

As Nick sat at his desk, going over his notes for the umpteenth time and adding his thoughts about this morning's hospital visit, he heard his phone buzz. He reached to the corner of his desk and pushed the intercom button. "Greer."

Nick recognized Rosa's voice. "Lieutenant, there's a Sue Kim on line two."

He looked to the front of the room and saw the playful grin on the receptionist's face. Without answering Rosa, he pressed the button.

"Good morning," he answered.

"Try afternoon," came a giggling voice from the other end.

Nick checked his watch. It was 2:15. "That'll work," he answered. "This day is flying by."

"You too busy to return my text?"

Nick retrieved his Android, saw the message notice, and pulled it down with one finger. "My place tonight?" It had been sent at 10:12 this morning.

"Sorry, I didn't hear it ring. Been covered up all day. I'll have to let you know later on about tonight. I gotta see how the day goes."

"Ahh. Getting tired of me already," she said in a playful tone.

"You know better than that. This case is getting more complicated every day. I gotta see it through."

"The priest?"

"Yeah, the priest."

"Anything I can do to help?"

"Don't know what, but thanks." He pursed his lips and thought for a moment. "Let's shoot for tonight. I'll let you know. Don't know what time or how much company I'll be. Got my mind all over the case."

She giggled. "I'll bet I can get your mind off of it for a little while anyway."

"No doubt you can."

She giggled again. "I should get out of here a little early. I need to get something from my safe deposit box before the bank closes. See you tonight."

Nick hung up the phone and deleted her text message. As he laid the phone on his desk, he thought about what she had just said. Safe deposit box! It was a shot.

Just then Sonny walked in and said, "Where ya been? I got the warrants you wanted. Now you wanna tell me what's going on? Why did the boss pull me off my cases? You gettin' weak? You need a real detective to show you how it's done?"

Nick laughed and said, "Have a seat, Sergeant Madison."

Sonny listened intently while his friend brought him up to date on the case.

"We gotta get something concrete before the bishop comes back," Nick stated. "The mayor is cooperating now, but that could change in a heartbeat once O'Malley gets to him."

Greer squinted as he pondered his next move. "I need you to do something." He reached into his drawer, pulled out a file, and handed it to his partner. "Here's everything I got on Beyers and Mignanelli. See if you can find a safe deposit box somewhere for either one of them. If you do, get a warrant."

"Where you gonna be?" Sonny asked.

"Gonna see how forensics is coming along with the car."

It was 2:55 when he entered the garage and saw the priest's smashed Camaro. The front end was resting on a pair of red jacks, and the car looked unattended. He saw two men dressed in blue overalls. Though their backs were to him, Nick could see that one was holding a long piece of copper tubing, pointing to it, and seemed to be explaining it to the other.

"I'm Lieutenant Greer," Nick said as he approached them. They turned in unison, and he recognized Paul Pratte. He had been with the department much longer than Nick, and he was considered one of the best at his trade.

"Hey, Nick," Pratte replied. "You the lead on this case?"

Paul Pratte was in his sixties and stood about five-ten. A blue PPD baseball cap sat on his completely bald head. His spectacled face displayed a little gray five-o'clock shadow.

"I am," the lieutenant answered.

Pratte looked toward his companion and said, "This is Rene Marquez. Rene, meet Lieutenant Nick Greer."

Rene was in his early twenties, about six feet tall with long, jet-black hair pushing its way out from under his cap. They shook hands, and Nick looked at Pratte and said, "Got anything for me?"

Pratte held up the copper tube for the detective to see. "Brake line."

"Tell me something I don't know," the detective said, smiling.

The mechanic pointed to one end and said, "See? Cut here."

"You sure?" Nick questioned.

Pratte looked at Greer as if he had just been insulted. He reached up, pulled his glasses to the end of his nose, dropped both hands to his sides, and stared out at the detective over his silver-rimmed glasses. His silence told Nick that the inspector was positive.

"Sorry," Nick responded with a grin.

"You should be," the mechanic smiled. He nodded once as he continued, "I should have the report for you by the end of the day."

"Thank you, gentlemen. Appreciate your help," Nick said as he turned to leave.

"Wanna know what cut it?" came the voice from behind him.

"If you know, sure."

"Small saw, probably a small hacksaw. Cut in a V from the top. It wasn't severed or pinched. Nice clean cut. Someone knew what they were doing. The fluid would leak as the brakes were pressed. It'll be in the report."

"Good job, Paul. Good job."

"Yeah, I know," Nick heard as he again turned to leave and smiled.

Returning to the squad room and expecting to find warrants for the safe deposit boxes, he saw none, so he phoned his partner.

"Madison." The answer came on the first ring.

"You got anything on the boxes yet?" Nick questioned.

"Nada! Still working on it."

"Where are you?"

"Just left Judge Connor. He's having the warrants typed up, just need the name of the banks. Can't find anything with the big banks. Gonna start on the little ones. How did it go with the car?"

"Somebody fucked with the brakes."

"For sure?"

Nick remembered the look on Pratte's face and said, "Oh yeah. For sure."

"Wow! Who would wanna kill a priest?"

"Two of them," Nick responded. "The second one got lucky. Sonny, I'm sure Pete will okay the OT on this. He wants something before the bishop gets back, so do what you can, okay?"

"You got it," Sonny answered and disconnected the phone.

Nick shut off his phone and laid it on his desk. With both elbows on his desk, he put his head in his hands, closed his eyes, and again went over the whole case in his mind. He went through every step from the beginning to now. Still no motive. Still no real suspect. He took a deep breath and exhaled. Then an idea hit him. He picked up his phone and hit redial.

"Madison."

"Try looking for Michael Kubic or BMK Enterprises."

"Got it," Madison replied.

Nick knew it would be difficult to obtain a warrant for Kubic unless he could show cause, and, as of now, he couldn't. As for BMK? Another shot in the dark.

"Uhhh . . . and see if you can get one more. 5478 West Desert Oasis Drive."

"Isn't that—?"

Nick cut him short. "Yeah. Make it cover everything."

He looked at his watch: 4:37. Looks like tomorrow is gonna be a busy day, he thought.

CHAPTER 37

It was Tuesday and Nick Greer was lost in thought about Sue Kim. His preoccupation with the case had caused him to leave her apartment early. She had understood and was very supportive of him, a trait Cassie lacked.

His thoughts were interrupted when Sonny Madison returned with the warrants. "Got 'em all," he said as he dropped them on his partner's desk.

"Good. Let's go for a ride. You're driving."

Sonny steered his Malibu into St. Michael's parking lot. Nick had arranged to meet Father Roman, who had agreed to provide a key for Mignanelli's house. The detective handed him the search warrant, but the cleric said, "I don't need it. Do what you gotta do. Just please return the key."

"I will," Nick said. He thanked the priest and returned to Sonny's car.

They arrived at the house, and Nick unlocked the door and punched in the alarm code that he had retrieved from his notes. Sonny followed him into the house. The lieutenant said, "Sonny, I have no idea what to look for. Forensics and I have gone through this whole house. Perhaps a fresh set of eyes may find something I missed. Go for it, my friend."

"What am I looking for?"

Nick shrugged and shook his head. "Something I missed! The warrant covers it all. Keys would be nice."

Sonny stopped, looked at the floor and then at his partner. "It's wet."

"What's wet?" Nick asked.

"The carpet! It's wet like it's just been steam cleaned."

Nick bent down and ran his hand over the carpet. "Looks like it. Just done. That ain't gonna help much."

Madison bent down and started unlacing his shoes. Greer asked, "What the hell are you doing?"

"Taking off my shoes," he responded in a matter-of-fact manner.

"Why?"

"They just had it cleaned. It's still wet. It's only right not to dirty it up," he said as he removed the second shoe.

"Well, the softer side of Sonny has emerged," Nick said as he kicked off his loafers and pointed to the room where the body had been found. "Let's start there."

With gloved hands, they thoroughly searched every nook and cranny throughout the west end of the house. The priest's belongings had been removed. All that was left were the furnishings. Nick showed his partner where the body had been. They went over his trajectory theory and the two bullet holes in the wall. Sonny agreed with his partner's findings.

Sonny made a remark about the room with the lone futon, and Nick told Sonny about the ones he saw at Beyers' home and at the condo.

The next move was to the living room. Sonny said nothing about how lavishly it was furnished; he just continued working.

Nick was working in the corner of the dining room next to the ebony china cabinet and as he ran his hands along the wall, he felt something uncomfortable under his foot. It felt like something was under the carpet so he bent down to look. He was surprised to find that the corner of the carpet was loose. He wondered why it was not tacked down as he easily pulled it away from the wall.

Sonny was working the other side of the room when he heard Nick yell, "Madison! You're a fucking genius."

Puzzled, Sonny stopped and walked to where Nick was crouched down in the corner and pointing to the floor. There it was, a floor safe!

"I haven't seen one of those things in ages," Madison stated. "What do you think is in it? Can you open it? And why am I a fucking genius?"

"Doubt it," Nick said. "It's got a combo. If I had shoes on, I never would have felt the carpet. Good move, Detective Madison. Good move."

"Guess we need a locksmith. The warrant covers it," Sonny stated.

Seeing that it was a three-digit combination dial, the lieutenant thought for a moment and pulled the paper that held the alarm code from his pocket. He looked at it: 4257.

Sonny snapped a picture of the safe with his cell phone as Nick began working on the combination. First he tried 425. No luck. 257. No luck. 752. "Got it!" He removed the heavy cover and sat it on the folded carpet beside him. Reaching into the safe, he pulled out a small brown notebook. Under it were several white plastic cylindrical containers. The lieutenant picked up one and was a little surprised by its weight. It was heavier than it looked. He twisted the lid and looked twice at the contents not believing what he saw.

"Sonny, look at this, will ya?"

"Holy shit," Madison exclaimed when he saw the Gold American Eagle coins! "If that thing is full, it's worth a bunch."

"You got a flashlight?" Greer asked.

Sonny retrieved a small flashlight from his pocket and shined it into the dark cavern.

The lieutenant asked, "What's gold worth today?"

"Uhhh . . . about seventeen hundred dollars an ounce, give or take, I think."

Nick looked at his partner. "I think we found our motive. We need to get a tech crew out here super pronto."

He grabbed his cell phone and began dialing. "Take some more pix with your phone, and neither of us leave each other's sight until they get here. If there's as much in here as I think, we don't want to trigger an IA investigation."

"Great time to have to piss," Sonny said.

Then Nick called Captain Mendoza and advised him of the situation. In about five minutes, two uniformed police officers came through the front door. The first one stayed at the door, and the other came into the room where the two detectives were. Neither spoke but both detectives knew why they were there and welcomed their presence.

They sat still for about twenty minutes before three crime scene techs came through the door. After conversing with the lead tech, they both got up, stretched, and went to the other side of the room. They watched the technicians process the scene, itemizing and listing the entire contents of the safe.

"Hey, Nick, the cavalry has arrived," Sonny said as Captain Mendoza came through the front door. Immediately he took his two detectives out of the room and into the kitchen.

The lieutenant explained the situation in detail. The captain carefully read the warrant and said, "Clean. The search is clean."

Nick requested that both he and Sonny be searched. Sonny agreed.

Mendoza motioned for the uniformed officer at the front door to join them. Both of the detectives emptied their pockets onto the table, and the uniform thoroughly searched them. Then Sonny asked to have his car impounded and searched. Pete agreed and made the phone call. Not knowing how much money was in the safe or if all of the containers were full, neither of them wanted to be accused of pocketing any of it.

"I assume Internal Affairs will want a full report from both of you," the captain stated. "I want to see them before you submit them. Now, let's get out of here."

As they got into Mendoza's car, Nick said, "Well, Pete, think we got motive?" He saw traces of a smile on his captain's lips as he put the car in gear.

As they pulled away, Sonny turned around and looked out the rear window. He saw a white sedan pull up to the house. He knew who it was. "Looks like we left just in time. The rat squad just arrived."

The ride back was silent.

CHAPTER 38

It was two p.m. and the two IA detectives had been in Mendoza's office for the last twenty minutes. Assuming that they would be questioned, the captain made his two detectives stay in the precinct. When the investigators left, they came over to Nick and Sonny.

The lead was a white-haired paunchy man, about five-seven, and his partner was a female, a couple inches taller than her partner. She was about thirty-five with short brown hair, and she wore a white blouse and a brown skirt.

"Lieutenant Greer, Sergeant Madison," the man said as he held out his hand. "I'm Lieutenant Catanese." He looked to the woman standing next to him. "This is my partner, Sergeant DeLuca." She nodded as the detective continued, "Good job. I read your reports. I see no problems. Just thought you might want to know."

Before either Nick or Sonny had a chance to say anything, both officers turned and left the room.

"They never interviewed us," Sonny said. "We never got to talk to them. How rude! I never got to tell them what bastards they are."

"That's probably best," Nick said and turned toward the captain's office.

Mendoza saw Nick coming and motioned for him to enter. Sonny followed and they both sat down. "That was pretty smooth. You both handled it well. Good job. IA is satisfied."

"Yeah, well, I'm not. How come they didn't talk to us?" Sonny asked.

"Madison, you're the last one I'd want them to talk to. You'd piss them off, and I'm the one who'd have to deal with it."

"What's the matter? You afraid I'd tell them what pricks they are?" Sonny grinned.

Mendoza shook his head as he looked at his detective. "Exactly! You know they're pricks. I know they're pricks. And what's more, they know they're pricks, and they don't need or like to be reminded."

"The bitch looked like a dyke," Sonny snuck in.

Mendoza shook his head again, reached for a manila envelope on his desk, and tossed it to Sonny. "Here, you guys concentrate on this."

They left their captain's office, crossed the room, and sat down at Nick's desk. Sonny opened the folder and dumped its contents onto the desk. There was a property form listing the contents of the safe and the small brown leather notebook.

Sonny read the contents sheet and let out a whistle. "Five containers. All full. Twenty American Gold Eagles in each. That's gotta be over a hundred and fifty grand!" He looked at Nick. "Where the hell would a priest get that kind of money, and why was it hidden in a floor safe?"

"Maybe this will tell us," Nick said as he pulled the notebook from its plastic bag and opened it. Each page had what looked like a nickname of some sort handwritten across the top. Below each name were numbers. Some had been crossed out and changed as though they'd been updated. Each time they got higher. The pages were labeled: Buffalo Bill, Lionheart, Tuck, Puzzleman, Viking, Indian, Napoleon.

Nick remembered his discussion with Father Beyers at the cabin in Prescott. Puzzleman! He said it was Father Kubic, and the bishop was called Napoleon. So this was some sort of accounting, most likely for the coins in the safe.

The first page said: Buffalo Bill with the numbers 2-3-5-6-7-10-11-13-15-16-18-19 all crossed out, and the final number 20. Each page was similar. The final number for Lionheart was 20, Tuck 10, Puzzleman 15, Viking 15, Indian 15. The final page labeled Napoleon was blank. Grabbing a pen from his desk, he added the numbers at the bottom of each page. 95. Then he wrote 5x20=100. "If this is what I think it is, there are five coins unaccounted for."

"Huh?" Sonny looked puzzled.

"Well, assuming that this book was the accounting for the coins and assuming each number was one coin, then either he didn't enter them all or there are five extra. You'll notice the page for Napoleon is blank." He pointed to the last page as he lifted the book up to Sonny.

"Napoleon?" Sonny questioned.

Nick told him about his conversation with Beyers and the nicknames.

"You think the bishop has the rest?" Sonny asked. "You think he's involved?"

"Don't know, but we need to figure out who the rest of these people are, that's for sure. I'm wondering if our dead priest was scamming more than just his parishioners. We gotta see if there's a safe deposit box somewhere, and I still wanna know where the hell his keys are. Sonny, can you work on that? I'm going to St. Joe's."

CHAPTER 39

Nick entered the hospital and was informed that Father Beyers was out of ICU and in a regular room. Riding the elevator to the fourth floor, he followed the signs to room 412. The drapes were fully opened and the priest was looking out the window, unaware that he had company. "Father Beyers, how are you feeling?"

The cleric was startled, and he quickly turned his head. The grimace on his face made it plain that he was in a lot of pain. "Uhhh . . . okay, considering."

"You up to answering a couple of questions?"

"Guess so."

"Do you know who would have wanted to hurt you?

He shook his head and told an obvious lie. "No."

Nick decided not to push it yet. "We found a notebook belonging to your deceased friend. Do you know anything about it?"

"What notebook?"

"Okay, it had some coded names in it. I hoped you might know who some of these are. You told me Puzzleman was Father Kubic, Tuck was Father Frank, and Napoleon was the bishop."

Though the detective thought he knew who some of them were, he wanted to test the honesty and cooperation of the priest. "There are some other names here: Buffalo Bill, Lionheart, Viking and Indian." Nick showed him the picture.

"I don't know anything about a notebook." Beyers stated strongly.

"I understand. It's the names in it I'm concerned with. Who are they?" Nick held the paper up in front of the priest, who responded by turning his head toward the window in silence.

The detective walked to the other side of the bed, and, blocking the priest's view of the window, said, "Father, your car going off the road was not an accident. Your brake line was cut. Somebody tried to take you out. They may very well try again. I can help you but I need your cooperation. I need you to tell me the whole truth."

The priest didn't seem surprised by what he heard. His face showed no emotion.

The detective shoved the paper in front of the cleric's face. "Let's try again. Buffalo Bill?" The priest was silent. "Lionheart?" Silence.

"Viking?" He turned his head away. "Indian?" Beyers squirmed in his bed. Nick knew he had hit a nerve.

The priest turned back to Nick and shook his head. "I . . . I . . . I can't. I can't help you. Please leave me alone."

Beyers was afraid of something or somebody. Did he think the car thing was just a warning? Nick again wondered if he should have a watch stationed on the priest's room.

CHAPTER 40

Mike Bradley had gotten a call yesterday afternoon from Lieutenant Greer who said he had some questions that Mike may be able to answer, so they agreed to meet at Rene's Coffee Shop at ten o'clock. When Mike arrived, the detective was already seated in a booth by the window along with another man he didn't recognize.

A young lady greeted him, and he pointed to the booth and said, "Thank you, but I'm meeting someone."

He slid to the middle of the red vinyl seat, and Nick looked to the man beside him. "This is Sergeant Sonny Madison, my partner. Sonny, Mike Bradley."

"Pleased to meet you, Sergeant."

"Call me Sonny." Grinning, he continued, "So you're the guy who started all this."

"Uhhh . . . started what?" He wondered where this was going.

"Never mind him," Nick said. "I want you to look at something."

Just then a server came over with a menu. "Just coffee. Black, please," Bradley said.

As the server walked away, Nick produced a large envelope, reached into it, removed a paper, and laid it on the table. "These are photos of pages from a notebook we found. It belonged to your ex-pastor. Do you know what any of these names mean?"

Mike picked up the paper and studied it. He shook his head. "No idea. Should I?"

"Hoped you would. We think they're nicknames, possibly other priests."

The server brought a beige coffee mug, set it on the table, and poured coffee into it. She turned and left. Nick took a sip of his coffee and Mike asked, "What's this all about?"

Nick explained the book and that he'd figured out some of the names but needed to get them all.

"Okay," Mike said, "Tell me what you've got. Give me an idea."

"We're pretty sure that Puzzleman is Father Kubic. He's supposed to be some kind of puzzle whiz. Napoleon, we think is the bishop. Tuck has gotta be the little fat priest, Father Frank. Can't figure who Buffalo Bill, Lionheart, Viking and Indian are. Any ideas? One of them has got to be Mignanelli. Father Blake Beyers is sure to be in there somewhere, too."

Mike looked at the names again and studied them for about a minute. "Father David could be Indian. It might be a reach, but he's from a town in Pennsylvania called Monaca. Their football team was called the Indians. I don't know. I guess that sounds kind of dumb, huh?"

"I don't know. Are you sure? How do you know?"

"I grew up in the area. It makes sense. Maybe Buffalo Bill is from the west, or maybe his high school or college mascot was a Buffalo. Maybe he's from New York, maybe even Buffalo. Maybe Viking is from Norway or maybe even Minnesota. Maybe his high school or college mascot was a Viking."

"Son of a bitch!" Nick exclaimed. He looked like he'd just had an epiphany. "Thank you, Mike. The coffee's on me."

Motioning to the server for the check, he rose, pulled his wallet from his jeans, grabbed a ten, and dropped it on the table. "I think I got it."

"But who?" It was too late. Nick and Sonny were already halfway to the door.

Waving to the server, Mike pointed to his coffee. "Can you make this to go?"

CHAPTER 41

Nick led a crew and searched the condo. Sonny took a crew to Beyers' home. Nothing had been touched in the condo since their last visit. He was hoping that Sonny was having better luck at Beyers' home when his cell phone rang. The caller ID said Sonny.

"What ya got for me?"

"Nada," came the response from the other end. "The place is clean. You?"

"Ditto."

"What's next?"

"It's late, Sonny. Go home. Spend some time with April and the kids. See you in the a.m."

Pushing the *end* button on his Android and stowing it in its case, he dismissed the crew, got into his car, fired up the engine, and headed back to Phoenix. He was thinking that he would stop by St. Joseph's Hospital and check on Beyers once more before going home when the ring of his cell phone broke through his radio speakers. The caller ID read Sue, so he pushed the *phone* button on his steering wheel and answered, "Hi, babe. What's up?"

"What's up with you? It's six thirty, and I'm home all alone and wearing a tee shirt."

"Okaaay," Nick responded, not sure where she was going with this. "Uhhh, what kind of tee shirt?"

"That's not important. But guess what I'm wearing with it, Mr. Detective."

"Uhhhhh. No clue."

She giggled, "Nothing! Annnd . . . I just got out of the shower!"

Nick remembered how sexy she looked the first night they made love. He pictured her perky, hard nipples pushing against the slightly damp, thin tee shirt. Beyers can wait until tomorrow, he thought.

"I was just getting ready to call you," he lied. "I'm in Scottsdale and I'll be there in a bit."

"Sure you were," she responded. "I'll order a pizza delivery."

"Just don't answer the door dressed like you are."

"Thirty minutes for delivery. Looks like you got twenty-nine."

CHAPTER 42

Sitting at his desk, reviewing his notes and trying to concentrate on the case, he found his mind wandering back to last night. Never before had he known anyone like Sue Kim, and his feelings for her were growing stronger each day. There was no doubt in his mind that he had loved Cassie, but this was a different feeling. It felt better, and, for a reason he didn't understand, it made him uncomfortable.

It was almost eleven o'clock when he felt a touch on his shoulder. He turned around to see his captain behind him, motioning with his finger to follow him. In silence they went in to the boss's office and sat down. Mendoza picked up a file from the center of his desk, opened it, and began reading. The silence was becoming uncomfortable for Nick, when his captain finally spoke without looking up.

"Where's Madison?"

"Working the case," Nick lied. Sonny had phoned and said he would be late because he had some personal errands. "Should be in soon. What's up, Pete?"

Still looking at the file, Mendoza answered, "The shit's about to hit the fan. The bishop is back, and, boy, is he pissed! He's been all over Murphy's ass." The captain's eyes widened as he looked directly at his subordinate and continued, "And that's gotta filter down to me. The chief already called once; wants to know why you searched the two priests' homes. The bishop is screaming church and state. Fortunately, the chief is backing us, at least for now. He told O'Malley that it was their personal residences, and it didn't come under that category. Actually, I'm not so sure about Beyers' place, since it belongs to the church. But your warrants were good, so I think we're okay for now."

The captain stared directly into his detective's eyes. "Please tell me you have something. *Anything!* The chief is running interference for us, but I'm afraid he's gonna shut us down if we"—he pointed directly at Nick—"*you*, don't come up with something we can use. So tell me something I wanna hear!"

"Well, the searches found nothing—"

"Tell me something I don't know," Mendoza interrupted.

"Pete, there's diocesan involvement of some sort here. I don't know if it goes all the way to the top or not. It might."

Mendoza listened intently to every word as his detective explained his theory about the names in the book.

"Here's what I think. Mignanelli and some of the others were involved in a scam of some sort. I think he, or they, used church funds to buy expensive merchandise from various stores in the valley. I think he, or they, would return it and pocket the money. There was over a hundred fifty grand in that safe, and it didn't come from baptisms and weddings. The coded names in that book are all involved in some way. I think I know who most of them are, but I can't figure out Lionheart and Viking. The Napoleon page is blank. I think it's the bishop, but I can't prove it."

"Might not be the bishop," came a voice from behind him. Startled, Nick turned as Sonny came in and sat down in the chair next to him.

"Hi, Pete." Sonny nodded to his boss. "I did some digging and found something interesting."

"Go on," Mendoza said.

"Nick, you remember our meeting with Bradley? He said the code for Mignanelli was from his hometown, right? The high school mascot bit?" Nick nodded.

"Okay, so on a hunch, I ran backgrounds on everybody on your list. Beyers is also from a town in Pennsylvania called Hopewell. Their mascot is a Viking. So, figuring that he's a Viking and looking where these guys are from, I found something interesting. You remember the janitor, Jamison?" Sonny didn't wait for an answer. "He has a sealed juvy record from—hold onto your seat—*Napoleon, Ohio!*"

Mendoza leaned forward as both policemen listened intently to Sonny. "So I dug some more—and though you're right about Tuck being Father Frank—if my theory is right, it may not be because he's fat. He's from, you ready? *Tuckerville, Colorado!* You may be right about the Puzzleman. We need to figure out who Lionheart is."

Pete looked at Sonny, and then to Nick. "Check out cities with the name 'lion' in them, maybe L-Y-O-N. Lionville, Lionburg. Could be a school mascot. Try Detroit. Hell, maybe there are Lions' fan in the mix."

Both detectives looked at each other and back at their captain, who motioned in a dismissing manner, and said, "Go! Go!"

As they left their captain's office and walked across the squad room, Sonny said with a sheepish grin, "There's more."

"Talk to me," Nick responded.

"BMK has a safe deposit box at Chase."

Nick looked at his partner. "Personal errands, huh?"

Sonny just shrugged.

CHAPTER 43

Armed with a search warrant, the two detectives entered the Chase Bank branch at the corner of Peoria Avenue and Sixty-Seventh. After presenting the warrant to the branch manager, they were escorted into the vault.

George Maravich, a tall man, well over six and a half feet in stature, had been running this branch for close to a year. He inserted two keys, turned them, and stepped back as Nick slipped on a pair of gloves, pulled the box from the wall, and lifted the lid. *Empty!*

Completely empty! Sonny let out a breath and shook his head when his partner showed him the empty box. Greer shoved the box back into its place, and the manager relocked the door and removed the keys.

Looking at his partner, Sonny asked, "Think we should have it dusted?"

"Maybe, but let's check something first."

Looking at Maravich, the lieutenant said, "I need to see the log for this box."

Nodding his head in assent, Maravich said, "Have a seat in my office. I'll get it for you."

About two minutes passed, and he returned with a small envelope and handed it to Nick, who removed the log, studied it, and asked for a copy. The manager took the log and left his office.

"Anything interesting?" Sonny questioned.

"Looks like Mignanelli was the last one here. The day before he was killed," Nick answered, as Maravich returned with the requested copy and handed it to the detective.

"Thank you," the lieutenant said as they rose to leave.

As the two detectives were leaving the manager's office, Nick stopped and asked, "You wouldn't know if anyone else has tried to get this box, would you? Maybe someone not on the list?"

"I don't think so, but if you hold on, I'll see if anyone might know."

As Maravich left the room, Sonny questioned Nick, "What you thinkin'?"

"I don't know. A shot in the dark. Probably nothing."

Maravich returned with a female employee. It had been she who had greeted the two cops as they entered the bank and had taken them to the manager.

"Beth, tell the officers what you told me." The young lady was African American, about five-two, and seemed nervous.

Nick said, "Don't worry. You're not in any kind of trouble. We just want to know if anyone tried access this box recently."

"A couple of weeks ago. It was a Monday," she said timidly. "A man was waiting when we opened. He had a key but his ID didn't match. I went to get a manager, and when I returned he was gone. A weird-looking guy."

"Can you describe him for me?"

"About six feet tall, white, long hair, looked like it needed washing. Kind of a creepy-looking man. He wore a dirty red hat."

"Would you recognize him if you saw him again?"

She nodded. "I think so. If he had that hat on."

"Thank you, Beth. You've been a big help."

The two policemen left the bank and got into their car. As Sonny started the engine, he asked, "Does that sound like anyone you know?"

"You betcha! We need to get a warrant for a certain janitor's residence and find out what he's doing with his dead pastor's key!"

"By the way, who are the signers on the account?" Madison asked.

"Mignanelli, Beyers, Kubic . . . and Victor Pinnetta."

"You gotta be shitting me!" Sonny exclaimed.

CHAPTER 44

Victor Pinnetta was a well-known and powerful attorney in Scottsdale. He had recently made an unsuccessful and highly contested run for State Senate. Losing by just one percentage point, he caused a recount. Though he was thought by some to be involved with organized crime, there was never anything to prove it. His record was clean; not even a traffic ticket. Was he involved in this scheme? If so, how? If so, why? The only thing connecting him at all was his being a signer on the safe deposit box. After they returned to the precinct, Nick decided he would pay Pinnetta a visit.

The law offices of Pinnetta & Associates was on the top floor of a plush building in Scottsdale. The detective was impressed as he entered into the large, nicely furnished lobby. A large glass desk sat in front of a wall on which was painted: Pinnetta & Associates. An attractive young lady greeted him from behind the desk.

"Can I help you, sir?"

Pointing to the badge hanging from his belt, Nick said, "I'd like to see Mr. Pinnetta, please."

"May I tell him your name and what it's regarding?" Her voice was pleasant and professional.

"Lieutenant Greer, PPD. It's a personal matter."

She pressed a button on her phone. "A Lieutenant Greer is here to see you." She listened for a moment and nodded. Standing up, she looked at him and said, "Please follow me."

She escorted him into a massive office that boasted of the financial success of its occupant. She looked to her boss and back to Nick. "Mr. Pinnetta, Lieutenant Greer."

"Thank you, Kelly," he responded. She left the room.

"Please have a seat, Lieutenant." His demeanor was gracious and welcoming as he looked at his guest and pointed to one of the plush leather chairs facing his large desk.

Victor Pinnetta was in his sixties with wavy gray hair. He wore a blue three-piece suit that the detective figured cost over a thousand dollars.

"I've been expecting you."

The statement caught the detective off guard. "Expecting me?"

"Yes. I understand you are looking into the death of my nephew."

The shock must have been apparent as the lawyer lightly nodded and smiled politely. "David Mignanelli is my nephew."

"Your nephew?" Nick repeated.

"Yes, Lieutenant. He was my sister's son."

"Why didn't you let someone at the department know?" the detective questioned.

"I don't know why it would be relevant. You people will do your job. There's nothing I can add. We weren't very close. I have nieces and nephews all over the country."

"How many are murdered?"

Pinnetta's eyes widened. "He killed himself! Why won't you let it be?" The defiance in his tone bordered arrogance.

The detective continued, "What is your relationship to BMK Enterprises?"

Pinnetta shook his head. "I don't know what you're talking about. Who is that?"

"You don't know who BMK Enterprises is?"

"I said, I didn't!"

"Then please explain to me why are you a signer on the BMK safe deposit account."

It was easy to see by the surprised look on his face that the lawyer had been caught off guard.

He breathed in, exhaled, and regained his composure. "Oh, is that the name of it? David asked me to sign it."

"Why?" Nick asked.

"I don't know. He just wanted me on it."

"Do you know what's in it?"

"Nope. No clue."

The detective looked straight at the man behind the desk. "Do you really expect me to believe that you, an attorney, would be a signer on a safe deposit box and not question its contents? Come on, Counselor."

"He said pictures and some memorabilia that was personal to him were in it. Nothing valuable. He shared it with another priest. He just wanted me on it because I'm family, I guess. I can't get into it. I don't even have a key. What's the big deal? I tried to call his friend, but he hasn't returned my call. I thought I'd send his stuff that was in it back home."

"Father Blake Beyers? Is that his friend?"

"Yes, I believe so."

"Who is BMK and what about the other signer? Father Michael Kubic?"

The attorney stood up and looked directly at his interrogator. The detective knew he had struck a nerve. "Why are you asking me all these questions?" His voice was raised and stern as he continued, "Don't you know who I am? I've had enough. Please leave." He pushed a button on his phone and said, "Kelly, please show the lieutenant out."

"I know my way." Nick said as he rose and left.

CHAPTER 45

"Take a look at this," Sonny Madison said as his partner walked through the door.

Nick reached for his messages. There was only one: See Sonny. Holding it up, he said, "I suppose I can throw this away. Can I sit down first?"

Sonny raised his left hand and motioned for his partner to come to him as he pointed to his computer screen. "Look. Check this out. Guess who's related to the deceased."

"Besides Victor Pinnetta?"

"How did you know?" Sonny asked.

"Just came from there. He told me. Nephew."

"Okay, smart-ass, I'll bet you didn't know that Reverend Michael Kubic and our deceased priest are cousins."

Nick rushed over to Sonny and looked at the computer screen. On it was Reverend David Mignanelli's obituary. Sonny explained, "Look, it says his mother was the late Annmarie Pinnetta Mignanelli. Okay, I guess you know that, but look here." He pointed to the screen. "Check out the grandmother." Sonny kept pointing as Nick looked at the screen: Mary Louise Kubic.

"So I did some more digging," Sonny continued. "It looks like our deceased priest was a late entry into the seminary. Most men go in right out of high school, but not our guy. Beyers was already out when Mignanelli went in. Both of them went to Seton Hall. Now, get this. There is no record of Kubic going to any seminary, at least not here. Not in this country."

Nick thought for a moment, turned, went to his desk, and sat down. With both elbows on the desk and his head in his hands, he sat there, thinking. Retrieving the card he had picked up on his way out of Pinnetta's office, he looked at the number on it and dialed.

"Pinnetta & Associates, Kelly speaking. How may I help you?"

"This is Lieutenant Greer. I was there a little while ago. May I speak to Mr. Pinnetta?"

"Yes, I remember. Please hold for a moment."

Nick waited. "Mr. Pinnetta is busy now. Would you like to leave a message?"

"Ask him why half the priests in this diocese are his relatives?" The phone went silent as she put him on hold.

"I'm sorry. Mr. Pinnetta has left for the day." This time her voice was shaky. "I'm sorry, but you'll have to call back at another time." The dial tone buzzed in his ear as the phone went dead. Nick looked at his watch; it was 12:20.

"Sonny, you wanna go and grab a bite?"

Nodding, he shut down his computer and said, "Sure. I'm starved."

Quite a family affair, Nick thought as they rode the elevator down to the main floor.

The lieutenant said to his partner, "Did you check to see if any of them are related to the bishop?" This was more tongue-in-cheek than a question.

Sonny answered, "Yes. And no."

CHAPTER 46

They had just returned from lunch, and Nick was contemplating his next move. He thought he would call Sue Kim first and reached for his cell phone but was interrupted.

"Gentlemen," came a familiar sound.

Sonny looked up. "Ahh. His Master's voice."

Captain Mendoza raised both of his hands and motioned for them to follow. They all sat down and the captain said, "Greer, do you know the governor?"

"Not personally," he answered.

"I just wondered because she's about the only one you haven't pissed off yet."

"The day's still young," Sonny commented.

Mendoza continued, "Victor Pinnetta? Big time attorney? Wants to be governor?"

Nick began to speak, but his captain held up his hand to symbolize silence.

"He's a sleazeball," Sonny snuck in sheepishly.

Mendoza shook his head and said, "Sleazeball or not, he called the chief. The chief told me to handle it. I called Pinnetta."

Nick interrupted, "He's supposed to be gone for the day. The sleazeball!"

Mendoza grinned. "Madison's rubbing off on you. Anyway, he's bitching about you harassing him. What did you do?"

Nick explained his visit and subsequent phone call. Sonny outlined what he had found.

"He threatened a harassment suit. I told him you were my best detective and that you were within the law. He yelled some nasty threatening stuff. I hung up the phone."

The captain looked at Nick and then at Sonny. "You know we've been trying to get something on this guy for years. You got anything?"

"Working on it," Nick responded. "I think he's hiding something."

Mendoza said with a hint of hope in his tone, "Be my heroes."

Nick left Mendoza's office, picked up his keys from his desk, jumped into his car, and raced to Scottsdale.

* * *

Holding up his badge, he marched into Pinnetta's outer office. Kelly reached for the phone, but stopped. "He's not here. He's gone for the day."

Nick turned toward Pinnetta's private office.

"You can't go in there!" She stood up.

Nick countered, "What difference does it make if he's not there?"

The detective went straight to the attorney's office. He threw open the doors and stopped dead in his tracks. There, sitting in a chair in front of the desk was a face he remembered from his first visit to the crime scene. The Reverend Michael Kubic.

Pinnetta sprung up from his seat. "You got a warrant?"

The detective was still recovering from the shock of seeing the priest sitting there.

"Didn't think so," Pinnetta yelled. "Get the fuck out! Now!" He picked up the phone. "Get me security."

He knew that since he had no warrant he must follow the order to leave. As he turned, he heard Pinnetta yell, "If you ever come back here, you better have a goddamn warrant!"

Nick stormed into the squad room and went straight into Mendoza's office. After telling his captain what had happened, he said, "I'm getting warrants for them all. Every fucking one of 'em. I'll get warrants for his dead grandparents if I have to."

"Don't bother." Mendoza reached to the left side of his desk and picked up the phone. "I'll get 'em for ya."

CHAPTER 47

As the morning sun peeked its rays between the slats of the mini-blind that covered the bedroom window, Sue Kim turned and wrapped her arm around him. Stirring slightly, Nick smiled and took her hand in his. The warmth of her body against his felt so good. His feelings for her were conflicted by the guilt he felt, but that guilt was waning as each day passed.

She got up and left the room. Returning a few minutes later, fully dressed, she kissed him and said, "Be back in a little while."

"Where are you going? Stay here. It's early. It's Saturday. We haven't even had coffee yet."

"That's the problem. You're out of coffee. I'm going to Starbucks for some. Be right back."

"I'll go if you want," he offered with sleepiness in his voice. "Or we can wait and get it later. Maybe I'll take you out for breakfast."

"I need my coffee now. I'll go get it and be right back, but I'll take you up on that breakfast."

Reaching over to the nightstand next to him, he groped for his car keys and handed them to her. "Here, take my car."

"Okay, but that's not gonna get you out of breakfast." She kissed him again and left the room.

* * *

Rolling over, Nick decided to sleep for a few more minutes. He had barely dozed off when his ears were pierced by a loud explosion, and the whole building shook violently around him.

He jumped out of the bed and into his trousers all in one motion and ran to see what had happened. Throwing open the townhouse door, Nick looked out and froze at what he saw. A car was engulfed in flames. His car!

"No!" he yelled as he saw his vehicle being consumed by fire. As he ran across the lawn and out into the parking lot, his eyes saw the motionless figure lying on the hard, debris-covered asphalt. He ran as fast as he could and knelt beside her. As he cradled her in his arms, blood gushed over her forehead onto her beautiful face. Her lips barely moved as she tried to speak.

His ears caught the distant sound of sirens. "Don't try to talk, baby. Help is on the way," he said gently.

In a weak whisper she forced out the words, "I love you," then closed her eyes. Her body went limp in his arms.

"No! No! Come back. Hold on. Help is coming. Don't go," he pleaded as he held her lifeless body in his arms. The sirens blaring in the distance were becoming louder as they neared. Still cradling her bleeding head in his arms, he looked up to the sky and yelled at the top of his voice, "Hurry!"

The front of his once-white tee shirt was now crimson, and each tiny second seemed like eons as he held her.

* * *

Finally, two vehicles sped into the parking lot. The first was a red ambulance with the familiar white lettering of Southwest Ambulance. It was followed by a Phoenix fire truck. A pair of EMTs, each one carrying emergency equipment, ran from the ambulance and rushed to the victim.

Though it was hard for him to let go of her, he knew he had to back away and let these professionals do their jobs. Helplessly, he watched as they worked in perfect precision. Positioning paddles on both sides of her chest, the male paramedic yelled, "Clear!" Her body convulsed as electricity invaded her tiny frame. They waited. Nothing happened. Again Nick heard: "Clear!" Once more her body shook violently.

The female EMT listened intently through the stethoscope she held against her patient's inner elbow, looked up to her partner, and shook her head. He turned the power up one more time and again yelled, "Clear!" Electricity was once again forced into her.

Nick's eyes welled up with tears when he saw the male EMT shake his head. Then he heard the female say, "Wait . . . I think I have a pulse . . . Yes . . . Weak, but a pulse. Get the gurney," she ordered.

Helping raise her onto the gurney, Nick watched them roll it into the ambulance. She was barely breathing, but the fact that she was breathing at all gave him hope.

The medic wiped the blood from her patient's face, placed a clear plastic mask over her nose and mouth, then turned the valve on the small green tank supplying life-sustaining oxygen.

Holding her hand in his, he didn't notice the firemen who were dousing his charred car as the ambulance pulled away from the complex. Red and blue lights flashed, and the siren screamed out its warning as it sped through the Phoenix streets. The female paramedic listened through the stethoscope that she now held against her patient's chest while her partner communicated with the hospital trauma center.

"Female approximately twenty-eight. Explosion. Cranial laceration. Breathing shallow. BP sixty over twenty. Eyes unresponsive. Skin molten. ETA eight minutes."

Seeing the EMT lay the phone down, he asked, "Is she going to be all right? Tell me the truth. I can take it. I'm a cop."

"I honestly don't know, sir. She's in shock. We need to get her to the ER. If we make it there in time, there's a good chance. Gotta get through traffic. Thank God, today is Saturday."

She looked back at her patient and said, "Come on, baby, hang on. Don't give up on me now. We're almost there."

As the ambulance turned into the Phoenix Baptist Hospital, he heard the female paramedic say to her partner, "Better hurry, Tom. It looks like she's gonna code again." She bent down and said gently into her patient's ear, "You gotta hold on, honey. Keep on fighting. We're almost there. You made it this far. You can do this."

Nick felt so helpless sitting there, watching. Finally he couldn't take it anymore and asked, "Can I talk to her?"

The paramedic looked up and nodded in assent. He bent down and whispered in her ear, "I love you, too."

Just then the ambulance came to a halt, and he moved back into the corner as the double rear doors of the vehicle flew open and two men pulled the gurney from its place. Nick followed closely behind as the two medics and the EMTs wheeled Sue Kim through the emergency room doors and down the hallway. As a pair of double doors automatically opened, one of the EMTs looked at him, pointed to a door, and said. "Sir, you'll have to wait in there."

"But—"

Sue Kim disappeared into the room as the doors closed behind her.

Nick just stood there. A feeling of helplessness penetrated his entire being.

* * *

The wait seemed like eons. It had been four long hours since Nick Greer watched the blood-soaked gurney disappear into the emergency room. Several times he had asked about her condition, only to be told that she was in the operating room and he would be informed as soon as they knew anything. Even the possession of a Phoenix Police Department badge didn't help him.

Sonny Madison, Pete Mendoza, and Jack Konesky had joined him at the hospital. They all waited as patiently as they could for the results.

Finally, Nick saw the door open, and a doctor came through it. He jumped up. "How is she? Is she going to be okay?"

The woman of Middle Eastern descent and dressed in green surgical garb appeared to be in her early thirties. Straggling strands of her black hair were sticking out from where they had once been tucked under her green cap.

"She had quite a shock to her system," the doctor replied in perfect English. "But she should have a full recovery. She has a concussion, but the MRI shows no signs of any brain damage. There is no bleeding or swelling, and there are no cranial fractures."

Nick couldn't hold back a sigh of relief.

The doctor continued, "Three ribs are broken and one of them punctured her lung. She'll be in a lot of pain for a while. There are no lacerations on her chest. It appears that she was struck in the chest by a piece of tire."

"But, her face. It was covered with blood," Nick interjected.

Holding both hands in front of her with the palms out, she responded, "The scalp laceration has been closed and sutured. There'll be some scarring, but fortunately it is above the hairline so it should be unnoticeable. The back was also sutured and should heal. Sometimes in these cases, the blood makes it look worse than is it."

"When can I see her?"

"She's in recovery now, then she'll go to ICU. You should wait until tomorrow. Go home and get some rest."

"Thank you, Doctor," Nick said as he shook her hand, "but I think I'll stick around for a while."

Pete, Sonny, and Jack had been standing beside him and heard everything. "I spoke with the chief," the captain said. "You have his complete cooperation and that of the whole department. The mayor is on board, and the bishop doesn't know what to make of it. He's backed off completely."

"Good! I'm staying here," Nick responded. "Her parents are in California. She has no one else. I need to be here for her when she wakes up."

Nick looked at his partner. "Sonny, you know what to do."

Sonny nodded.

Nick sat down and waited.

CHAPTER 48

He knew what his partner and friend meant when he said, "Sonny, you know what to do," so he left the hospital. But on his way back to the precinct, Sonny Madison decided to make a detour and headed for St. Joseph's Hospital. He dodged the yellow tent signs warning of a wet floor. A worker listening to his iPod through earphones was busy mopping and oblivious to his surroundings.

As he opened the door to Father Blake Beyers' room, he saw what looked like a nurse reaching up to the IV tube that led to the patient's arm. Startled by his entry, the medic dropped a syringe on the floor.

"Sorry, I didn't mean to scare you," Sonny stated.

A man in hospital clothing looked at Sonny and said, "I'll get another one." He kept his head down and seemed in a hurry to exit.

Sonny thought it odd that he didn't pick up the syringe from the floor, then saw that he wasn't wearing a name tag. "What's your name?"

Like a flash, the man shoved the cop against the wall and ran out the door. Sonny quickly recovered and began to chase the subject down the hall. He was gaining on him when the man hit the unsuspecting worker still mopping the floor, and knocked him to the ground. Then he kicked the water bucket, knocking it over. Its soapy contents swiftly spread across the tiled floor.

The detective tried to stop, but his feet slid out from under him and he hit the floor.

* * *

When he came to, a light was shining from one eye to the other. Sonny tried to sit up but felt a hand on his chest and heard a voice say, "Please lie still, sir."

He shook his head and squinted a few times as his vision began to clear, and then he forced himself up from the floor and stood for a few seconds while his equilibrium returned.

"Sir, please. You hit your head. I need to check you out." It was the same voice.

"I got a hard head. Let me go." He looked down the hallway. No sign of his quarry. He turned and headed back to Beyers' room.

He woke the sleeping patient and shoved his badge in his face. "I'm Sergeant Madison. You know my partner, Lieutenant Greer. I just saved your life. Now you're gonna talk."

A box containing surgical gloves was hanging on the wall. He pulled out one glove, bent down, and retrieved the syringe from the floor. Holding it up to the priest, he said, "Do you believe in guardian angels?" Not giving him a chance to utter a response, Sonny continued, "I'm yours! Now you're gonna tell me who's trying to kill you and why. And I got one helluva headache so you better make me believe you!"

CHAPTER 49

Sonny Madison spent the rest of the afternoon at home popping Tylenol and working at his computer, reviewing all of Nick's notes along with his own. He checked and cross-checked, rerunning backgrounds. The thoroughly frightened priest had revealed the whole story to Sonny.

The theory about Father David buying and returning merchandise was only the tip of this iceberg. They were also stealing credit card information from some of the wealthier parishioners, and it wasn't limited to St. Michael's.

It was a brilliant scheme. Mignanelli and Beyers were running the scam alone until Kubic figured it out. Then somehow the word leaked to the others, and the only way to keep from getting defrocked was to cut them in. It's sometimes amazing how honest people can be turned to the dark side, even priests, Sonny thought. These priests were savvy enough to know that even if they got caught, the church/state thing would make criminal prosecution hard without the bishop's support, and if anyone ever protected their lair, Bishop James Francis O'Malley did.

Beyers said there was someone else involved, someone with lots of power who may be calling the shots. He said David knew who it was but never told him. He didn't think it was the bishop; however, he thought the bishop knew that something was going on.

Beyers said he knew nothing about a safe, but knew that his friend kept the records. They took the money and bought gold bullion. They kept it in a safe deposit box at Chase Bank. As far as he knew, it was all still there. They divided it up periodically, and they were about to do so again. When asked who the signers were, the priest said, "David, me, and Mike." He didn't know of any others, nor why there would be. The detective asked him if he knew Victor Pinnetta. The priest denied knowing him.

That fateful Saturday, Father Blake Beyers had found himself on the west side of town and had decided to visit his friend. It had been around four o'clock. He had a key and knew the alarm code, and he went in when no one answered the doorbell. When he found the body, he was spooked. There had been rumblings within the group that the phantom power was unhappy with a couple of them. He knew not who or why, but when he found his friend, he thought he might be next. He'd gone home, packed a bag, and went to the only place he could think of—the cabin in Prescott. He had called Mike Kubic and reported what he had seen.

That explains, Sonny thought, how the two priests showed up at the crime scene as quickly as they did. Their motives may not have been as innocent as they were meant to appear.

Sonny knew he now had more than enough to support the warrants, but he also knew the bishop would fight it. He decided to call his captain at home.

Victor Pinnetta was somehow involved, but there was no discernible connection to any of those in the dead priest's notebook.

While reviewing Jamison's file, Sonny discovered that he was ex-military. Further digging showed he had received a medical discharge from the army. His training was in ordnance!

More research found that Victor Pinnetta came from a town in Pennsylvania. Lyonsville! It was a stretch, but could he be Lionheart? If so, how to prove it.

CHAPTER 50

The phone rang and Julie picked it up. "Sure," she said, then handed Mike the phone. "Your cop friend again. Doesn't he know it's Sunday?"

"Hello, Nick. What can I do for you?"

"This is Sergeant Madison. Lieutenant Greer is tied up. He asked me to call you. It appears we could use your help."

"Sure, whatcha need?"

The detective explained that he was going to need to pick up St. Michael's janitor for questioning. This would happen at the church, and he needed someone to familiarize him with the entrance and exits of the premises just in case he bolted. "I hope he's there."

Mike's immediate concern was that school would be in session, and there would be kids around. "Sergeant, did you know there's a grade school there? The place will be crawling with kids. I'm not comfortable with this at all. Can I talk to Lieutenant Greer?"

"Lieutenant Greer has had an emergency, uuhh, a family emergency. I'll be handling this for now. I forgot about the school, but I have an idea. Do you know this Jamison guy? Do you know what kind of car he drives?"

Mike thought for a moment. "I only met him a couple of times, but I think he drives a white pickup. The bed has one of those smooth covers over it. I don't know what they're called.

"But how will that help?" he added. "It'll still be at the school. Can't you pick him up where he lives?"

"We tried that. He moved. No forwarding address. His PO doesn't know where he's at either," Sonny answered. "Look, Mr. Bradley, I think he's about to run. He may already be in the wind. This may be our only chance. We're gonna take him if he's there with or without your help, but I have an idea."

"I'm listening," Bradley stated. The sergeant explained his plan.

It was 9:15 when they arrived at St. Michael's. Mike had explained to Sonny that the hall doubled as a cafeteria when school was in session and that the church building would block the view of the north parking lot. So they met there; two black and whites, Sonny's Malibu and Mike Bradley.

Looking to the east parking lot, they saw Jamison's pickup parked in one of the diagonal spots. Luck was on their side. The spot in front of the pickup was empty, and Mike drove his SUV into it and killed the engine. Sonny parked his car several spaces away, just far enough not to be easily seen. Reaching under the dashboard, Mike pulled the hood lever, got out of the car, and raised its hood. Retrieving a set of jumper cables from the rear of his SUV, he headed for the hall.

The cafeteria workers were busily going about their morning duties as Mike entered the large room. The custodian was leaning against the wall by the kitchen door talking to one of the workers.

Pointing to the east lot, Mike called out loudly, "Anybody got a white Chevy pickup parked over there?"

Jamison looked up. "Yeah. I do."

Walking over to the custodian, Mike held up the jumper cables and said, "My car won't start, and I'm right in front of your pickup. I think it's the battery. I got these things." He held them up to be seen. "I need a jump. Can you help me?"

Jamison shook his head like he was disgusted.

Mike said, "There's twenty bucks in it if you help me."

"Sure." Jamison answered.

Following Sonny's instructions, Mike kept the custodian's attention focused on him as they walked to their vehicles. Lifting the gnarled cables out in front of him, he said, "I really appreciate your help. I don't know much about this stuff. I'll bet you know all about fixing cars. I don't know which side of the battery is which."

"I thought every guy knew how to jump a battery." The disdain in his voice was obvious.

"I work in an office," Mike answered.

Jamison shook his head in disbelief as he went to the front of his pickup, reached into the grill and tripped the hood latch. The hood raised a couple of inches and he lifted it. Grabbing the tangled cables out of Mike's hands, he stretched them out and reached under the hood to attach them to the terminals.

Sonny Madison appeared out of nowhere, grabbed him, and threw him to the ground just as the two black and whites arrived on the scene. As Jamison lay face down on the asphalt, four uniformed officers rushed to them. Sonny pulled his subject's arms behind his back and cuffed him. "You're under arrest for the murder of David Mignanelli!

You have the right to keep your mouth shut. Anything you say can and will be used to hang your sorry ass. You have the right to a lawyer. Better get a good one, you priest-killing bastard."

Expecting to see a bunch of people watching, Mike looked around. No one. The parking lot was empty. Two of the uniforms picked the subject up off the ground, and, as per Sonny's instructions, put him in the back of one of the cruisers. Sonny motioned to one of them. "Be sure to read him his rights again. I don't always get it right."

CHAPTER 51

They had been in the interview room for three hours. Sonny had interviewed his share of uncooperative witnesses before, but this guy was something else. Up until now he was silent except to ask for a glass of water and utter something about Sonny being a stupid pig.

Just then the door sprang open. "Mr. Jamison. Do not speak. I'm your attorney." He looked at Sonny. "With what are you charging my client?"

The detective answered, "Uhh, let's see, we can start with parole violation and add destruction of property. Then, how about attempted assault on a police officer? Now let me think." He scratched his head like he was thinking. "Attempted murder, yeah, that's a good one. And, oh yeah, how about, oh, what's it called? You know, the one that sends you to that death row place. I think that's called"—he tapped his forehead with his fingertips several times, and looked up at the attorney—"Ooh yeah. I remember! Murder one! And I'm thinking about throwing in being an asshole, just for good measure." He stared at Jamison with fire in his eyes as he bent down with his face so close to the suspect that their noses almost touched. "But what do I know? I'm just a stupid pig!"

The door flew open again and Sonny was shocked to see Nick Greer walk in. "I'll take it from here. Everybody out!" He looked at the lawyer and said, "Out!"

"Oh, no, you don't," the man objected. "I'm his counsel. I'm not going anywhere."

Nick nodded to Sonny who stood up, took the lawyer by the arm, opened the door and pushed him through it.

Sonny turned to come back in. Nick looked at him and said, "You too, Sonny."

"I'm stay—" He never got to finish his sentence. There was a look on his partner's face he had never seen before. He didn't think he liked it.

"Go!" Reluctantly, Sonny left the room.

Nick saw the lone microphone in the center of the table, picked it up, ripped it from its cord, and threw it against the wall. Bending over the table, he looked the suspect in the eyes and said, "There is a very sweet and innocent young lady lying in a hospital bed. She almost died because of you. Did you know she works in one of our labs? Did you know the whole department adores her? Your life is over. I'm going to bring your attorney in here, and you're gonna sing like a flock of robins on a spring morning. If you don't, I'm going to release you, and your picture will be in front of every police officer in town. They'll all know that it was you who blew up the car! So here are your choices. Tell me what I want to hear, and I'll talk to the ADA, and maybe, just maybe, she'll take the death sentence off the table. If I release you, we won't need it, and it'll save the county some money."

Fear along with a look of puzzlement appeared on Jamison's face. "What car? I didn't blow up no car! I killed the priest, but I didn't blow up no car. I didn't hurt no girl."

Nick motioned toward the two-way mirror, and the door opened. Sonny came in first, followed by the attorney, Pete Mendoza, and ADA Shelly Kisler.

Nick pointed to Jamison, then looked at Shelly and said, "Do your thing." He left the room and Sonny followed.

CHAPTER 52

Nick returned to Phoenix Baptist Hospital. She had been moved to a regular room. He was oblivious to the two people who were sitting against the wall facing her bed as he came in and kissed her on the cheek. "How you feeling, kid?"

"Like I've been hit by a bomb," she answered.

"You were." Nick's answer was serious.

"Oh yeah." Nodding to the people in the chairs, she said, "These are my parents."

Nick's face turned red with embarrassment as he turned and saw a man and a woman, both of Asian descent. They nodded as Nick reached out his hand and was about to speak.

"This is my . . . friend. His name is Nick. He's a policeman," she said before he had a chance to speak.

Her father stood up and shook his hand. Nick said, "Pleased to meet you, Mr. Kim."

The man looked insulted as he stated, "Lee. Meesta Lee."

Looking back to the gentleman, he said, "Please accept my apologies, Mr. Lee."

Lee answered, "It's okay fine. Not to worry."

His wife uttered something in what Nick thought was Japanese. Sue Kim answered her in English, "It's okay. I'm not one of his either."

Nick looked at Sue, who shrugged and answered, "It's a cultural thing."

"Cultural?" Nick asked.

She nodded.

Nick's mind flashed back to a conversation he once had with her. She had said that her parents would be furious with her if they knew she was dating a non-Asian. They were a proud and strict family. He wondered what they thought when they saw this tall, white, round-eyed man come in and kiss their daughter.

"When are they going to release you?" Nick questioned.

"The doctor said in a day or so."

"Good. You can come to my place. I'll take care of you. I have some time coming—"

She reached up and put her fingers over his lips. He looked at her with questioning eyes.

"Nick, I need to tell you something."

He could tell he wasn't going to like what he was about to hear.

Tightly squeezing his hand, she said, "I'm going back to California for a while."

"What?" He pulled his hand from hers. "Why?" He looked at her parents. "Whose idea is this?" Looking back to her, he said, "I can take care of you. It's no problem. I want to."

She looked at him with a tender sadness in her eyes. "You know I care about you, but my father thinks it is best that I go back home for a while. Please understand."

With an ache in his heart, he asked, "What's a while?"

She shrugged.

CHAPTER 53

It was Tuesday morning, and Nick was suffering from a tremendous hangover. Though he had tried, he was unable to convince Sue Kim to stay in Phoenix. After receiving the news that she was leaving, he'd left the hospital, drove to the neighborhood where he grew up, and sat in the park, reflecting back on his days there as a child. After a while he looked at his watch. He had been there for hours. He thought it was odd that the whole time he was there his cell phone never once rang, so he pulled it from his belt and saw that he had forgotten to turn it on after he left the hospital. He pushed the power button, and the instrument came to life. There were three messages waiting for him. The first was from Sonny: Where you at? Got something to tell you. The next one was from Captain Mendoza: Call me. The third was a text from Sue Kim:

> Nick,
> Please don't be mad. I care about you, but it's best that I go.
> If you truly care for me, please don't come here. It would only make things worse.
> Just know that I will always cherish our time together.
> Love, Sue

Tears came to his eyes as he read the text. Getting into his car and resisting the deep temptation to return to the hospital, he headed for home. He would honor her wishes. He saw Charley's Place, a local bar, and decided to stop and have a drink. I haven't gotten drunk in years, he thought.

The rest of the night was a blur.

* * *

Sonny Madison came over to Nick and said loudly, "Good morning, Lieutenant Greer!"

Nick put his right hand to his head and said, "Please, Sonny. Not now."

Seeing the pain in his friend's bloodshot eyes, he said, "Be back in a jif."

Nick put his head in his hands and wondered how he got home. The car he had been issued from the motor pool had been parked in its normal place at the townhouse, but he had no idea how it got there. He doubted that he would drive drunk, but he had been pretty well plastered. He looked up and saw Sonny standing in front of him with a fizzling glass of water in one hand and two Tylenols in the other.

Nick downed them. "Thanks," he said as he looked up at his friend. "I don't even know how I got home last night."

Madison chuckled. "Sonny's friendly taxi service. You're a lousy tipper." Seeing the puzzled look on Nick's face, Sonny said, "Charley called me. He said you were shit-faced and trying to find your keys. Charley had taken them off the bar and called me. I took you home and threw you in bed. You puked on my shoes!"

They didn't notice Shelley Kisler as she passed them and went into Captain Mendoza's office. She dropped an envelope on his desk, causing him to look up. "Confession?" he asked.

"Thought you'd want a copy," she said as she turned to leave. She stopped and turned to the captain and said, "Legal, but a bit unorthodox, don't you think?"

Knowing that she was referring to the manner in which his detective obtained the confession, he just looked up and shrugged. "He owes us for a microphone."

Opening the envelope, he removed its contents and read the summary:

About a month ago, Jamison had overheard a discussion between two of the workers about the comings and goings at their pastor's residence. He began watching what was going on there, and the day before the murder, confronted Mignanelli, who became irate and fired him on the spot.

Jamison threatened to turn him in, citing pictures and times and dates that he had recorded. He demanded a piece of the action. Mignanelli reluctantly agreed. Jamison demanded cash on the spot, but Mignanelli told him that the cash was kept in a safe deposit box, and he would go to the bank the next day and get it.

The next day Jamison followed Mignanelli. He watched him go into Chase Bank and come out with a paper bag in his hand. That afternoon he went to Mignanelli and demanded his money. The priest was working at his computer and told him it was still at the bank, and he wasn't giving him a dime until he saw the proof that he claimed to have.

Jamison left and on his way out unlocked the sliding door. He went to his truck and retrieved a unregistered .38 cal Smith and Wesson that he had hidden under the seat. He returned through the back door. Music was playing, and Mignanelli never heard him as he approached from behind.

Being left-handed, he held the gun to the left side of the victim's head and demanded his money. Mignanelli elbowed Jamison in the groin and the gun went off.

Jamison saw the victim's keys sitting on the edge of the desk, and, remembering the safe deposit box, grabbed them.

He then took the gun, wiped it off, and put it in the victim's hand. He cupped his hand around the victim's, picked it up, and fired into the open closet, knowing this would put GSR on the victim's hand. He used a pocketknife to dig the bullet out of the closet wall and closed the door.

He then lifted the victim's lifeless head with one hand, and, knowing his fingerprints were on file, he took a handkerchief, put it over his fingers and typed, "I'm sorry" on the laptop.

Jamison then went to his truck and retrieved one bullet and returned to the house via the back door. Using the handkerchief, he emptied the gun and wiped off all the bullets and casings. He reloaded the gun and put it back in the victim's hand. He left by the back door after wiping his prints from the handle.

Jamison stated that he never intended to kill anyone. He just wanted to scare him into giving him his money.

He denied any involvement with the demolition of Lieutenant Greer's car.

CHAPTER 54

Mayor Murphy and Bishop O'Malley were already seated and Chief Morris had just entered the room when the three police officers arrived. Captain Mendoza looked at his watch and saw that it was 10:57. His instructions were to meet in the mayor's office conference room at eleven and to bring the investigating officers with him.

Taking care to follow proper protocol, the mayor introduced the bishop to the chief, then to the captain and then to the detectives. They took their seats and the mayor began.

"Gentlemen, as you know this is a delicate situation. Chief Morris has assured me and the bishop of your cooperation in protecting the reputation of the church in this matter." He nodded to the man to his left and said, "Your Excellency."

Bishop O'Malley looked to the mayor and said, "Thank you, Mr. Mayor." He looked back and forth between the three policemen as he continued, "It is understood you will be investigating ordained Catholic priests attached to this diocese. Your discretion in this matter will be expected and appreciated, and, in return, you will have the full and total cooperation of my office. It has been agreed upon by your superiors that I am to be informed in advance of any warrants or arrests."

A surprised Chief Morris looked at the mayor and then to his subordinates. "What? That's not gonna happen." Looking to the mayor for support, he saw that he wasn't about to agree.

Murphy was about to speak when Lieutenant Greer said, "Your Excellency, please know that it's not the intention of any of us to bring any dirt down upon the church. You have two and a half Catholics on this side of the table."

The bishop repeated, "Two and a half?"

Nick answered, "I don't go anymore but that's not the point. We have a job to do and getting your permission is not part of it. Now, I must ask you a question though, if you don't mind."

The bishop nodded.

"Father Michael Kubic?"

"What about him?"

"He's not a Father."

"What do you mean?" O'Malley questioned.

"How well have you checked his credentials? Where was he ordained? What seminary did he attend? Do you not screen all your priests?"

"I believe he went to Seton Hall. He was ordained in Baltimore, I think. Bill Denkens would know. He's the Vicar General. He's in charge of the priests."

"What would you say if I told you that we ran a background check on him, and there is no record of him ever attending a seminary in this country. *Annnd* . . . he was not ordained in Baltimore, D.C., Philadelphia, or Pittsburgh.

"We're going to pick him up for questioning. If you would like advance notice, I hope this will do." He looked at Sonny. "When will we be picking him up?"

Sonny looked at his watch. "About forty minutes ago, I believe. He's waiting for us. I told him we had a meeting with his boss, but I don't think he believed me."

Chief Morris nodded to Mendoza, rose, and looked at the mayor and said, "If there is nothing else, my officers have a job to do." Neither the mayor or the bishop said a word as the three policemen left the room.

Nick and Sonny went straight to the interrogation room. Kubic was sitting at the table along with a man in a very expensive suit. Greer introduced himself and his partner. The man handed Nick his card and said, "James Seever, Counsel for the Reverend Michael Kubic. Please explain why he's here and why he's been sitting here for the past two hours."

Nick looked at the card, showed it to Sonny, who looked back at his partner and commented, "Figures." The card read: James P. Seever, Esq. Law Offices of Victor Pinnetta & Associates.

"What figures?" Seever asked with an indignant look on his face.

Ignoring the question, Nick pointed to the microphone in the center of the table.

"Please state your name, date of birth, and occupation for the record."

Seever nodded and Kubic said, "Reverend Michael A. Kubic, January 12, 1961, vicar of finance for the Roman Catholic Diocese of Phoenix, Arizona. Will you please tell me why I'm here? I'm a priest. I didn't break any law."

202 – C. P. Holsinger

"Wow! Two lies in one sentence!" Sonny exclaimed. Looking at the priest he asked, "Tell me who hears your confession? Do you confess to yourself? Oh, wait a minute! You can't." Sonny got in his face. "Because you ain't no priest!"

"Excuse me?" he said as he pointed to his collar.

The attorney asked, "Where are you going with this?"

"Where did you get your law degree?" Nick asked the lawyer.

"Ohio State University. Why? And what does that have to do with my client?"

"Can you prove it?"

"Of course, but what . . . ?"

"He can't." Nick said, pointing to Kubic.

The barrister was confused and frustrated by what he was hearing. "He can't what?"

"He can't prove that he's a priest," Nick said as he stared into Kubic's eyes. "Can you?"

Madison took over, looked the man in the eyes, and said, "Where did you go to the seminary?"

"Seton Hall," he answered nervously.

"*Eeeeeee*, wrong answer," Sonny challenged.

Seever tried to speak but Nick said, "Shut up, Counselor. You might learn something."

Sonny continued, "Where were you ordained?"

"Baltimore."

"*Eeeeeee*, wrong again. We checked. There's no record of you at Seton or any other seminary in this country. I spoke with them myself, and they assured me that no one by the name of Michael Kubic ever applied there. *Aaaannnnd*"—he looked at Seever—"hold onto yourself, Counselor, this ride ain't over. I spoke with the bishop's office in Baltimore. They assured me that no one by the name of Michael Kubic was *ever* ordained in the Baltimore diocese, *EVER*."

Sonny looked at Nick. "Your turn."

The lieutenant took over. "We have your diploma, or certificate, or whatever it's called. We got a warrant, and it was picked up while we met with your boss this morning. It's in the lab as we speak. How much you wanna bet, when the results come back it'll say, *FAAAAKE*?"

The attorney spoke up, "May I have some time to confer with my client, please?"

Nick looked at him and said, "Sure, take all the time you want."

As the two detectives left the room, Sonny stopped, turned, and said to Seever, "By the way, Counselor, don't let him hear your confession. I kinda doubt it'll count."

As they left the two alone, Nick said to Sonny, "Vicar of finance, huh? Maybe the bish needs to audit himself."

* * *

The two detectives were outside in the hall talking with ADA Shelley Kisler when Pete Mendoza came up to Nick and handed him a note. He read it and looked back to his boss and nodded.

The door opened, and the attorney came out with his client and said, "We're finished here. It's time to release my client. His credentials are the bishop's concern, not yours."

"Counselor, let's sit back down. I have a couple more questions."

They all sat at the table. Greer reached out and turned on the microphone again and said, "Fath . . . , excuse me, Mr. Kubic, who owns BMK Enterprises and what is its purpose?"

"Uhhh, David, Blake, and me." Confusion covered his face. "Purpose? We have joint ownership in a condo. It's all legal."

"Anyone else involved?" Nick questioned.

"Just us."

"According to the Corporation Commission, BMK Enterprises is owned by Lionheart Holdings."

The suspect was silent.

"It says here the CEO is . . . hmmm." Shock came over the face of the lawyer sitting across the table when Nick looked at him and stated, "Victor Pinnetta!"

The detective then looked at the suspect and asked, "How is your uncle anyway? You know, the one who wasn't there in his office talking to you when I went in last Friday?"

Seever looked at his client and then to Greer. "So what does that have to do with anything?"

"Hang on, Counselor, I'm just getting started." Nick looked back to Kubic and said, "You were in the first Gulf war, I see."

Kubic nodded.

"What did you do there?"

"Chaplain corps."

"Hmmm. I'm having difficulty understanding something. Perhaps you could enlighten me. Why would a chaplain, a man of God and a man of peace, be trained in explosives? Can you explain that?"

Kubic sat in silence.

"OK, we'll get to that later," the detective said. "You, your cousin David, and Blake Beyers have been running a scam on your parishioners for years. We already know that. But there's someone else, isn't there? Someone with the power and resources to make it work without detection, someone who has been running the show from the beginning."

The detective looked at Seever and said, "You might want to hurry this interview because the feds just picked up your boss. He's being charged with money laundering, tax evasion, and conspiracy to commit murder. He might be needing your services."

Seever's face turned white and his mouth opened as the detective's words permeated his being.

"Now, as for you, Mr. Kubic. You're being charged the same as your dear uncle. The feds are on their way here to give you a ride. You can expect to spend a *looonnng* time in federal prison. By the way, we'll be adding attempted murder of a police officer. And my partner here says you look a lot like the guy who tried to inject some bad shit into Father Beyers' IV. That would be another attempted murder charge, and I'll bet we can prove you made a trip to Prescott the night before Father Beyers' car went off the road. I can probably come up with a couple more goodies, but I think that's enough to put you away for a long time. Who knows, maybe you and your beloved uncle might share a cell. Wouldn't that be ironic? A family plan!"

Nick looked at Sonny. "Do they have a family plan at the Florence pen?"

Sonny chuckled.

Fear consumed Kubic as Greer stood up and said, "You have the right to remain silent. Anything you say can and will be used against you in a court of law." He looked at Seever and then back to Kubic. "You have the right to an attorney. It looks like this guy is going to be busy so if you can't afford an attorney, one will be appointed for you at no charge. Do you understand these rights?"

Sobbing like a baby, Kubic nodded.

"Book him!" Nick said to Sonny, who cuffed the subject and escorted him out of the room.

Just then ADA Shelley Kisler came in along with a man in a blue suit. She looked at Nick.

"All yours," he said.

"Counselor, let's talk," Nick heard Shelley say as he left the room.

CHAPTER 55

Nick Greer was clearing his desk. It was Friday morning. He was going home, to try to relax for a while before he headed for Prescott. He was excited that he was going see his kids tomorrow.

His call to Phoenix Baptist Hospital revealed that Sue Kim had been discharged. His calls to her all went to voice mail. He was deciding whether to honor her request to leave her alone or whether he would try and see her once more when ADA Shelley Kisler came into the squad room.

"I just thought you'd like to know," she said with a triumphant glow. "We got Pinnetta! Kubic told all. The feds have him in protective custody and agreed to protect him until it's all over. They had to make a deal though." She looked at Nick. "We dropped the attempted murder charges in exchange for his testimony. I had no choi—"

"Don't worry about it," Nick interrupted. "I expected something like that. "Where's Pinnetta now?"

"The feds have him. His bond will be in the millions, and his assets have been frozen. He ain't goin' anywhere soon." She smiled as she left.

* * *

Nick gave in to his emotions and decided to go to Sue Kim's apartment. As he rapped on the door, he was approached by a white-haired man wearing jeans and a work shirt.

The man asked, "Can I help you?"

"I'm here to see—" He never got to finish.

"She's gone. Left a couple of hours ago. Came to the office, paid off her lease, and turned in her key. Said something about California." Holding up a ring of keys, he continued, "I'm maintenance. Just checking to see how the place looks. Gonna miss her. Nice kid."

Just then, Nick's cell phone rang. It was a text from Sonny. Nick's eyes widened as he read: Southwest Flight 245, Gate 17, 2:26. Better hurry.

He looked at his watch: 1:57. Nick ran to his car and headed for the airport. With his lights flashing, he drove as fast as he could darting in and out of traffic. He ached to see her one more time before she left, even if only for a moment.

He pulled into Phoenix Sky Harbor Airport and followed the signs to terminal four. His tires squealed as he slammed on the brakes and darted into a spot next to the curb.

Killing the car's engine, he got out and opened the trunk. He grabbed the Glock from his belt, reached out into the open cavern, and dropped the magazine and the gun into the trunk. Remembering the .32 on his ankle, he bent down, removed it and tossed it into the trunk with the others. As he closed the trunk, a young uniformed police officer saw him and yelled, "Sir, you can't park there."

The lieutenant flashed his gold badge, and the officer nodded assent.

Running as fast as he could through the terminal, he followed the signs to the gates servicing Southwest Airlines. There was a long line waiting to be screened. Thinking he would surely miss her, he ran to the front of the line, held his badge up and said, "Screen me. I gotta hurry."

Showing the screener that his cell phone worked, he grabbed a gray plastic container and tossed his badge, keys, wallet, loose change, and his cell phone into it.

He passed through the metal detector without incident, retrieved his belongings, and ran as fast as he could up the sloped ramp.

There is was! Gate seventeen. Almost out of breath, he ran into the gate area. He stopped. He looked. It was empty except for a lady and two small children standing at the window and waving. The Jetway doors were closed.

He rushed to the window and saw the servicing vehicle drive away. Could she see him? It was useless to wave, he thought. The tears welling up in his eyes clouded his vision as reality set in. Sue Kim was gone. It was over.

He thought, I could use my badge to get on the plane. At least I could say goodbye.

Just then, the doors to the Jetway opened. He looked up and saw her. A large carry-on bag hung from her right shoulder and a purse from her left. Her long, black hair fell over her shoulders as she looked at him, shrugged, and smiled.

Nick ran to Sue Kim and hugged her. The grimacing look on her face reminded him of her delicate condition and to be gentle. She stood on her tiptoes and met his kiss as he bent down to her.

Nick took the large bag from her shoulder. She put her hand in his and said, "Mama and Papa are pissed. Papa more than Mama. Everything I have is on the plane, even my cello."

"I'll buy you another one," Nick replied as they began their walk out of the gate area to his car.

She laughed. "Not on a cop's salary."

Nick looked at her. "Can I ask you a question?"

"Sure."

"What changed your mind?"

She reached into her purse, pulled out her cell phone, and pushed the power button. A few seconds later it came alive. She pushed another button, then handed the phone to Nick.

It was a text from Sonny Madison:

He's on his way. He loves you. Don't blow it!

ACKNOWLEDGMENTS

Thanks to:

R. T. French, mentor and friend

My wife, Judy, for the lonely hours
she spent while I wrote this book

Foremost Press, for their patience